Praise for Frank Leslie
and *The Lonely Breed*

"Frank Leslie kicks his story into a gallop right out of the
gate . . . raw and gritty as the West itself."
—Mark Henry, author of *The Hell Riders*

"Frank Leslie writes with leathery prose honed sharper than
a buffalo skinner's knife, with characters as explosive as
forty-rod whiskey, and a plot that slams readers with the
impact of a Winchester slug. *The Lonely Breed* is edgy, raw,
and irresistible."
—Johnny D. Boggs, Spur Award–winning author
of *Camp Ford*

"Explodes off the page in a̶̶ ̶ ̶ntertaining burst
of stay-up-late, read̶ ̶ ̶ ̶wing flurry of
page-turning ̶ ̶ ̶rivals the very
best on W̶ ̶

̶r of *Lawdog*

"Hooks you̶ ̶ ̶uc characters and sin-
soaked villa̶ ̶ ̶ ̶ ̶heart of gold and an Arkansas
toothpick. If̶ ̶ ̶er Peckinpah to Ang Lee, this one's
for you."
—Mike Baron, creator of *Nexus*
and *The Badger* comic book series

"Big, burly, brawling, and action-packed, *The Lonely Breed*
is a testosterone-laced winner from the word 'go,' and
Frank Leslie is an author to watch!"
—E. K. Recknor, author of *The Brothers of Junior Doyle*

Also by Frank Leslie

The Wild Breed
The Lonely Breed
The Thunder Riders

THE SAVAGE BREED

Frank Leslie

A SIGNET BOOK

SIGNET
Published by New American Library, a division of
Penguin Group (USA) Inc., 375 Hudson Street,
New York, New York 10014, USA
Penguin Group (Canada), 90 Eglinton Avenue East, Suite 700, Toronto,
Ontario M4P 2Y3, Canada (a division of Pearson Penguin Canada Inc.)
Penguin Books Ltd., 80 Strand, London WC2R 0RL, England
Penguin Ireland, 25 St. Stephen's Green, Dublin 2,
Ireland (a division of Penguin Books Ltd.)
Penguin Group (Australia), 250 Camberwell Road, Camberwell, Victoria 3124,
Australia (a division of Pearson Australia Group Pty. Ltd.)
Penguin Books India Pvt. Ltd., 11 Community Centre, Panchsheel Park,
New Delhi - 110 017, India
Penguin Group (NZ), 67 Apollo Drive, Rosedale, North Shore 0632,
New Zealand (a division of Pearson New Zealand Ltd.)
Penguin Books (South Africa) (Pty.) Ltd., 24 Sturdee Avenue,
Rosebank, Johannesburg 2196, South Africa

Penguin Books Ltd., Registered Offices:
80 Strand, London WC2R 0RL, England

First published by Signet, an imprint of New American Library,
a division of Penguin Group (USA) Inc.

First Printing, June 2009
10 9 8 7 6 5 4 3 2 1

*This book is dedicated to the memory of
renowned Houston meteorologist, Nam veteran,
beloved husband, father, grandfather,
and friend and champion to many, including this writer
—Robert S. Smith*

Chapter 1

Faith . . .

He'd etched her name into the crude plank headboard with a barlow knife and a chisel.

He'd done nothing to treat the wood to keep the sun from bleaching it out and the rain from rotting it. The name would be legible for a few short years here in the high, dry desert air of what remained of his ranch—their ranch—at the foot of Mount Bailey.

Then it would weather. The board would turn gray, fall down, and rot. In ten years there would be little left of the board but slivers, nothing left of the name but the screaming echo inside his head.

In time that too would fade, as would the memory of her face—her blue eyes, straight nose, long, full mouth. The way one of her eyes narrowed slightly whenever she smiled, which she used to do a lot. Or the dry way she used to roll her eyes at him, or tuck in her bottom lip when she stepped into her saddle.

The timbre of her voice when she called his name. The sound of her slow, contented breaths as she slept beside him in their cabin . . .

The memory of her lying dead in his arms outside Bill Thornton's burning roadhouse, her lifeless eyes staring up and over his shoulder at the black night sky, as though in awe of the vastness that had so suddenly claimed her.

All that would fade, as her body was now fading, returning to the earth in its grave up in Colorado Territory. For natural, practical purposes, he'd been unable to haul her back to their ranch here in Arizona. He'd returned here alone to place a marker with her name on it beside the grave of her brother, Kelly, on a sage-tufted knoll behind the cabin. Here, where they'd all three had a home for a time, and where they'd known happiness for a shorter time than most, longer than some.

Still, he felt cheated. He felt hollowed out and parched by anger and grief all the more keen for his knowing that he had no one to see about it. The men who'd killed her were dead, leaving him with nothing but rage and loneliness and this worthless scrap of lumber in his hands, into which he'd spent several hours the previous night etching her name, knowing that like her, it would not last . . .

Yakima Henry set the board at the foot of the rocks he'd mounded as a monument to Faith. Holding it up with one hand, he took some of the stones from the top of the cairn and placed them behind the board, in a wedgelike shape that would for a time hold the board against the weather.

The rocks would last. In a hundred years someone might even remove them to see what or whom had been buried beneath the pile, only to find nothing but dirt. And they'd wonder why someone would go to the work of piling heavy rocks like this on top of nothing, capped by a few remaining shreds of disintegrated pine.

Faith . . .

He knelt on one knee, his left hand resting atop the board engraved with her name. This would be her grave now. Not that place near Thornton's in northern Colorado where he'd buried her body. When he needed to be close to her and to recall the memories, to try to summon the fading images of her face and the sound of her voice and remember the happy times, he would come here, where they once stood hand in hand to watch the sun fade behind Mount Lemmon in the west.

He knelt there for a long time, till the sun was angling westward and the heat on the back of his neck reminded him that he did not want to spend another night here. No point in enduring a sunset here alone, with only these rocks and that board with her name on it.

He would start for Saber Creek, thirty miles south, where he intended to drink himself drunk, break up a couple of saloons, find a woman who would help him forget for a night or two, and figure out where he would go and what he would do next.

Faith . . .

Yakima stood, staring down at the headboard. "Adios, girl."

He glanced at her brother's grave, told the boy goodbye, and then turned to his black stallion, Wolf, saddled and waiting nearby, reins dangling. He glanced down the hill at the ranch yard, turned away, then turned back again.

Nothing more than mounded ashes. His cabin, corrals, stable, and springhouse. Ashes. Sometime after he'd pursued the gang that had killed Kelly and kidnapped Faith to bring her back to the venomous old roadhouse proprietor Thornton, who'd thought he owned her, a band of Apaches had burned the ranch.

Just as well. There was nothing here for Yakima anymore.

He toed a stirrup and swung into the saddle. He glanced down at the two mounded graves once more, then clucked to the horse and heeled the big stallion down the hill and into the ruined ranch yard. He didn't stop to look over the place but turned south onto the old horse trail that had first brought him here two years ago, and put Wolf into a lope across the rolling, sage-stippled clearing toward the blue-green pines beyond.

He'd ridden only a couple of hundred yards from the ranch before he checked the stallion down suddenly. As Wolf stood, rolling his eyes back with incredulity, blowing and twitching his ears, Yakima narrowed an eye against the sun, looking around.

He had the shoulder-raked feeling that eyes were on him, watching him. No one around, though. Just the breeze-ruffled bluestem and sage and a lone coyote trotting across the clearing to the left, bushy gray tail down, glancing back over his shoulder with defiance and caution in his eyes. It was the same coyote Yakima had fed when he'd built the cabin; he was no doubt still sniffing around for the venison scraps Yakima used to throw him.

The half-breed had been gone too long, however. The brush wolf no longer recognized him.

When he'd had a good look around, Yakima clucked to the stallion again and continued across the clearing, the uneasy feeling riding across the back of his shoulders, prickling the hair under his collar. As the horse drifted into the pines and began descending the long grade toward the valley below, the rider shucked his Yellowboy Winchester repeater from its saddle boot beneath his right thigh.

One-handed, Yakima levered a fresh shell into the breech, then set the hammer to half cock and laid the rifle across his saddlebow.

Ready for whatever his senses were telling him was out there.

The long-muscled half-breed—who knew he looked ten years older than he had a year ago because he'd seen himself in flophouse mirrors over the past winter he'd spent knocking about Denver—rode halfway down the mountain from his ruined ranch. Below the level of the pine forest, where the cracked and sun-bleached rocks, greasewood, and saguaros started, he camped in a dry wash between boulder-strewn hills.

When he'd tended his horse, giving Wolf a long rub-down and curry while the stallion watered and grained, he gathered piñon and mesquite branches and built a small cook fire. Darkness settled quickly, leaving only a few lingering pink streaks over the black western mountains. Coyotes yammered from distant ridges, and a javelina thumped through the brush, snorting softly as it grubbed. There was the distant screech of a hunting eagle.

While his tea water heated, Yakima tramped around the

camp, climbing a couple of low hills with his Yellowboy repeater in his hands, taking a long, careful look around. Listening as well as watching and scrutinizing the ground for fresh sign. There was a spring in the wash. Water attracted people, and down here you avoided Apaches as you avoided bobcats, mountain lions, and grizzly bears, though Yakima thought he'd prefer wrestling a mountain lion to a Coyotero Apache.

He saw nothing but rock and saguaro shadows and the kindling stars over the surrounding escarpments.

He took advantage of the spring by filling his two canteens, then stripping down and taking a sponge bath. He ran his last sliver of lye soap across every inch of his cherry-hued, oak-textured body, scrubbing hard at his corded loins and slablike chest. Last, he lathered his long black hair—the hair he had received from his Cheyenne mother's side of the family, while the green eyes set deep in his wide, flat, broad-nosed face had been handed down from his German prospector father.

Both long dead.

Yakima had been alone ever since he stood half as tall as he did now—nearly six feet—with a horrific boardinghouse in the beginning, then a handful of odd jobs, a few women here and there. Mostly he'd been alone. Riding, working wherever and whenever he could, then riding on.

He'd figured the ranch and Faith would be the end of that aimless trail. He hadn't figured on Thornton sending riders way down here to even the score for the bullet she'd drilled through his belly when she'd escaped him the first time, when she and Yakima had first met up in Colorado and run away together after becoming lovers.

A sporting girl and a half-breed swamper and stable-boy . . .

Boy, that had piss-burned Thornton good. The roadhouse proprietor had been in love with Faith, and he'd been fool enough to think she'd been in love with him. Finding out it wasn't true, he'd sent bounty hunters. . . .

Yakima doused his hair, then whipped his head around

to get the water out. Standing at the bottom of the wash in the starlight, he dried himself slowly, enjoying the cool night air pushing against his sun- and windburned skin, his tired, worn-out body.

If it could only get inside his head and cool his brain . . .

Naked, he sat by the fire and roasted a big jack he'd shot earlier. He ate the greasy meat hungrily, sprinkling salt on it from a small canvas pouch and washing it down with green tea, which he'd acquired a taste for while working to lay rail with a Chinese man. After supper, donning only his moccasins, he picked up his rifle and scrambled around the ridges once more, scouting. He squatted on rocks to look and listen and sniff the freshening breeze tinged with sage and piñon.

That hunted feeling was still there, but he could find no reason for it. Maybe it was only the angst that had constantly ridden his shoulders since the bounty hunters had raided his ranch and taken his woman . . . his life.

Later, he checked his horse, which was standing contentedly near the spring, tied to a cedar; then Yakima returned to the fire. He kicked dirt on the flames, leaned his rifle against a rock, within easy reach of his bed, and rolled up in his blankets, leaning his head back against his saddle. Consciously he suppressed his inexplicable unease and purged his mind—at least for a time—of the excruciating thoughts that had haunted him since last fall. He took a deep breath, released it slowly, and went to sleep.

He woke at first light, dressed in his summer underwear—cutoff long johns minus the top—faded blue denims, red and black calico bib-front shirt, and undershot stockman's boots with spurs. A leather thong strung with curved grizzly teeth hung around his neck—a trophy from the bruin that had attacked him near his ranch. After he was dressed he walked down the wash a ways to check his stallion.

Wolf nickered as he came closer, twitching his ears as he glanced back toward his approaching owner.

"Breakfast in a minute," Yakima said, patting the horse's rump.

He was unbuttoning his fly to evacuate his bladder when the horse whinnied more shrilly. Yakima gave a start and looked back over his shoulder. "Damn it, Wolf, I told you . . ."

He let his voice trail off as two men stepped around a gnarled cottonwood at the edge of the spring, one moving in from the right, the other from the left. They were hatted shadows in the misty light, but the revolvers they both aimed at Yakima were plain as day.

"Hey, fellas, get a gander at this," growled the man on the right. "We done skeered the half-breed so bad he near pissed hisself!"

Chapter 2

Wolf whinnied again, causing both men in front of Yakima to jerk and cast quick looks behind them. Yakima was about to reach for the staghorn .44/40 holstered low on his right thigh, but the unmistakable click of a cocking gun hammer sounded behind him—crisp and clear on the still dawn air.

"Uh-uh, breed," a voice said. Gravel crunched and a spur trilled softly. "That wouldn't be advisable. Get those hands up."

Yakima stared straight ahead at the first two men, who were walking slowly toward him. Hearing the third approaching from behind, he raised his hands shoulder-high. "Figured you weren't Apaches," he said. "Wolf would have fussed more at Apaches. How long you fellas been shadowin' me?"

"Shut up," ordered the man on the right as the man behind him snagged Yakima's Colt from its holster.

"I don't have any money."

"Did we say we wanted money?"

Yakima just stared at the man who'd spoken. The gent ahead and to the left was Yakima's height, with thick curly hair puffing out around the brim of his shabby bowler. He wore a ratty suit coat and baggy pin-striped pants. His ugly face was covered with a four- or five-day growth of curly beard, and a matchstick protruded from the right side of his thin mouth. He spoke with an accent Yakima recognized as Australian.

Yakima heaved a sigh. "What, then?"

"Personally," said the man behind him, nudging Yakima's left foot with his own, "I like them boots." There was a soft *whoosh* as the man spun the half-breed's Colt on his finger. "Fine-lookin' weapon, too. I could use a new hogleg. Mine hasn't fired right since I dropped it down a privy hole last summer. Think it gummed up the firing pin."

The man ahead and to the right—a string bean in a battered black and gray sombrero and deerhide vest—canted his head toward the campfire. "Personally," he said in a faint Spanish accent, "I like that Yellowboy repeating rifle." Grinning, he glanced at the curly-haired Australian. "What about you, McMasters, huh? What would you like the mestizo to offer *you*?"

McMasters held his leering stare on Yakima as over the barrel of his cocked Dragoon horse pistol with engraved ivory grips he said, "I kinda been off my feed since both you and Randy Earl got yourselves them good hosses. Yessir, I sure would like to get me a good hoss." He glanced over his shoulder, squinting one eye. "Believe I'll take me the black stallion off your hands, mate. You wouldn't mind, would you, mate?"

Yakima's gut tightened but he kept his face stony. "Horse stealin's a serious offense . . . mate."

"Only if ya get caught, mate." McMasters winked.

Yakima heard the man behind him draw a sharp breath. On the ground beside him he saw the man's shadow move as he raised his arm above his head.

Yakima reacted instantly, bounding straight up off his right foot while raising his left leg and pinwheeling to face the man behind him—a big man with a fleshy pocked and pitted face that had shaggy brows and small, deep-sunk eyes. He wore a black felt slouch hat with a hawk feather poking up from the brim.

The man's eyes snapped wide and his jaw fell slack as,

holding his Smith & Wesson above his head by its barrel,
butt down, he saw Yakima's foot rushing toward him. The
man had no time to do anything but grunt before the boot
slammed into the side of his head, spur first.

"Jesus Christ!" exclaimed one of the men now behind
Yakima.

The man he'd just kicked toppled like a windmill in a
cyclone, screaming, arms and legs akimbo, the Smith &
Wesson hitting the ground behind him. As Yakima rushed
toward the pistol, the downed man swung both heavy legs
sideways, roaring curses. One of his ankles clipped Yakima's right boot, tripping him.

A gun barked. The slug spanged off a rock just ahead of
Yakima, blowing up dust.

"What are you doin', Trujillo?" the Aussie bellowed.

Down on all fours, heart racing, Yakima lunged for the
Smith & Wesson as the big man continued shouting curses
as he flopped around on the ground, holding his bloody ear.

Running footsteps sounded.

Yakima wrapped his hand around the revolver's butt. He
turned, thumbing the Smithy's hammer back.

He'd only just caught a glimpse of the Aussie standing
over him, the man's right hand whipping toward Yakima
from the Aussie's left shoulder. The butt of the big Dragoon
in the man's hand slammed against Yakima's right temple.

Yakima felt as though a train had hit him. He squeezed
the trigger, and the Smithy's belch was the last sound he
heard before the world went dark and quiet.

Yakima had no idea how much time had passed before
something woke him—some raucous sound that, he realized
as his marbles rolled slowly back into their rightful pockets,
he'd been hearing for a long time and had been wishing
would go away. Tightening his face against the searing pain
in his head, he opened first one eye, then the other.

A magpie crouched in the gnarled cottonwood, staring at
Yakima and opening and closing its black, white, and aqua-

marine wings. It had a hungry look in its pellet-sized, oily black eyes.

As Yakima lifted his head with a groan, touching a hand to his battered temple and fingering the torn flesh and dried blood, the bird gave another raucous cry. It spread its wings and clumsily flew up from the branch, screeching as it whooshed off into the distance.

Other magpies also flew up from around Yakima, raising the din to a veritable Indian powwow in the half-breed's head as they left in search of other carrion.

"Sorry to disappoint you fellas."

When he had both eyes open and his senses as well as his memory had returned, he jerked a look again toward the tree. Wolf was gone.

Yakima's heart thundered in his chest, increasing the drum thuds in his head. Wincing, he shuttled his gaze to his camp.

The fire was out, and around the ash-heaped fire ring, only rocks remained. His gear was gone. Including his prized Yellowboy Winchester repeater. His heart thumped even harder.

The Yellowboy with engraved brass receiver and long octagonal barrel had been a gift from a Shaolin monk whom he'd called George and with whom he'd laid railroad track several years back. George of course hadn't been the whiskey-swilling monk's real name, but it was as close as Yakima could get to forming the actual sound in Chinese. Not only had George given Yakima the rifle, which he'd won in a poker game, but he'd taught Yakima the fine, graceful, deadly art of Eastern fighting.

George had been one of Yakima's few friends. The rifle, along with the black stallion, was one of his few prized possessions.

This wasn't the first time he'd lost both to trail-haunting peckerwoods . . .

Yakima dug his heels into the dirt as he began to rise. He stopped, looked down at his feet, wriggled his bare toes.

It appeared that this time he'd lost not only his horse and his rifle but his boots as well.

"You mangy coyotes."

The boots were old and worthless. Over several years of constant wear, they'd molded like gloves to Yakima's feet. They wouldn't fit anyone else. The only possible reason for stealing them was to slow Yakima down.

If the thieves had wanted to slow him down, though, why hadn't they just put a bullet in his head?

Gaining his bare feet, he strode over to the fire, one hand to his aching temple, and looked around to see if he'd missed anything. Only his low-crowned, flat-brimmed black hat remained, lying wedged between two rocks. It had probably tumbled out of his bedroll when they'd gathered his gear and cleaned up the camp like thieving gnomes.

Bastards hadn't even left him a canteen.

Again he couldn't help wondering why they hadn't killed him. Unless the miserable trail rats had wanted to leave him to the Apaches or to the May sun that at the moment hovered at around ten o'clock in the morning sky . . .

Yakima rolled his head on his shoulders, trying to loosen the kinks in his neck, as he tramped over to the spring. He knelt and put his face down close to the mossy black rocks, lapping water like a dog from a stone cup.

He drank the cold, mineral-tasting liquid until he had his fill and then some. It was a good thirty-mile walk to Saber Creek, which was likely where the thieves were headed, as it was the only near settlement, and the day was heating up. He would lose moisture fast.

When he'd cleaned the two-inch gash in his temple, wincing at the sting in the tender flesh, he began following the four sets of horse tracks the thieves had left in the prickly orange caliche. The iron-shod hooves rose up and out of the wash, angling due south through the lime green chaparral that spiked the burnished orange desert under a clear, sprawling, brassy sky. Bald ranges rose in all directions—toothy, misty, savage, and silent.

Yakima continued south, pacing himself and watching for cactus and the small spiked seeds called goatheads that would cut up his feet quickly and miserably.

Sure enough, the bastards were heading for Saber Creek. Now all Yakima had to do was stick to their trail and hope the Apaches were sticking to the mountains, where General Crook and Al Seiber had chased most of them, last he'd heard.

When he reached the main trail—the only trail, really—to Saber Creek, he was glad he was still on the trail of the thieves. He recognized his stallion's shod hoofprints, and he followed them closely, stuffing his rage down in a deep pocket in his chest and letting out just enough at a time to keep going in spite of all the sharp stone and thistle pricks to his bare feet, in spite of the sunlight blazing down on him and the intense heat that broiled him—a heat so dry that it sucked up his sweat as soon as it popped out on his forehead and back.

At midday the sand burned his feet like hot coals, and he rested for a half hour in the shade of a rocky overhang. When the sun started angling westward, he continued, striding purposefully, stalwartly forward, swallowing the dry knot in his throat. He continued to dribble out the rage that kept him going in spite of his howling feet and the sun burning through his hat and practically setting his hair on fire.

Occasionally a sweat bead would evade evaporation and trickle through the dust on his cheeks, though not one ever reached his jaw.

After his nooning under the rock, he left the trail only twice, both times to avoid horseback riders who were clomping up behind him and heading in the same direction. Judging by their shabby, dusty trail clothes, both small groups were composed of ranch hands from area spreads, likely heading to town for an evening of tail stomping and mattress dancing.

He didn't bother asking for a lift or even for a drink of water. Most men around here mistook him for a reservation

Apache, and he didn't want to have to dodge lead or a lasso. Those who knew him knew him as a troublemaker. Conflict not of his choosing seemed to follow his every trip to town, leaving a demolished saloon in his wake. He knew the jail well enough to have counted the exact number of stones in its back wall.

His real trouble, as Faith had told him, was he couldn't control his temper. Unlike a good reservation Indian, he didn't take to being branded.

The sun was about another hour from the far western mountains by the time he saw the little sunbaked sandstone village rising out of the chaparral ahead of him. His mouth was so dry that it didn't even water at the smell of the supper fires rife with the aroma of seasoned meats, beans, and chili peppers.

His stomach rumbled above the light, crunching thud of each footstep that brought him nearer the outlying corrals and goat pens. Little adobe huts pushed up out of the greasewood and gnarled cedars, the roofless, crumbling hovels long since abandoned by the first Mexicans who'd founded the *pueblito* of Sable Riachuelo, long before the gringos came and made it a modest ranching and stage-coach hub.

Shadows angled. The air cooled. Doves cooed softly.

As Yakima entered the main part of the town, the brick-adobe shops showing pink and salmon in the dwindling light, he could hear the revelers in the saloons ahead. He saw the horses clumped at various hitch rails and the wan lamplight now competing with the dwindling sunlight on the gray, dusty, dung-littered boardwalks.

In one of the Mexican cantinas on a near side street, the bittersweet notes of a guitar rose in stark contrast to the savage growls of a distant dogfight and a woman yelling in Spanish.

He angled toward the open doors of the Federated Livery and Feed Barn, and the cool, soft dirt and manure under the peaked roof felt good against his burned, chafed soles. The smell of fresh ammonia engulfed him while female groans and sighs rose from the tack room housed in a side shed and separated from the main barn by a narrow curtained doorway.

Male grunts and epithets wheezed in Spanish accompanied the woman's groans and the creaking of the tack bench over which the barn's manager, Miguel Gomez, was bending his current *puta*.

Yakima made for the horses stalled at the back of the barn. Their silhouetted heads hung over their stall partitions. "Miguel!" he said as loudly as he could, his throat parched as ancient leather.

"Mierda!" the man said behind the curtained doorway.

The woman laughed.

Ahead of Yakima, a horse whinnied shrilly and tossed its silhouetted head. Wolf turned toward him and shook his head and rippled his withers eagerly. His eyes stood out in the shadows—white-ringed and wild.

Miguel Gomez yelled from the tack room. "Who is it? Can't you hear I'm busy? Take your horse and leave your money on the feed barrel!" The woman sighed, and Gomez added in a slightly higher-pitched voice, "Don't forget a gratuity, if you please, Senor. . . ."

The black stallion was stalled beyond two paints and a buckskin. The paints regarded Yakima owlishly while the buckskin pushed his snout toward Yakima's chest as though looking for a handout. Ignoring the horse, Yakima grabbed Wolf by his thick jaw and scrubbed the stallion's dusty cheeks.

The horse nickered and twitched his ears and bobbed his head with joy.

Relief mixing with his barely restrained fury, Yakima turned again toward the curtained doorway showing dimly in the side wall behind barrels of miscellaneous tack. "Get out here, Miguel!"

"Shit!" he heard the man groan. "Yakima?"

"Where's my rifle, you Aztec dung beetle?"

Yakima peered into Wolf's stall. His saddle and saddlebags lay in the back corner. Opening the stall door, he pushed the snorting and nickering stallion out of his way, stepped through the straw, and shifted the gear around. His war bag and his boots were there, but there was no sign of his guns.

He kicked around in the straw, breathing hard and cursing. Finally he grabbed his boots, his socks stuffed inside, and pushed back out of the stall and into the barn's main alley. Miguel Gomez was moving toward him from the shadows, holding a heavy striped saddle blanket around his thick waist.

The man's black hair was mussed on his nearly bald head, and his thin lips stretched a phony smile, his round, coffee-black eyes dancing in the waning light from a window. "Yakima . . . it's been a long time, uh?"

Yakima leaned against a feed barrel as he pulled his right sock on his scratched, burned foot. "Don't act like you're surprised to see me. That's my stallion and you know it."

Gomez glanced at Wolf as though seeing him for the first time. "Oh . . . *sí, sí*! I thought he looked familiar."

"Where are they?"

The liveryman frowned. "Who?"

Yakima jerked a sharp look at the squat, puffy, half-naked Mexican standing before him, who was wide-eyed with phony innocence as he held the saddle blanket closed behind his back. Gomez stepped abruptly back, flinching and dropping his eyes to the floor. "I believe they said something about . . . the Saguaro Inn."

"The Saguaro Inn, huh?" Yakima had pulled his right boot on his swollen foot, wincing at the pain shooting up into his leg. Now he shook out his other sock and stuffed the other foot into it. "Figured as much."

The Saguaro Inn was favored by the area's rawest element because of the good, albeit expensive liquor and the comeliest whores north of the Mexican border. Before Faith had come into his life for the second time a year ago, Yakima had preferred the place for the same reasons, though he usually chose ale over hard liquor, as hooch often brought out the atavistic warrior in him.

"Yakima, *por favor*," the liveryman said, twisting his round face with beseeching. "My brother-in-law, Giuseppe, still works at the Saguaro Inn. Please do not cause trouble for him. His nerves have been bad ever since . . . you know . . . the trouble with Bandolier Bob . . ."

"Bob's the one that shot that notch out of Giuseppe's nose, Miguel."

"*Sí, sí.* I am not blaming you." Gomez held up his free hand, palm out, stretching his lips back from his tobacco-stained teeth. "But you were playing cards with Bob when the trouble erupted, as it so often does whenever . . . well, whenever you are in town." The liveryman lurched back another step. "*Por favor*, Yakima! I mean no offense."

"None taken," Yakima said, grunting as he stomped his swollen foot into the corresponding boot, making the spur ring. As he headed toward the barn's open front doors, he growled without turning his head. "Rub Wolf down good. His coat's a mess. I'll be checking."

"*Sí*, Yakima." The liveryman sighed behind him.

As the half-breed approached the front of the barn, the shapely silhouette of a full-bodied *puta* appeared, leaning seductively against the doorframe to his left, thrusting her breasts out underneath her sheer sleeveless cotton shift. Her brown legs were bare, her feet clad in rope-soled sandals.

She took a drag off the cornhusk cigarette in her hand, the coal glowing brightly in the barn's shadows. As she blew out the smoke, she said huskily with a coquettish smile, tossing her long, thick hair back from her face, "*Hola*, Yakima."

"Rose." Yakima strode stiffly, painfully past her in the too-tight boots, angling across the street toward the side street on which the Saguaro Inn lay.

"Love to stay and chat," he said, "but I have to see some men about a rifle and a horse."

Chapter 3

A short blond gent in a charro jacket burst out the batwing doors of the Saguaro Inn, staggered to the edge of the boardwalk—causing a dog that had been drinking from a stock tank to yip and run off—and fell to his knees. His shoulders jerked, his head dropped, and up and out came all he'd eaten that day and no doubt a good quart of tequila in a frothy lime green mess.

Yakima stopped in the street in front of the man, near the half dozen horses tied to the hitch rails. The man continued convulsing, and Yakima stepped around him, a grim look on his broad, tan face. "A little early for that, ain't it, fella?"

The only reply was another seizure and splattering sound as the man continued airing his paunch into the dust and shit of the street while the horses eyed him curiously.

Yakima pushed through the batwings and stopped just inside the low adobe-brick saloon and pleasure parlor. Smoke wafted throughout the large candle- and lantern-lit main hall in which a sizable crowd milled and roared. A three-piece band was playing at the rear-left corner, and above the band was a balcony on which half-dressed doxies were ushering men to and from their rooms.

More girls were mixing with the crowd below, making the rounds and drumming up business while a hodgepodge of Mexicans, white men, and a handful of blacks played poker or stood at the bar running along the saloon's right wall, conversing and drinking tequila, pulque, or ale. The haylike smell

of marijuana mixed with the odor of harsh black tobacco.
Two apron-clad Mexican bartenders were sashaying around
behind the mahogany bar like trained dancers.

Ahead and to the right of Yakima, five big, bearded Irish
miners in overalls and hobnailed boots argued loudly over a
game of five-card stud while they guzzled ale from tin
buckets and spewed stogie smoke at the ceiling.

Yakima's attention was drawn to the table behind them,
around which the three men he was looking for were playing cards with a dude in a black clawhammer coat, paisley
vest, and string tie. The Aussie, McMasters, and the dude
faced Yakima from the other side of the round table, which
fronted an adobe-brick wall. The dude had a beautiful
black-haired *puta* in a sexy, skimpy red dress on his lap.
The girl's arms were around the man's neck as she watched
him flip cards, coins, or bank notes onto the table. A long
black cheroot protruded from between his lips.

The other two men—the string-bean Mex and the big
man, Randy Earl, who had a bloody white bandage
wrapped over his ear—sat with their backs to the half-
breed.

Yakima's prized rifle leaned against the table between
them.

Yakima stepped down off the three entrance steps and
angled past the Irishmen's table. None of the three men he
was after had spotted him yet. They were too captivated by
their game, smokes, tequila, and the whore, who had the
intermittent attention of all four as she squirmed and wriggled around on the dude's lap and occasionally threw her
fine head back on her bare shoulders to send a sexy laugh
above the din.

It was the girl who saw him first. She frowned curiously
as Yakima strode up to the table, reached between Randy
Earl and the lanky Mexican, and grabbed his Yellowboy. He cocked the repeater loudly, causing the bearded,
bowler-hatted McMasters to lift his head suddenly and the
string-bean Mex and Randy Earl to jerk in their chairs with
starts.

The dude raked his eyes from the whore's well-formed breasts, which were all but exposed by the low-cut dress and alluringly highlighted by several colorfully beaded necklaces. When he saw the big sunburned Indian standing over his table, holding a Winchester across his chest, broad nostrils expanding and contracting, jaw set hard, the dude's face turned the color of skim milk.

"Ah, hell!" McMasters exclaimed, his fat stogie dropping from his mouth to spark as it hit the table. The Aussie's eyes were rheumy from drink. As he glared up at Yakima, his right hand dropped over the big silver-chased pistol lying beside his ashtray.

Randy Earl and the string-bean Mex looked around and up at Yakima, incredulity and fear showing behind the tequila glaze in their eyes.

Yakima squeezed the rifle in his hands. His chest rose and fell slowly.

The Mexican leapt up from his seat and, twisting around toward Yakima, tripped over his chair, nearly fell, caught himself on the table, and sidled away, holding his hands above the two revolvers thonged low on his denim-clad thighs. One was Yakima's own staghorn .44, poking up from Yakima's well-oiled tan holster.

Randy Earl made the same move, kicking his own chair out of the way. He backed around to the left side of the table, holding his hands shoulder-high, fingers curled toward the palms, a wary look in his eyes. Blood had dribbled down from beneath the bandage and dried on his neck.

Yakima stepped straight back from the table, giving himself plenty of room to work with the Winchester.

Suddenly, the din around him died so that only the guitar, fiddle, and brass horn were sounding. Then, as all heads swung toward the big Indian standing menacingly over the table in the room's far right corner, the music dwindled, one instrument after another, until the room was so quiet that a woman could be heard outside, yelling in Spanish for a boy named Paco to come inside for supper.

The pretty whore sat tensely on the dude's lap, her large

round brown eyes fearful. She said beseechingly, "Yak-ima . . ."

The dude frowned indignantly as he removed the cheroot from between his teeth. He was a blond-haired, strong-jawed, overly handsome man, clean-shaven and in his late twenties, with several large rings on his fingers. "What the hell's your problem, hombre?"

The last word had barely left the dude's mouth before McMasters kicked his chair back with an angry wail and lifted both ivory-gripped Dragoons above the table. Rocking his Yellowboy's hammer back, Yakima raised the rifle's stock to his shoulder, aimed quickly, and fired. McMasters screamed as the slug plowed through his upper right chest, throwing him straight back in his chair as he dropped one Dragoon and triggered the other one into the pile of playing cards and money.

As coins and table slivers flew in every direction and the whore screamed and leapt from the dude's lap to the floor, Yakima calmly but quickly racked another round into the Yellowboy's chamber and drilled another slug through McMasters's forehead.

The Aussie's head snapped back to reveal the blood- and brain-splattered wall behind him. The rest of the man's body followed a quarter second later, the chair tipping over and the man's spurred cavalry boots flying up above the table.

"Why, you bastard!" Randy Earl yelled.

Before the big man could get his Smith & Wesson clear of its cross-draw holster, Yakima shot him in the belly. Randy Earl screamed and staggered straight back against the wall, raising his Smithy and triggering a shot into the ceiling before, clutching his blood-oozing gut with his free hand, he fell to his butt bellowing like a speared grizzly.

A revolver barked to Yakima's right. The bullet seared a line across the nub of his right cheek.

He whipped around toward the string-bean Mex, who was backing away while aiming and recocking his smoking saddle-ring Schofield. Before the man could get the gun's hammer back, Yakima seated fresh brash in the Yellowboy's chamber, aimed from the shoulder, and fired.

The Mexican groaned as, twisting sideways, he took Yakima's bullet high on his left shoulder.

The man sort of danced and pirouetted between nearby tables, sending bystanders running and kicking over chairs. Spinning back toward Yakima, he bellowed something in Spanish and raised his Schofield again, his mustached face a mask of raging terror, eyes bulging grotesquely.

The whip crack of Yakima's Yellowboy sounded like a cannon blast in the close confines.

The bullet took the Mex through the throat. The man triggered his pistol into a chair as he flew two feet up in the air and then straight back, landing butt down on a table behind him, glasses and bottles flying and shattering across the floor.

The man gurgled, grunted, and arched his back as he tried to suck a breath down his torn throat. Failing that, his body fell slack against the table, arms and legs dangling over the sides. His right hand opened. His Schofield hit the floor with a thud.

Blood dribbled down a table leg, dark as spilled molasses.

Yakima ejected the spent cartridge, heard it clatter to the floor behind him and roll, then levered a fresh bullet into the Yellowboy's chamber as he turned back toward the thieves' table. The blond dude sat back in his chair against the wall, looking around in shock at his dead poker opponents. When he saw Yakima's rifle aimed at him, he gave a startled grunt and threw his hands up to his shoulders, palms out, one blue eye twitching nervously.

The heavy silence following the gunfire and the screams was broken by one of the Irishmen, who rasped, "Bloody hell . . ."

Then the others in the room who'd taken cover behind chairs and tables started to slowly gain their feet and turn their chairs upright, keeping their wary gazes on the rifle-wielding half-breed.

The young *puta* had fallen to the floor several feet from the dude's chair, her legs curled beneath her. Her dress was drawn up to her waist, exposing long, fine, tan legs. She'd lost both of her black stiletto-heeled shoes. Holding one hand to her breasts, she looked around through the wafting powder smoke.

She whipped her head toward Yakima as the half-breed lowered his rifle, draped his holstered Colt and cartridge belt over a shoulder, and strode toward her around the table. "Yakima," she said thinly, frowning fearfully up at him. *"Christo!"*

He reached down and grabbed the girl's arm. She gave a startled shriek as he pulled her over his free shoulder and straightened. "Yakima, put me down! *Maria y Jesus!"*

She pounded his back as he swung around and, holding her over his shoulder with one hand, his rifle in the other, moved around the table and threaded his way to the back of the room. The murmurs around him grew quickly to a tremulous din. Glasses clinked and coins clattered.

The fiddle started up again with a buoyant Mexican tune, and the guitar and horn soon followed, the players trying with all their might to reinstall merriment on the premises. Yakima headed up the broad wooden stairs at the back of the room, wincing at the additional pressure on his tender feet. As he rose along the room's rear adobe-brick wall, the girl quit pounding his back with her fists and dug her hands around his belt, holding on tightly as she sighed and groaned her protests.

The liveryman's brother-in-law stood halfway down the stairs, staring slack-jawed at Yakima rising toward him with the girl on his shoulder. "Haul me up a bath, Giuseppe?" Yakima continued past the swamper. "I'll be in Angelina's room."

The notch-nosed Giuseppe watched in awe as Yakima gained the top of the stairs and turned down the candlelit hall, several half-dressed men and whores watching him with similar expressions, the shooting having brought them out of their rooms in a hurry. One man—a burly muleskin-

ner known as Tin Cup Pete—held only a shabby feathered
bowler over his privates.

"Yakima Henry—what in Sam Hill? We figured you was
dead!" the man exclaimed as Yakima strode past him.

Yakima threw open the fourth door on the hall's right
side, staggered in, kicked the door closed behind him, and
tossed the whore on the bed. She gave a wail as she bounced
on the lumpy mattress, dress rising up her legs, beaded
necklaces dancing across her breasts.

"What do you think you are doing, you crazy Indio?"
she spat, rising up on her elbows, her brown eyes flashing
at him like sunlit ebony. "You can't treat a girl that way!
Haul her around like a sack of corn to feed your pigs!"

Yakima threw his pistol belt on a chair and sat on the
edge of the bed. He hiked his right boot onto his knee and
began pulling it off. It felt two sizes too small, and he bit
his lip with the painful effort. "You never minded before."

"He had money, Yakima."

"The dude?"

"*Sí*. A whole walletful. *Muy* greenbacks and a bag of
coins!"

The boot came off with a jerk, and Yakima set it aside
and started on the other one. "Must be a cattle buyer from
Tucson. I don't think he's in the mood, anyway, Angelina.
His face looked a mite on the pasty side after he saw them
horse thieves go down."

"What kind of a ranchero are you when you cannot keep
track of your horses? You are always having to chase them
to town!" The girl was still propped on her elbows, frowning and flushed, her mussed black hair in her face. She was
the most beautiful *puta* Yakima had ever seen—delicate,
even features, with large pear-shaped breasts—and he remembered now how, before Faith, he'd once hungered for
her.

The hunger was back with a vengeance.

"Good question." Yakima chuckled, dimpling his cheeks
as the second boot slipped free of his heel.

The girl climbed off the bed, making the springs squawk,

and padded barefoot toward the door. Her voice was loud and sharp. "Besides, I heard you had a woman up there at your flea-infested coyote den." She stroked her hair and squinted sarcastically. *"Bonito rubio."*

"You got that right." Yakima sat with his hands on his thighs, wincing at his stocking feet as he flexed his toes. "You can pull your horns in. She's dead."

Angelina stopped with her hand on the doorknob. She stared at the door, then turned to look at him over her shoulder. A thin red strap hung down her left arm, leaving the fragile shoulder bare. The side of one full breast was visible beneath her arm. The anger leached slowly from her eyes.

"What happened?"

"An old friend came calling. He sent bounty hunters." Yakima looked down again at his feet. "I went after her, but I didn't get there in time."

Angelina removed her hand from the knob and walked slowly back toward the bed. She stopped before him, tucked her hair behind one ear, then swept Yakima's own hair back from the broad, rugged face the sun had browned to the color of an old saddle.

"Can't keep a woman any better than you can keep your horses." Angelina clucked her disapproval, holding his hair behind his head in one hand and rubbing her other thumb across his cheek. "What are you going to do with yourself, you crazy, lonely Indio?"

"I was thinking about heading to Mexico. Wanna come?"

"What will you do in Mejico?"

Yakima reached up and swept the other strap down her arm, letting the front of the low-cut dress slide slowly down her breasts to just above her nipples. "What will I do here?"

All anger had left her now. Her eyes were smoky, alluring. She pursed her lips, dimpling her cheeks. She shook her head slowly. "A lonely, wild coyote . . ."

Yakima pulled the straps a little lower on her arms. The dress slid over the pronounced nipples to her waist, laying bare the delectable, pear-shaped orbs, the undersides of which displayed gooseflesh though it was warm in the room, which smelled faintly of piñon and the subtle perfume she always wore.

Yakima cupped the breasts. Her nipples pebbled beneath his fingers. She cooed and groaned, her eyelids growing heavy. Sliding his hands to her shoulders, he pulled her down to him, and as she straddled his thighs, facing him, he brought her mouth to his and kissed her slowly, passionately, her head higher than his, her naked breasts pressed against his chest.

There was a soft knock at the door. Yakima slid his hand up the girl's naked thigh to his .44, removed the gun smoothly from its holster, and rocked the hammer back.

"Who's there?"

"Giuseppe, Senor. I bring your bath."

Yakima eased the hammer down against the firing pin. "Come in."

The door opened a crack, and a black eye stared into the room, which was lit by only one window and a candle. Staring over her bare shoulder at the door, Angelina chuckled. "I have never known you to be so polite, Giuseppe," she teased in Spanish.

The swamper pushed the door wide and entered the room carrying a copper bathtub in one hand, a wooden bucket of steaming water in the other. A big mestizo, a half-breed Mexican, followed with two more buckets of water, one cold, one hot.

"It is not to be polite that I knock," Giuseppe said in English, casting an indignant glance at Yakima. "It is so that I am not to be shot again by the crazy gringo Indio."

"If you remember," Yakima said, canting his head to see around the bare-breasted *puta*, "it was Bandolier Bob that carved that notch in your nose, Giuseppe."

The swamper set the tub near the bed and fingered the scar. "*Sí*. But it was you who started the pistol works!"

"Bob was dealin' from the bottom of the deck, and three of my best green-broke mustangs were ridin' on that jack.

Besides, I may have shot first, but Bob was the first one to claw iron."

"All I know," Giuseppe said, pouring his bucket of water into the copper tub while the silent mestizo, in his red bandanna, buckskins, and moccasins, stood by the room's single dresser, holding his own buckets, "is that where Yakima Henry goes—and I mean no offense, I am only stating a truth!—trouble follows like mites on a chaparral cock."

"Here!" Yakima flipped the man a silver dollar. "Go buy you and Yanni there a bottle or a cheap whore. I'd like a little privacy." As the swampers finished filling the tub and filed out of the room, closing the door behind them, Yakima continued to Angelina, "I'm dirty and tired and I got one hell of a wild edge that needs filing."

As he leaned forward to nuzzle her breasts, the beautiful *puta* groaned and reached down between his legs. "Don't worry. I will file it for you. Like I used to, huh?"

Chapter 4

Both before and after his bath, the beautiful *puta*, Angelina, filed Yakima's edge and then some.

It was a wild night in the whore's little room. While Yakima rarely imbibed anything stronger than ale, he threw down his share of the tequila that Angelina ordered up from the saloon downstairs. It didn't seem to dampen his desire any. He and Angelina frolicked on the bed as well as on the floor in front of a small charcoal brazier, and even once over the washstand before returning to the bed, spending themselves with one last mad coupling before collapsing, naked and entangled upon the knotted, twisted, sweat-damp sheets.

Whump!

Yakima jerked his head up from the pillow, as a little Apache inside his head fired poisoned darts at the backs of his eyes, to see the door of the whore's room slam back against the wall, the metal latch breaking and wooden slivers flying in all directions. The concussion shuddered the whole room and knocked a glass of tequila off the dresser to shatter upon the floor.

Lying prostrate and naked beside Yakima, Angelina groaned and lifted her head slightly from her pillow, looking around frowning, the picture of living agony, her mussed hair in her eyes.

Blinking, Yakima watched as two tall, mustached figures stepped side by side through the open door and into the room, each holding a silver-plated Remington revolver in his right hand. In unison, the figures stopped just inside the door and, aiming their Remys at the bed, reached behind them with their free hands. Yakima blinked and squinted, and suddenly the two figures slid together to become one as the lone man in a funnel-brimmed hat and whipcord trousers sent a pair of tarnished metal handcuffs tumbling end over end through the air toward the bed.

Yakima flung a hand up. The three chain links slapped his palm, and the cuffs danced around his fingers. Holding the cuffs up above his head, he closed one eye and opened the other to get a better look at the tall, rangy man standing before him, one fist on his hip, the Remy aimed negligently straight out from his waist. The five-pointed sheriff's badge on the man's cowhide vest flashed in the golden morning sunshine angling through the window, making the little Indian in Yakima's head spit more arrows with a vengeance.

"You're slowin' down, Speares," the half-breed growled, smacking his lips and bringing the cuffs down to his naked hip. "I expected you hours ago."

"Was out of town chasin' rustlers till exactly two hours ago," said the sheriff of Saber Creek, Mitch Speares, his silver-blond mustache hanging long and shaggy over his mouth, obliterating his lips. His eyes were tobacco-brown, and his scarred, sun-seared face owned a self-satisfied expression. "Took me a little nap. Figured you wouldn't be goin' anywhere. Usually takes you a while to get movin' after one of your dustups."

Yakima held up the shackles. "We really need these?"

"Don't know about you, but I do."

"Mind if I get dressed first? I normally need my hands . . . less'n you wanna march me through the morning streets buck-ass naked."

"Do it." Speares flipped the Remington into its holster and stood there, one heel out, one fist on his hip, inspecting Yakima grimly as Angelina grunted and groaned and lay her head back on her pillow. "Damn it, breed, it's been so long since I last seen you, I thought you was dead."

Yakima dropped his legs to the floor and took his throbbing head in his hands. "I'm workin' on it."

"What's with the whore?" Speares asked, plucking Yakima's gun belt off a chair and draping it over his shoulder. He canted his head toward Angelina, who lay with her face turned toward them, mouth open slightly, breathing softly. Sunlight glistened across her round, firm bottom. "You already give that blonde I met the boot?"

Reaching down for his underwear, Yakima looked up at the lawman, anger burning in him. Speares must have seen the hardness in Yakima's eyes and jaws. The smile dwindled on the lawman's face, and his brows beetled. "Apaches?"

Yakima sat down on the bed and began pulling on his wash-worn longhandle bottoms. He'd told Speares, when he and the sheriff were on friendly terms, which they sometimes were, the story of how he'd rescued Faith from Thornton's roadhouse only to have the old pimp send a posse to chase them into the Rockies. How they'd gotten away, separated for a time, and gotten together again down here when Faith had needed Yakima to break her brother out of a Mexican prison.

"Our old friend in Colorado sent bounty hunters. Killed her brother. Left me in a snake pit." Yakima stared at the wall above the broken dresser, then raised his hands and pulled his long hair back from his temples. "Me and Brody Harms chased 'em all the way to Colorado, and we killed Thornton and every last one of the bounty hunters."

He chuckled dryly as he turned to the sheriff, who was staring at him stonily. "Thornton had beaten her up bad by then, and she died in my arms outside the burning roadhouse."

"Shit." Speares stared at the floor as Yakima continued dressing. "A couple prospectors in town last week told me Apaches had burned your ranch."

"That's where I was comin' from when the three dead men downstairs bushwhacked me and stole my horse."

"Sorry to hear that. I'm turnin' the key on you just the same."

"They were horse thieves, goddamn it." Yakima was pulling on his shirt. "Took my rifle and left me barefoot."

"Sorry to hear it." Speares stepped back against the door and pursed his lips, holding Yakima's rifle in one hand across his chest. "I'm takin' you in, Yakima, because if I don't turn the key on you after your little show last night, I'm gonna lose even more respect than I've already lost. Thanks to you and all the saloons you've busted up and all the business you've given to the undertaker in the past year and a half, that's a barrelful of respect I'll never see again. The only way I'll win the next election is if nobody runs against me."

Yakima knew Speares wasn't going to change his mind. He had a stubborn streak, as Yakima had himself. Speares would hold him for a day or two, until the dead men had been buried and the blood washed out of the saloon. He wouldn't charge him with anything except breaking up the Saguaro Inn. Again.

"I hope you have the coffeepot on over at the jailhouse," he said as, sitting on the bed, he put his boots on. The swelling in his feet had gone down, but his soles still felt as though he'd walked over miles of hot coals.

"Don't forget the cuffs."

Yakima looked at the handcuffs on the bed beside Angelina's naked, wonderfully curved right hip. "You sure we need those?"

"I'm sure."

Yakima chuffed, ratcheted the cuffs around his wrists, and gained his tender feet.

Speares stepped to one side, canted his head toward the door. As Yakima turned the knob and stepped into the hall, Angelina stirred on the bed behind him, lifting her head and squinting her eyes. Her tan breasts sloped toward the sheets. "Yakima," she purred groggily, "where are you going?"

"To jail," Speares growled.

Angelina slid her narrowed eyes between the two men for a second, figuring it out. *"Sí."* She dropped her head back down on the pillow and was fast asleep again.

In the Saguaro Inn's main drinking hall, Giuseppe was down on all fours, scrubbing one of the several large bloodstains out of the puncheons with a heavy brush and a bucket of soapy water. He was the only one in the dingy, cavernous room in which the smell of tobacco and gun smoke still lingered.

As Yakima passed the man, weaving around the tables upon which chairs had been upended for sweeping, Giuseppe merely glanced at him over his shoulder, a loosely rolled quirley smoldering in one corner of his mouth. The swamper scowled, saw the half-breed's cuffed hands, grunted, and continued scrubbing.

Outside, the day was already heating up. Ranch supply wagons and riders on horseback were on the move, and a couple of dogs were fighting over a boot in the street outside the Saguaro Inn. Squinting against the sun, Yakima and Speares followed the boardwalks to the main drag. A couple of business owners, sweeping the dung and dirt and blown tumbleweeds from their boardwalks, paused in their work to regard Yakima grimly and nod approvingly at Speares.

"If I was you, Sheriff," said a well-dressed gray-haired man passing in a leather buggy, whom Yakima recognized as one of the county's prominent ranchers, "I'd put a bullet in the breed's head and give Milt Wade two bits to throw his mangy carcass in the nearest ravine." As the buggy was drawn behind Yakima and Speares by a couple of matched bays moving at a spanking trot, the rancher turned his head back to exclaim around the stogie in his big white teeth, "Save you a hell of a lot of headaches in the long run!"

With that, the rancher turned forward, flipped the reins over the bays' backs, and disappeared in a churning cloud of dust and horse manure.

"He's got a point," Speares said behind Yakima.

"I reckon I won't be invited to his daughter's wedding," Yakima said as he crossed an alley mouth and approached the intersecting main street.

As both men angled across the street toward the squat stone jailhouse fronted by a stock tank and two hitch rails and a bare patch of ground shaded by a brush arbor, Speares glanced at a lanky old gent crossing the street to his left. "Hey, Fritz, you wanna earn two bits?"

Fritz turned. He was the town's odd-jobber. He'd once owned a livery barn, but after a walloping by a half-broke Mexican mustang left him without a memory or the ability to cipher figures, the bank sold his business and Fritz took to odd-jobbing for drinking and whoring change.

"When don't I?" The man grunted. He had a face like a gnarled mesquite trunk, and his rheumy hazel eyes bespoke a preceding night not unlike Yakima's own, though likely minus the quality bed partner or even a quality bed.

Speares fished a coin out of his vest pocket and tossed it to the befuddled old man, who caught it against his chest. "Fetch three plates of huevos rancheros from Fettig's. Tell the cook to go easy on the chili peppers on one of 'em."

When Fritz had turned to shamble northward toward the café, Yakima continued toward the jailhouse. "Three orders? Generous of you, Speares, but I ain't that . . ."

Yakima tripped the metal and leather latch on the jailhouse door and strolled slowly into the room's dank shadows, frowning. At the back of the room were three jail cages. The right and middle cages were empty, their doors halfway open.

In the cage on the left stood the blond-headed dude from the previous night—the man who'd been gambling with the three thieves that Yakima had turned toes-down in a hail of hot lead.

The dude faced Yakima, looking sharp in the same outfit he'd worn last night, a crisp brown bowler perched on his head. A woman stood outside the dude's cage, half turned now toward Yakima, tears streaming down her face. She

was a full-figured blonde in a pink velvet lace-edged summer frock, with a little decorative box hat and a parasol
resting on the spool-back chair beside her.

Yakima stopped a few feet in front of the jailhouse door
and turned to Speares, who was tramping in behind him.
"Didn't know I'd have such cultivated company," the half-
breed said. "If he's wearing the cheap cologne I smelled on
him last night, you'll have to leave the door open."

"Is this the one?" the woman sniffed, glancing at the
dude. Her red lips were the epitome of bee-stung. Her eyes
were the blue of a Minnesota lake.

"That's him."

The two stood staring at Yakima as Speares crossed to
the desk, where he dumped Yakima's rifle and pistol belt.
The sheriff jerked open a desk drawer, pulled out a key
ring, and canted his head toward the middle cage. "After
you."

Yakima gave the woman a bold up-and-down, and her
hourglass figure, with creamy breasts pushing up from the
low-cut corset like giant scoops of fresh-churned ice cream,
assuaged the throbbing in his head and the cramped boots.
She had a small mole high on her right breast, near her
cleavage. Stepping through the cage door, Yakima lifted his
gaze to her eyes. They were not pleased.

"This *savage*?" she asked the dude in the cell beside
Yakima's.

The dude grinned. "That's the one, all right."

Chapter 5

Speares closed the half-breed's cell door. It rattled all the other cages. When the din died, Speares said, "Yakima Henry, meet Cleve O'Shannon. This is his lovely bride, Mrs., uh . . ."

"Ashley," the blonde sniffed.

"Mrs. Ashley O'Shannon." Speares turned the key in Yakima's door and sauntered back toward his desk. "Mr. and Mrs. O'Shannon, meet Yakima Henry."

Yakima sagged down on his cot and rested his elbows on his thighs. He was about as interested in these two—apart from how well the woman filled out her corset—as he was in the occasional ants and spiders scurrying across the jail's stone floor. He gave a grunt and swept his hair back from his forehead, trying unsuccessfully to quell the hammering pistons between his eyes.

Speares tossed his key back into his desk, kicked the door closed, and dropped into his swivel chair, making the chair squeak like a mouse caught in a trap. He loosed a long sigh and regarded the buxom blonde and her husband, both eyeing Yakima through the bars with faintly worried expressions on their faces, as though observing a strange, newly discovered kind of bobcat. The woman dabbed at her cheeks with a pink silk handkerchief.

"You wanna tell him why you're here?" Speares asked, hiking a boot on his knee, regarding the couple with a self-satisfied expression on his broad, mustached face. "Or should I?"

Yawning, Yakima leaned back on his cot, resting against the opposite barred wall. "Did I miss something? I don't know either of them from Adam's off-ox."

"They know you," Speares said. "They came to town two weeks ago, lookin' for someone to guide 'em—Mr. O'Shannon, that is—into Mexico. I told 'em their best bet was you, if you were still kickin', that was. Otherwise, they'd have to wait for old Moondog Scully to make his way up from his diggin's south of Tombstone."

"We got word that Mr. Scully had fallen on a Mojave green rattler." O'Shannon had moved over to peer through the bars. He had a long black cheroot in his beringed right hand. "Dead as a post within two hours."

"The savage ain't interested," Yakima growled. He glanced at Speares. "Where's that coffee?"

Speares got up with another squawk of his chair, blew into one of the several stone mugs on his desk, and moved to the potbellied stove in the middle of the room. A dented black pot sat on top of the stove, steam rising from its spout. Speares filled the mug and shoved it through Yakima's door.

"You haven't heard the whole story," the sheriff said, that grim, slightly mocking grin in place. "This mornin', Mr. O'Shannon tells me that he—"

"I'd like to tell the story, Sheriff." O'Shannon turned to Yakima. "What I told the sheriff this morning, to try to keep you out of jail where you would be no use to me, was that I sent the three men out to find you." O'Shannon drew deeply on his cigar, blew smoke at the ceiling, and continued with a slightly chagrined air. "If and when they found you, I instructed them to challenge you."

"Challenge me?"

"Challenge you," Speares said, standing between the two cages, looking like the cat that ate the canary.

Mrs. O'Shannon had sagged down onto the spool-back

chair, parasol in her lap, regarding Yakima now with a wary sidelong look.

O'Shannon glanced at Speares with an expression of strained tolerance, then returned his gaze to Yakima. "I wanted to know what kind of man you were, because the kind of man I need to help smuggle a hundred thousand dollars in silver ingots out of Mexico needs to be the toughest, meanest sonofabitch I can find."

Speares chuckled as he swaggered back to his chair. Yakima was eyeing the dude, O'Shannon, through the wafting cigar smoke, anger burning in his belly. Before he could respond, the door opened and Fritz came in, carrying a tray with three oilcloth-covered plates.

Speares and Fritz passed the plates through feeding slots to the two prisoners, including a mug of coffee for O'Shannon, apologizing to Mrs. O'Shannon for not ordering her a plate as well, but he was running a jail, not a hotel restaurant. Yakima sat back against the wall again, hanging his crossed legs over the edge of the cot, positioning his plate on his lap. He immediately went to work on the rich, spicy breakfast, dousing the works with the runny egg yolks.

Speares was the first to resume the conversation, eating at his desk with his back to the two cells. "Anyway," he said, obviously enjoying the entertainment, "O'Shannon figures you'll do, Yakima. So what do you say—how does foggin' the sage down Mexico way sound to ya?"

"No."

O'Shannon looked up at him from where he sat at the edge of his own cot, eating off his lap. "No? You haven't even heard the offer yet."

"Don't need to. I oughta kill you for what you did. If I'd known it was you who put those three privy rats up to leaving me barefoot thirty miles from town, I'd have killed you last night. You'd have gone first."

Ashley O'Shannon turned to Yakima, her blue eyes beseeching. "Please, Mr. Henry. It was an impetuous, indefensible move, but my husband and I are desperate. You see, Cleve's brother is trapped with the silver atop a mesa in the Sierra Madre. Jason's cut off from any chance of escape by a pack of Mexican desperadoes who are after the silver as well as my brother-in-law's woman."

Yakima and Speares stopped eating to say at nearly the same time: "Woman?"

"One of the lobos thinks Stella is *his* woman," O'Shannon said. "We can talk about that later. The gist is this—I need you to guide me to the mesa where Jason holed up with the silver when the desperadoes chased him away from our mine. It isn't that I don't know the way, but revolutionaries are running wild just now, wreaking havoc on all the known trails. They kill *norteamericanos* on sight. Alone, and only just *barely* knowing the country—Jason works the mine and I manage the books from my office in Prescott—I'd be a dead man. I need someone who can ride and shoot and isn't afraid of killing. Once we've reached the mine, I'll need you to lead me and Jason and Jason's men—about twenty or so hired guns—back out of the canyon to the Texas border."

Yakima swabbed the last of his egg yolk and beans from his plate with a tortilla wedge and popped it into his mouth.

Chewing, he stared through the bars at the blond dude and his buxom blond wife. He set his plate aside and rose slowly. Uncoiling like a panther, he moved to the other side of the cell. His broad, tan face was implacable.

As Yakima pushed his face up to within ten inches of O'Shannon's, the dude uncurled his hand from a bar of the cell wall and took one step back. A flush rose in his pink cheeks.

Yakima stared hard at the man, resisting the urge to reach through the bars and wring his neck.

Finally the half-breed said, still staring at O'Shannon, "Speares, how long I gotta sit here with this hog-walloping sharpie?"

"Ah, hell," Speares said, frowning over his shoulder as he chewed. "Why don't you take the job? I'd like nothing better than to get shed of both o' you. Because, frankly, I don't know what to do with either of you."

"Let us outta here," Yakima said.

"I arrested him for horse-stealin'."

"He didn't steal my horse." Yakima's eyes burned holes through O'Shannon's while O'Shannon's woman stared at Yakima as though at a rampaging grizzly, dropping her fragile lower jaw and drawing a slow gasp.

Speares set his silverware on his plate and turned around in his chair, holding his mug of steaming coffee in both hands. "He sent them that did. You don't wanna press charges?"

"Nope."

Yakima continued staring at O'Shannon. O'Shannon stared back at Yakima, frowning warily and sort of sidelong, frightened. O'Shannon's wife stared at Yakima, too, bee-stung lips shaping a perfect O, one hand to her bosom. Her peaches-and-cream complexion was flushed.

Speares cursed again and squawked up out of his chair. He opened his desk drawer, grabbed his keys, and tramped over toward Yakima's cell, boot heels clomping on the uneven flagstones, spurs chinging. He sighed as he stuck the key in the lock, then jerked the door open angrily. Punishing a man for killing horse thieves would be setting a bad precedent.

"All right, get outta here."

Yakima glanced at him, befuddled.

"Get outta here!" Speares yelled, stepping away from the door.

Yakima shrugged, grabbed his hat off his cot, and walked out of the cell. He shaped a half grin as he moseyed over to the desk, upon which his cartridge belt and holster were coiled, and against which his rifle was leaned. The sheriff had thought he'd rid himself of two troublemakers in one fell shot. Yakima had called Speares's bluff.

The half-breed canted his head toward O'Shannon's cell. "What about him?"

Speares went in and grabbed Yakima's empty plate, tossed it on a shelf, and returned to his chair with another angry chuff. "He's gonna stay right where he is until you leave town." He narrowed his eyes at Yakima. "You have till sundown."

Wrapping his cartridge belt around his waist and cinching it, Yakima shook his head. "Gonna need another night to rest up and earn some money for trail supplies." He had no idea where he'd head. His woman was dead, his ranch was burned, he was walking around with what felt like an Apache war lance in his gut and a fire between his eyes, and this town had obviously had its fill of him.

"Sunrise!" Speares barked, leaning forward in his chair. "Not one minute later!"

"Fair enough." Yakima picked up his Winchester and slung the Yellowboy across his shoulder as he tramped to the door. He set his hand on the latch and canted his head toward O'Shannon again, staring at him mutely through the bars of his cell door.

His deep, calm voice teemed with barely restrained, savage fury. "Gonna let him out anytime soon?"

"Not till you're clear of here. If you track him, you better track him to the next county before you kill him."

Yakima glanced again at O'Shannon staring warily at him through the bars. Then the half-breed pinched his hat brim at the woman, his face still as implacable as granite, and opened the door.

"Yakima?"

He glanced over his shoulder at the sheriff leaning back in his chair, hands entwined on his belly, a sober look on his face. "Sorry about the woman."

Yakima went out.

He spent the rest of the morning in a bathtub behind Stendahl's Tonsorial Parlor, because he didn't know what else to do with himself and he figured it would be the last bath he'd get till the next blue moon. After he'd scrubbed a month's grime from his hide, he trolled the town for a poker game, borrowed into a couple but made only enough to pay back the stake.

He'd never been a pasteboard artist, but he'd usually been able to win enough to cover a few days' worth of trail supplies. Problem tonight was he just couldn't hold the game in his head. His gut was tied in knots, and that fire between his eyes was fanned by the perpetual town noise, with whores laughing, gamblers arguing, wagons squawking, dogs barking, and the privy stench wafting on the hot, dry wind.

He considered saddling Wolf and riding out with the few beans he had in his saddlebags, but he couldn't decide which direction to drift. North, south, east, or west? He could find ten reasons for heading in each one, just as many for not. Added all up, they paralyzed him.

Several times that day, he thought he saw Faith in the crowd, and he had to restrain himself from chasing her, to steel himself to keep his knees from buckling, dropping to the boardwalk or the street or a sawdust-littered saloon floor and crying like a kid goat searching for a mother it knew had been hit by a lumber dray and was never coming back.

After supper he gave up on gambling and decided to get drunk in one of the Mexican taverns behind the large brown cathedral out in the scrub that was quickly overcoming the Mexican part of the growing gringo ranching hub. He had two stone mugs of pulque and didn't get so much drunk as numb and disinterested, as hollowed out as an old tree stump. Not even spoiling for a fight.

He watched a bloody cockfight for a few minutes, then tramped through the lamp- and torch-lit back streets, with whores beckoning from dark balconies, toward the center of town. He felt more comfortable among the Mexicans during the day, but at night a strange desperation closed down over the adobe huts, the makeshift whores' cribs, and cantinas.

There, after sundown, he became a dislocated white man. In the Anglo section he was just as out of place, but he figured he had a better chance of finding a hotel in which he wouldn't wake up the next morning with his throat cut for his tobacco pouch, though the irony of what had occurred earlier was not lost on him.

He was heading for the livery barn to sleep with his horse when he remembered that a hotel proprietor named Sam Campbell owed him for a load of split cordwood. Thus he landed a free room in the Arizona Hotel and Saloon, where he normally couldn't afford a beer and a plate of beans even if, as a half-breed, he'd have been allowed to dine and imbibe with the more respectable clientele.

Such fancy furnishings as those in his room—brocade-upholstered chairs, velvet drapes, and a wagon-sized cano-pied bed appointed with silk sheets—were to him a foreign and frivolous waste of *dineros*. He'd likely be bedding down with the snakes and scorpions for the next few months, till he landed a job with a ranch north or south of the border or wrangled a position as shotgun rider for a stage line, and the proprietor owed him, so why the hell not pretend he was Jay Gould for a night?

He'd stripped down to his summer underwear and was about to blow out the lamp on the hulking dresser when someone tapped on the door. He grabbed his stag-butted .44 from his holster, tramped to the door, and tipped his head toward the varnished panels.

Sam Campbell had probably come to inform him that the other customers had complained about the presence of an Apache on the premises and Yakima would have to bed down with his horse after all. The half-breed grinned devil-ishly as he cocked the .44.

"What do you want?"

He kept the gun down low by his thigh as a soft, sensu-ous female voice said, "Please let me in, Mr. Henry, for heaven's sakes!"

Chapter 6

Yakima recognized the voice. But why not have a little fun?

"What do you want?"

In a tone of strained patience, the voice said, "It's Ashley O'Shannon. Please let me in."

Yakima turned the key in the lock, opened the door. Mrs. O'Shannon stood in the hallway in a hooded black cape and a long, silky, midnight blue skirt that shimmered as though lightly brushed with silver and gold. Her cheeks were flushed, and her fine lips were pursed.

She glanced quickly, nervously, up and down the hall around her, then brushed past him into the room.

"To what do I owe the pleasure?" Yakima said when he'd shut the door behind her.

She stood staring at him, holding her cape closed as though she was afraid he'd rip it from her shoulders. "You're obviously a half-wild man, Mr. Henry. Probably more at home out among the Apaches and banditos than mixing with civilized folks in civilized environs. Thus you can understand how shocked I was to see you prowling these halls as I was coming up from the dining room downstairs."

"I'm dead-dog tired."

"Isn't there any way I can convince you to help my husband and me?"

"What do you have in mind?"

Offended, Ashley O'Shannon frowned and gripped the cape tighter. "I thought I'd try to entice you by telling you how much we're offering. A thousand dollars. Surely even a man like you could find a use for that kind of money."

Yakima strolled toward her. "You're right. Even I might be able to find a use for that much cash. But I'd like something else thrown in."

The frown cut deeper into Mrs. O'Shannon's forehead. "What . . . is . . . it?"

"You."

Yakima reached forward and ripped the cape away from the woman's chest. It wasn't buttoned, and she didn't have nearly as strong a grip on it as she'd been pretending. As Yakima whipped the garment onto the bed, her naked breasts jostled—full, pale, and pear-shaped. The pink nipples stood semi-erect. Under his gaze, gooseflesh rose across those delectable orbs and her belly.

She did not lift her arms to cover herself.

"You always lurk the halls with nothing on under your cape, Mrs. O'Shannon?"

She bunched her lips and raised her hand to strike him, but he caught her wrist six inches from his face and fought her arm down. He flung her straight back, and she dropped down onto the bed. She twisted around and pushed up on her elbows. A flush colored her cheeks, and her breasts rose and fell heavily as she breathed.

"You son of a bitch," she snapped.

"No games tonight." Yakima shoved his summer underwear down his thick, muscle-corded thighs and let it drop to his ankles. "This was what you came here for, wasn't it?"

She said nothing. Her throat moved as she swallowed. Her breasts swelled as they rose and fell. Her eyes dropped to his crotch, widened slightly, and scuttled back to his face.

"Wasn't it?" he repeated, louder.

"Yes."

She dropped her eyes again, shoved farther back on the bed, then reached down to unbutton the skirt at her waist, kicking off the delicate little slippers on her feet. They hit the floor with light thuds.

She shucked each side of the skirt away from her hips, so the fabric lay flat against the bed, like the covers of an open book, exposing her long, slender, coltish legs and the nap of honey-colored hair between her thighs. She lifted one leg slightly and angled the knee toward the other as she gazed up at him, her blue eyes glowing in the lamplight.

Yakima stared down at her, curling his upper lip. His desire for her grew—a raw male desire that knew only the need for release.

He moved to the edge of the bed and she scuttled slightly back, fear showing fleetingly in her eyes before the desire returned once more. As he climbed onto the bed, she spread her arms and legs for him, then, as he mounted her, she wrapped her limbs around his back.

Ashley O'Shannon moaned as he began thrusting savagely against her.

Yakima jerked his head up from his pillow. He'd had the uneasy sense of something—whether heard or felt, he wasn't sure.

But half a second later, the staghorn Colt was out of the holster hanging from the front bedpost and in his hand, its barrel aimed at the bedroom door to his right. After the hammer's click had resounded off the burgundy-papered walls, which midmorning light painted with an ethereal illumination, a woman said, "Easy, fella. No one here but me."

Belly down on the bed, Yakima swung his head to the left. Ashley O'Shannon lay on her side, facing him, her fine blond head resting on the heel of her hand, which in turn was propped up by her elbow. She was as naked as she'd been last night when Yakima had at long last crawled out from between her silky thighs damp with perspiration.

The woman's pink-nippled breasts sloped toward the twisted sheets. The windows behind her, the shutters thrown open to the din of the midmorning traffic and wafting dust, gilded the thick, rich hair piled loosely atop her head.

Yakima squinted at her. He depressed the Colt's hammer and slid the iron back into its well-oiled holster.

He rolled around to face her, smacked his lips, and sighed. "Figured you'd have left by now."

The corners of her mouth rose slightly. "I would have if I'd been able to walk." She moved her right hand from her hip, slid it across the bed. Her hand closed around him, and she blinked slowly, like a cat in the sun. "I thought maybe we could spend a little of the morning together."

"Don't think it would help your stride any." He rolled over and dropped his legs to the floor, sitting up. He hadn't drunk enough to get drunk but just enough to set up an irritating throb behind both eyes.

Wincing against the pain, he reached down, grabbed his underwear, and stood to pull it on. As he continued to dress in his worn Levi's and calico shirt, dropping the leather thong adorned with the long bone-white grizzly teeth down over his neck, he felt her eyes on him. He ignored her, because he didn't want to spend any time on her in the sane light of morning—she was married after all, and, as beautiful as she was, she wasn't Faith, and what's more, he really didn't much like her—until he turned back to the bed to grab his shell belt and holster from the front post.

She was in the same position as before, smiling faintly, her smoky eyes on him, ever so slightly pressing her feet together . . . every bit like a cat in the sun.

Yakima wrapped the belt around his waist. "You best run along if you don't want stories told about you. Even if you weren't married to that dude, I'm not too popular around here."

She hiked a shoulder. "No one knows me around here. I figure I'll sleep in. Moving on, are you?"

"Nah." As he headed for the door, Yakima checked his Colt to make sure he had five pills in the wheel and an empty chamber beneath the hammer. "Think I'll go over and see about your husband."

Ashley O'Shannon frowned. "Whatever for?"

Yakima draped his saddlebags over his shoulder and

picked up his Winchester from where it leaned against the dresser. He glanced over his shoulder at the naked pink woman on the rumpled bed. "A roll like that would convince any man. I'm gonna lead the poor cuckolded sonofabitch to Mexico."

Yakima went out. Just as he closed the door he heard the bed springs squawk and the woman intone with shrill surprise: "You *are*?"

He tramped down the papered hall, digging a canvas pouch of chopped tobacco and rolling papers from his shirt pocket. The building was silent around him, only one man— a drummer probably—yawning loudly behind one of the closed doors adorned with gilded numerals.

The half-breed smiled at the fancy numbering. He couldn't remember ever having stayed in a hotel with gold numbers on the doors. Mostly, he stayed in flophouses without much for doors at all besides woolen blankets strung from ropes, so that you could hear the rannie and the cheap whore in the other "room" so clearly they might as well be in bed with you.

He moved down the staircase, which was as wide as a livery barn, his worn boots cushioned by the two-inch-thick, wine red carpeting. The rug was so soft he kept getting his heels caught in it; he ran his hand down one of the varnished rails, preventing a fall, and struck a lucifer to life on his cartridge belt.

Crossing the saloon's broad main hall, puffing the quirley, his boots clomping dully and his spurs ringing like small copper bells, saddlebags slung over one shoulder and his Yellowboy repeater in his right hand, he attracted several sour looks from the well-heeled, derby-hatted breakfasters as well as from the two dapper Mexican waiters.

A hacendado with sweeping gray mustaches, who was attired in a gold-embroidered charro jacket, looked up from his huevos rancheros. He let his eyes catch on the rough-garbed half-breed, glanced at the two ornately dressed vaqueros around him, and shook his head, sneering.

Madre Maria, these gringos allow an Apache into their

finest establishments. America won't last another fifteen years!

Yakima stepped through the batwings, letting smoke trickle through his broad nostrils and glancing to the right along the sunlit street. He was trying to figure out when he'd decided to lead the dude into Mexico—before, during, or after the man's wife's visit?

Before, he decided, chuckling to himself.

Hours before.

The woman had wasted her time and risked her reputation, if she had one, for nothing.

O'Shannon had played a dirty trick on him, and by rights the man should be dead. But Yakima had to admit it hadn't been a half-bad distraction.

And besides helping the man who'd played the trick on him, what the hell else was he going to do? He hated cattle wrangling, and that was about all there was to do out here, unless he wanted to try his hand at rock breaking for gold again. And he wanted to do that about as much as he wanted to play wet nurse to a herd of bullet-stupid cattle and live in a bunkhouse with twenty farting, yammering, bellowing white men who would regard him as one rung up from a privy-sniffing coyote.

Besides, he felt a raking urge to put as much distance as he could between himself and that night last fall when he'd held Faith in his arms for the last time. There was no outrunning hard times and bitter memories, but only one part of his mind knew that. And Mexico was as good a place as any—better than most, in fact—for venting the white-hot fire of horror and outrage blazing just between and behind his eyes.

It could very well get him killed, but he'd never felt so unafraid of dying.

He took another deep drag off the quirley, adjusted the saddlebags on his shoulder, and tramped southward along the street's west side, wincing against the bright morning sun whenever he left the shade of the brush arbor for open ground.

The stone jailhouse came into sight on the opposite side of the street—its sun-bleached stones fairly glowing, white smoke trickling from its square chimney rimmed with black soot. Yakima stepped out from the shade of Grolsch's Barber Shop, paused to let a couple of saddle tramps and a small ranch wagon pass, then angled across the street to the jailhouse.

He sucked one more long drag from the quirley, then flicked the unraveling stub into the adobe-colored dust, where it bounced and sparked. He tripped the latch with his Yellowboy's barrel and pushed the door wide with its butt.

"Speares?"

He'd barely stepped over the threshold before the sheriff bounded up from a spool-back chair parked outside O'Shannon's jail cell, between the cell and a small wooden table on which cards and coins were scattered around two tin coffee mugs. With five pasteboards fanned out in one hand, Speares wheeled and unholstered his long-barreled Remy with the other, thumbing the hammer back with a loud ratcheting click. He held the gun out from his waist and narrowed his steely eyes.

"Oh, no, you don't, goddamn it!" the sheriff snapped while O'Shannon, sitting on a chair inside the cell, peered through the bars at Yakima. "I told you to get outta town, Henry!"

Yakima held up his hands, palms out. "Pull your horns in, Sheriff. I'm not here to ventilate the man."

Speares blinked and cocked his head to one side. "You're not?"

"I'm here to accept his offer. I'm gonna throw in."

"You are?" Speares and the dude said at nearly the same time.

Yakima shrugged. "I got to thinking, after I soaked in a tub and rested up, that I don't have nothing else to do. Always was sorta fond of Mexico, in spite of all the scrapes I been in down south of the border. And I could damn sure use the money." He stared at O'Shannon staring incredulously back at him through the cell door. "We're gonna have to come to an agreement on terms, but if they sound right, I'll go."

The blond, blue-eyed gambler brightened as he slowly gained his feet, holding his own cards in his right hand, a fat stogie in the other.

"Hold on," Speares growled, keeping his head cocked to one side as he strolled slowly toward Yakima. He gave a wolfish grin that dimpled his cheeks on either side of his sandy-colored soup-strainer mustache. "I think you're lyin'."

"I ain't lyin', Speares."

"I don't believe you."

Yakima frowned.

"I think you're concoctin' to pull ol' Cleve here outta his cell, haul him out in the dry beyond the town, put a bullet in his head, and leave him for the coyotes." Speares glanced over his shoulder at the gambler, who was twitching his cheek with mild chagrin. "Hell, after the stunt he pulled, I can't say as I'd blame you. But I'm not gonna allow it."

"You know me better than that," Yakima said. "If I wanted him dead, he'd be dead. Let him out. We gotta discuss terms, and then we'll be ridin' outta here and leave you alone." Yakima chuffed as he slid his glance between the sheriff and the gambler. "Cleve, is it? You two become friendly."

"Only because he won sixty-three dollars off me since sundown last night," O'Shannon groused through the bars. "Never met a sheriff so good at the pasteboards."

"Speares hasn't always been a sheriff," Yakima said snidely. "Speares here has been a lot of things."

His face flushing, Speares dropped his cards down by his side but kept his Remy aimed at Yakima's belly. "What do you mean by that?"

"Let him out, Speares," Yakima said impatiently. "If it gets much later, we're gonna have to spend the night here in town again and start fresh in the morning. And I know you don't want that. Remember, you're up for reelection soon."

"All right, all right."

Speares dropped his revolver into its holster and dug the key ring out of the desk. "But if you kill the sonofabitch, you better do it a good long ways from town, and you better bury him good and deep."

He turned the key in the lock and swung the door wide with a loud chirp of rusty hinges. "If I get a whiff of it, I'm comin' after you, and I'll hang you out there on the main drag for the whole town to see. Give myself some job security."

O'Shannon dropped his cards on the table, rose, and grabbed his bowler off his cot. "I appreciate your concern for my welfare, Sheriff."

"Anytime." Speares plucked his coffee cup from the table and sauntered over to the percolator chugging atop the potbellied stove. "Your gun belt and that wicked little pigsticker are in the top drawer of the filing cabinet. Take 'em and both of you go."

O'Shannon moved to the file cabinet standing against the wall opposite the desk, left of the hanging gun rack in which two old Springfield rifles, a Henry, and a double-barreled shotgun were chained.

"You had breakfast yet?" the gambler asked Yakima.

"You're buying."

"With what?" the gambler said, cinching his gun belt around his waist and regarding the sheriff wryly. "Pocket lint?"

Speares stood near the stove, lazily holding his coffee cup, his hat shoved back on his shaggy head, his snakelike eyes slanting as he grinned with satisfaction. "You fellas have you a good time down in Mexico. Don't let the banditos, Indios, federales, rurales, or revolutionarios get you, now, hear?"

"We'll send you some chili peppers," Yakima said, turning toward the door.

He stopped suddenly as none other than Ashley O'Shannon stepped up between the hitch rails, heading toward him but looking down as she held her skirts above her ankles. When she looked up and saw Yakima in front of her, she stopped as abruptly as Yakima had and sucked in a startled breath.

"Oh!"

"Ashley," O'Shannon said, stepping up beside Yakima and carefully adjusting his bowler so it sat at a rakish angle over one eye. "Good news. The half-breed here—I mean, Mr. Henry," the gambler corrected, flushing slightly—"has agreed to guide me back to the mine."

The pretty woman's eyes flicked to Yakima, then back to her husband, her cheeks coloring slightly as she gave her walnut-handled pink parasol a nervous, wild spin. "Oh, you don't say!"

She flicked her eyes between the men once more, and, judging by the heat in his head, Yakima figured his face was probably as red as hers, though likely less conspicuous beneath his natural tan.

"So, anyway, I'm free," O'Shannon said, then leaned over to peck his wife on her rosy cheek. "We're going to have breakfast and discuss the nuts and bolts of the venture. Why don't you go on back to the hotel and lie down for a while, pet?" He continued frowning back at his wife as he stepped out from beneath the jailhouse's brush arbor and started into the street. "You look as though you didn't sleep well."

Yakima smiled at the woman as he stepped around her. She glanced at him again, then quickly, sheepishly, lowered her eyes and continued to nervously spin her parasol over her shoulder.

As Yakima started off after the gambler, he thought he heard Speares chuckling in the jailhouse behind him.

Chapter 7

"On paper, it's a fairly simple proposition," Cleve O'Shannon said as he cut into his thick, bloodred steak, upon which he'd carefully placed one egg, sunny-side up.

He was meticulously cutting around the edges of the yolk, apparently saving the yellow center until after he'd finished the white.

"We ride into the Sierra Madres, to a formation called Mesa de Almas Perdidas—Mesa of Lost Souls. It's on the border between Sonora and Chihuahua. Big tabletop sonofabitch. We'll see it from fifty miles away. That's where my brother holed up with the silver when he was chased away from his mine."

O'Shannon chewed, swallowed, and frowning down at his plate, added with an offhand air, "I have a sizable interest in the mine, so I guess you could say it's our mine—Jason's and mine. Anyway . . . as I told you before, Jason's being pinned down by a party of Mexican cutthroats who want the mine—and all the silver Jason's smelted and poured into a hundred thousand dollars' worth of ingots—for themselves.

"You and I will sneak back to the mesa, atop of which sits an old Jesuit church, and help Jason get the silver off the mesa and across the rough desert country to Texas. We have a bank in El Paso waiting for it.

"Most of Jason's men are Mexican roughnecks. Their leader was wounded in one of the attacks, and without a firm hand to guide them, they're like a pack of rabid lobos. That's where you come in. You'll lead them and guide us off the mesa and back to Texas."

The dude glanced across the rough wooden table at Yakima, frowning as the half-breed continued to eat his beans, eggs, and medium-well steak without having once looked up during O'Shannon's entire sermon.

With an annoyed, perplexed air, the dude carved another piece of egg white and steak, forked it, and stopped it half-way to his mouth, giving Yakima another glance over the top of it.

"How I found out that Jason and his men were pinned down was through a courier. A half-Apache desert rat named Gabriel Dumas. Some French blood, I guess. Anyway, Dumas found a way off the mesa and past the revolutionaries surrounding it, and literally shot his way out of Mexico. When he arrived at my dwelling in Prescott, he was half-dead. The poor soul barely spoke a lick of English, but he came bearing a letter from Jason, explaining the situation.

"That was two weeks ago. Jason believes he and his men—about twenty when he wrote, cut down from thirty originally—have about three months' worth of provisions and ammunition. There's a well up there, and the church's padre raises goats and a garden. The walls of the mesa are fairly steep and exposed, so there's only one way in and one way out—a narrow saddle rising gradually from the desert below. Jason has enough men, ammunition, and food to hold the top of the mesa for a time, but he can't hold it forever. Time is of the essence."

O'Shannon shoved the forkful of egg white and meat into his mouth and narrowed an eye at Yakima, who swabbed beans up with a warm tortilla and, true to the course of their breakfast, did not look up at the gambler.

"Are you hearing what I'm saying, or are you in some sort of trancelike state?"

Yakima swallowed and nodded and cut off another hunk of steak. "I heard."

"What do you think about all this?"

"Sounds good to me."

"You haven't asked a single question."

"Like you said," Yakima said, chewing and finally shuttling his gaze up from his plate to the gambler's piqued eyes, "it's a fairly simple proposition."

"On paper. On the trail it's going to be fairly dangerous. Like I said—"

"Plenty of Injuns, *revolutionarios*, and banditos out there," Yakima finished for the man, nodding and continuing to shovel food into his mouth. It was likely the last big meal he'd have in a long while, and he was going to take full advantage since the gambler was buying. "I been down there before. Seen the Mexican elephant, you could say. Danced with a few revolutionaries and even some rurales. Hell of a dustup, but I made it. I'm not a leader of men, but if there's a way down from the mesa"—he nodded speculatively— "I'll find it."

O'Shannon was chewing. "What about money?"

"What about it?"

O'Shannon continued to chew and study Yakima, sizing him up. He swallowed and took a deep breath, pursing his lips. "I'm prepared to pay you one thousand dollars after we've reached El Paso in one piece . . . with every ounce of the silver."

"All right."

O'Shannon looked as though he'd been smacked on the back of his head. *"All right?"*

Yakima stopped eating and looked up, crumpling his brow with incredulity. "Ain't it?"

"Well, hell . . . it's fine with me. But don't you want to dicker a little?"

Yakima shoved the last of his meat into his mouth and, chewing, said, "How much are you willing to pay?"

Chuckling, O'Shannon said, "I was prepared to raise my offer to two thousand."

"Okay, I'll take two thousand. Full payment due when we reach El Paso in one piece." Yakima set down his fork and leaned forward to swab his plate with the last scrap of tortilla, then said with his mouth full, "Won't have any use for money before then, anyway, since you'll be paying for all the trail supplies."

O'Shannon narrowed an eye at him, staring at him suspiciously for about fifteen seconds, his fork hovering between his plate and his mouth. His plump pink, even-featured face owned a day's growth of blond beard stubble. "You aren't . . . uh . . . planning on killing me as soon as we get out into the desert, are you?"

"Nope."

"That's it, isn't it?" O'Shannon smiled knowingly. "That's why you're so uninterested in the details of the trek. You don't even plan on taking it." He leaned forward over his fork and gave Yakima a level stare. "I might look like a copper-riveted fool fresh out of his father's drawing room or some Maryland boarding school, but I warn you, mister, I've been to West Point. I've fought Indians up in Dakota Territory. I can handle myself pretty damn well."

"I don't doubt you can," Yakima said. There was, indeed, something about the dude that wasn't entirely dudish. It was in the way he carried himself—assured without being cocky like so many of his station—and the level look in his eyes.

If the man hadn't sicced the three cutthroats on him, Yakima would have felt ashamed for diddling his wife.

"Now," O'Shannon said, running his blue-eyed gaze across the half-breed's thick, muscular neck and broad shoulders that tapered into well-rounded arms, "you might be stronger and more desert-savvy, but if you try to kill me, you'll have a fight on your hands. Unless you're a back-shooter. And I don't take you for a backshooter."

Yakima leaned across the table, crinkling his eyes at the corners. "Like I told Speares, if I wanted you dead, you'd be dead. And if I still wanted to kill you, I wouldn't accept the job. Now, why don't you finish your breakfast so we can go rustle up some pack mules and supplies and hit the trail before we have to wait till tomorrow?"

With that, Yakima rose from his chair, set his battered hat on his head, and shouldered his rifle. When he'd grabbed his saddlebags, he swung around and tramped through the dingy little eatery toward the open, brightly lit front door.

"Hold on," O'Shannon said, quickly but delicately sliding his fork under his egg yolk, which now sat alone on his plate, so the yolk wouldn't break.

He'd raised it to within three inches of his mouth when the yolk, which wasn't quite centered on the fork, slid over the edge, hit the plate, and burst.

"Now look what you made me do!"

Once outside the eatery, Yakima and Cleve O'Shannon split up, O'Shannon heading for the mercantile to purchase trail supplies and Yakima branching toward the livery barn to spring Wolf and to buy a horse for O'Shannon. He was also going to pick out a good pack animal to haul the supplies they would need for their two-week trip to the Mesa of Lost Souls.

Damn, that had a fitting ring to it . . .

When Yakima had accomplished his own task, he rode Wolf toward the south end of town, trailing O'Shannon's mount and a big, rangy mule, upon which he'd strapped a wooden pack frame and canvas panniers. He pulled up to the mercantile to see O'Shannon outside on the loading dock, smoking one of his ubiquitous black cheroots and kneeling beside the small mound of merchandise he'd obviously purchased and which he was tallying up with the mercantile proprietor, Frank Padilla, who was scribbling figures on a notepad.

"That comes to forty-three dollars and sixty-two cents," the proprietor said around the cornhusk cigarette clamped between his permanently tobacco-stained lips. Padilla's three-legged calico cat was rubbing up against his leg and humping its back at Yakima's approaching mounts and pack mule.

As the gambler and Padilla settled up, Yakima inspected

the supplies mounded on the mercantile's dock, pleased as
well as surprised that the man hadn't made the rube's mistake of overbuying for the trail. In fact, O'Shannon hadn't
bought more than Yakima himself would have bought—
aside from the expensive black cigars, shiny new Henry
repeater, and a sheathed knife forged in the bowie style.

When they'd packed the coffee, jerky, side-pork, ammunition, and other possibles into the panniers, which didn't
take them much over five minutes, O'Shannon scooped the
new Henry off the dock, opened the breech, and peered
inside.

"What do you think?" the gambler asked, hefting the
piece in his hands.

Yakima stepped into his saddle. "Personally, I prefer my
Yellowboy. Your Henry fires sixteen rounds but it'll jam on
you, and a slingshot is more accurate."

"Personally, I prefer the Henry." O'Shannon closed the
sixteen-shooter's breech and slid the rifle into his saddle
boot, glancing at the half-breed's oiled Winchester stock
jutting from Yakima's saddle boot under his right thigh. "I
saw your weapon last night, while you were using it on my
men." The gambler chuckled. "A mighty impressive piece.
The receiver's engraved, if I remember. Mind me asking
where you got it?"

"A friend," Yakima grunted, reining Wolf away from the
loading dock. He didn't care to reminisce just now about
George or anyone else in his bloody past. "We're burning
daylight . . ."

"Just one more stop," O'Shannon said. "I have to tell my
wife good-bye and make sure she has passage to El Paso."

"You're sending her on the stage alone?" Yakima asked
incredulously as they gigged their horses northward along
the dusty main street, threading around a couple of hay
carts pushed by bare-chested young peons in ratty straw
sombreros.

"She may not look like it," O'Shannon said, patting his
new horse's right wither and twisting around to admire the

roan's muscular hindquarters, "but Ashley can take care of herself."

Yakima chuffed to himself as he angled Wolf toward one of the hitch rails fronting the sprawling, gaudy Arizona Hotel and Saloon. "Oh, I reckon she can . . ."

As O'Shannon stepped down from his saddle, Yakima heard a familiar woman's voice say from above, "Cleve, what on earth . . . ? You're not leaving *already*, are you?"

Ashley O'Shannon peered out the open shutters of her second-story window, frowning, her silky hair hanging in golden swirls around her delicate shoulders, which were clad in a gauzy cream-colored wrap.

O'Shannon stopped beside his horse, squinting against the midmorning sun as he gazed up at his fetching wife. "My guide is not a man for lingering, pet. Which suits me. The sooner we can get to Jason, the better. I'll be right up."

O'Shannon mounted the hotel's covered porch and pushed through the mahogany batwings. Blushing down from her window at Yakima, Ashley O'Shannon gave a tentative wave, sliding her open palm stiffly to one side.

Yakima snorted and fidgeted around in his saddle, grinding his molars. Last night he'd merely used the woman, as she'd used him. This morning he had no time for her. In fact, her synthetic beauty repelled him. He turned to squint southward, where the dun and lime green chaparral rolled off under the brassy heat haze toward Old Mexico.

What a relief it would be to drift deep into that fabled, sinister land. He had the half-formed notion that he could somehow lose himself there, along with his haunted past, and his misery . . .

He was glad when he heard O'Shannon's voice in the room above. Mrs. O'Shannon turned away from the window and disappeared into the room's shadows. Yakima could hear them up there, conversing in soft tones, though he couldn't make out what they were saying. He waited, bored and impatient, until Ashley appeared in the window once more, smirking.

"Good luck." The woman glanced furtively over her shoulder, then turned back to Yakima, holding her hand to the side of her red-lipped mouth as she said, "I'll be waiting in El Paso."

With that, she winked and drew the window shutters closed with a soft thud and a click of the inside latch.

Yakima grunted, scowling, and turned to regard two little boys chasing a goat across a nearby intersection. He was glad to hear O'Shannon's spanking stride echoing from within the hotel's main saloon hall. The man surfaced from the shadows, pushed out the batwing doors, and crossed the porch with a brown leather war bag in his right hand and matching monogrammed saddlebags draped over his left shoulder.

While upstairs, he'd changed clothes. Instead of the gaudy gambler's attire complete with pinky ring and paisley vest, he now wore far more sensible trail duds, including a cream slouch hat, red neckerchief, pinto vest, and brown whipcord trousers, the cuffs of which were stuffed inside his high-topped, low-heeled cavalry boots. Though recently polished and shined, the boots had obviously seen some wear.

"Ready," he said, throwing his saddlebags over the rump of his roan and quickly tying his bedroll behind his saddle. Toeing a stirrup and pulling himself into the hurricane deck, he glanced at Yakima, showing a full set of glistening white teeth through his perpetual annoying grin. "Let's head to Mexico."

Why did he have to act so damn peppy?

"'Bout time," Yakima growled as he heeled Wolf into a westward gallop.

Chapter 8

Yakima and Cleve O'Shannon pushed their horses and the pack mule hard the rest of the first day.

They fogged the chaparral, heading due south between two bald, craggy sierras that shifted back and forth along both sides of the old smugglers' trail they were following. The sun-blasted and -bleached rock formations changed shape and dimension as the molten, brassy sun passed over them, shunting liquid shadows this way and that, delineating their varied aspects so that from hour to hour the jagged crests and runneled, boulder-strewn slopes acquired the aspect of different sierras altogether.

When they'd passed between both ranges, Yakima knew from having traveled this way several times in the past—the last time with Faith and her brother—that they were nearly in Mexico.

At eight o'clock that night, they stopped in a dry wash sheathed in mesquites and a few gnarled cottonwoods, with a church-sized boulder giving protection from the southeast. As they were still in relatively safe country, with the Apaches holed up farther south and west and banditos prowling closer to the international line, Yakima shot a couple of big jackrabbits for supper.

He and O'Shannon ate hungrily, washing the sinewy but tasty meat down with hot black coffee. O'Shannon's attempts at conversation were largely ignored by the taciturn half-breed, who found the man's sunny disposition and

loquaciousness especially bothersome in light of his own
burning emptiness.

Yakima was here to do a job, and that's all he wanted.
He didn't want conversation. He neither wanted nor needed
any feeling of friendship or camaraderie. He really cared
very little about the job, in fact, so he felt no need to inquire
about the many as yet unexplained aspects of it.

His job as guide and pack leader was merely something
for him to do while trying to vent the raging fire burning
deep in the hollows of his soul, to quell the unquellable
sorrow and loss that followed him like mad, yellow-toothed
warlocks nipping at his heels, allowing him no surcease
even in sleep or, like last night, between a woman's legs.

Except as a way to pad his and Wolf's bellies regularly,
and to keep his weapons filled with ammunition, he didn't
even care about the money. What the hell would he do with
two thousand dollars? Retire and move to Monterrey and
buy a fishing boat?

After supper he and O'Shannon checked on their horses,
evacuated their bladders, rolled up in their soogans, and
slept, relying on their horses to stand watch over the bivouac. Yakima woke a few hours later and prodded the gambler with his boot toe.

"Up and at 'em. We're burnin' moonlight."

O'Shannon snapped his arm down from his forehead
and lifted his head from his saddle with a start, glancing at
the moonlit night-black sky. He stared up at Yakima in disbelief. "It's not even dawn!"

"That's right." Yakima knelt to roll his soogan. "We
travel at night, sleep during the day. We're damn near to
Mexico. We travel when the desert's cooler and the cutthroats are holed up in their lairs."

Yakima tied his bedroll, grabbed his sheathed Yellowboy, and strode off to where the horses were nickering
among the moon-pearled mesquites and cottonwoods.

Fifteen minutes later, they were both saddled and riding
through the eerie, shadowy, opalescent nightscape, the air
velvet soft and fresh in their faces. The night was so quiet

that their hoof clomps seemed to resound off distant, un-
seen ridges, and the yammers of coyotes and wolves seemed
to float straight down from the moon, filling all of Mexico
and Arizona.

Sage, piñon, and Sonoran wildflowers perfumed the
breeze with their unmistakable musk, while saguaros
stood with their black arms lifted as though in perpetual
surrender.

Over the next several days, they saw no one except a
couple of distant, slow-riding cow waddies and a lone prospector dry-panning a wash near a formation called Finger
Rock. They were close enough to the old desert rat that
they could hear the man talking to himself in low tones as
he inspected a horse blanket he'd likely laid over the wash
the night before, to attract gold dust from the chill rocks
and gravel of the streambed.

But if the prospector heard Yakima and O'Shannon's
horses, he didn't let on. He continued to inspect the striped
wool blanket as though for loose weaves, muttering while
his gray bib-beard, fine as cotton, blew to and fro in the hot,
dry breeze.

A week's travel found the two *norteamericano* sojourn-
ers deep in rugged, canyon-gashed, sierra-stippled Sonora.
They angled gradually southeast toward the massive purple,
cloud-obscured reaches of the Sierra Madre. The Mother of
Mountains humped over the low, shadowy hills pleating
and folding around them, like massive thunderheads gathering to wreak havoc on northern Mexico.

Every day they stopped traveling around ten in the
morning and slept, kept watch, and tended their horses over
the course of the long, hot, wind-seared afternoons.

During their sixth night of travel, with the moon a
thumbnail careening behind velvety black northwestern
ridges, they stopped around four a.m. to blow their horses
and to fill their canteens from a rock tank at the southern
end of what had seemed an endless, barren playa—the
bleached remains of an inland lake.

The night was cool at this higher altitude, and they'd

donned their coats—Yakima, a sheepskin vest and O'Shannon, a corduroy duster with a fox collar.

"Let's have some coffee," the gambler said with a weary air.

He was a good horseman, and Yakima was surprised by his stamina, but over the past twenty-four hours he'd sunk lower and lower in his saddle. The two blue eyes staring out of his blistered sun- and windburned face weren't nearly as bright as when the men had started out. Yakima wasn't complaining; it made O'Shannon less talky and grating.

"Go ahead," the half-breed said, slipping the bridle bit from Wolf's mouth under a willow bush. "I'm gonna take a walk over those hills yonder. I thought I heard a hoof clomp a while back."

"You think someone's trailing us?" O'Shannon asked, dabbing at his chapped cheeks with a moist handkerchief.

"Don't know. That's why I'm going to take a look around."

As Yakima shucked his Winchester and stepped out away from the horses, O'Shannon slung his canteen over his saddle horn and said with an ironic wheeze, "Been nice chatting with you."

Yakima looked around at the cracked white ground and the boulders piled around the shore of the lake bed. The rocks, too, shone ominously pale in the starlit darkness. He traced a jagged gap through the boulders, heading south of the playa. The cool breeze made the Spanish bayonet plants rub together with sounds that unnervingly resembled gun hammers clicking to full cock.

Off in the massive jumble of strewn stone, a lone owl hooted. At least, it sounded like an owl . . .

Yakima moved into a high-walled corridor of jagged rock, setting each foot down softly, looking around and listening. His many years alone on the frontier had honed his senses to a fine edge, so that he could hear not only the yodel of a distant coyote but the stone the animal loosed from the scarp it was perched on.

He climbed a low boulder that gave him a good view of

the night-shrouded southwest and hunkered there on his haunches, unmoving, swinging his head slowly from left to right and back again. When he was about to start down from the rock, satisfied that he and O'Shannon were alone out here, two quick pistol shots rent the silence.

A third shot followed, the muffled crack echoing off the jumbled stones.

"Henry!" O'Shannon shouted.

Yakima pushed himself up and leapt off the boulder, landing bent-kneed. Heart thudding, holding the Winchester in both hands across his chest, he sprinted back the way he'd come.

A low fire flickered along the playa, where he'd left O'Shannon. Beyond the fire was only the willow shrub. Both horses and the pack mule were gone.

An icy knife ran up along Yakima's spine as he ran back, following the tracks of the horses and the mule—two sets now, one coming, one returning at a gallop.

A figure appeared out of the darkness just ahead.

Yakima stopped.

"They took the horses!" O'Shannon's boots made thumping, cracking sounds on the playa hardpan.

"Who?"

The gambler stopped in front of Yakima and bent at the waist to catch his breath. Smoke curled from the maw of the revolver in his hand. "I didn't see them. I was gathering more wood. When I returned to the fire, the horses and the mule were gone."

"You let 'em sneak up on you?"

Yakima couldn't see the gambler's face clearly in the darkness, but he sensed the man's chagrin. "Are we going to stand here and argue or go after them?"

"Get your rifle."

"It's on my horse," O'Shannon muttered through a weary sigh.

Yakima brushed past the gambler and started jogging along the edge of the playa, following the tracks of seven shod horses—Yakima's and O'Shannon's own mounts and those of the three thieves leading them. He could hear O'Shannon following, breathing hard from the altitude. They were probably at around seven thousand feet and would be rising higher . . . if they ever got their horses and mule back.

Jogging, following the tracks as they swung west of the playa over a low hill, then angled straight south, Yakima cursed his lousy luck. Horse thieves were the bane of his existence. As much as he wanted to believe otherwise, he was as much to blame for this current debacle as the gambler was. Somehow he'd let himself be tricked into believing they were circling around him from the south.

"Jesus," O'Shannon rasped behind him, after Yakima had jogged for nearly twenty minutes. "I gotta . . . rest . . . or I'm . . . gonna have . . . heart stroke."

Yakima stopped then. He was feeling the altitude as well. Leaning on his rifle, he knelt over the tracks etched in the sand and gravel, meandering around creosote shrubs and patches of buckbrush, disappearing in cedar thickets only to reappear on the other side.

He tried to suppress his own anxiety, but it burned at him anyway. Judging by how easily they snuck up on the bivouac so that even Wolf hadn't whinnied an alarm, the bandits were likely professionals. If Yakima lost their tracks and couldn't run them down, he and O'Shannon were dead men.

Their bones would merely be added to those of the myriad other fools who'd ventured too far south of the Mexican border.

He heaved himself to his feet, which still hadn't fully recovered from his long walk to Saber Creek, and began hoofing it forward toward the long swell of rolling, rocky, chaparral-bristling hills. O'Shannon muttered a curse behind him as the gambler started walking as well.

"I guess we should look on the bright side," he said.

Yakima glanced over his shoulder.

"At least they're going in roughly the same direction as we are."

Yakima turned his head forward and started jogging.

"All right," O'Shannon said wryly behind him. "I'll shut up."

The whitewashed adobe-brick casa sat in a hollow sheathed in craggy ridges that shone like molten iron in the mid-morning sun.

It was a long, low, L-shaped affair, with a red-tile roof and smoke unraveling from a broad brick chimney. A floury white two-track trail snaked past the place—obviously a roadhouse, as guitar strains and occasional female laughter sounded from inside—and on the other side of the trail were a small, straw-roofed stable and two rickety corrals built of skinned cottonwood poles. Ten or so horses milled around inside one of the corrals, including a blaze-faced black stallion, a roan, and a bulky dun mule.

"You sure they're ours?" O'Shannon asked.

He and Yakima were crouched atop a rocky hill, staring down toward the roadhouse's brushy, boulder-strewn backyard.

Yakima's field glasses were in his saddlebags, which the bandits had robbed when they'd made off with Wolf. But he could recognize the clean-lined, blaze-faced black stallion from half a mile away. "They're ours." He spit dust from his lips and continued squinting around the barrel of his Yellowboy, held butt down before him. "And we're about to get them back."

Chapter 9

Yakima started to rise. O'Shannon grabbed his arm, frowning. His face was peeling from the sun and wind they'd endured on their five-hour walk after the horse thieves.

"What should I do?"

Yakima's feet were blistering inside his boots. He, too, was sun-seared, tired, thirsty, and hungry. What's more, he felt like a copper-riveted fool for having let the thieves sneak up on him, even though the gambler was supposed to have been watching their flank.

He jerked his arm free of the blond man's grasp. "Just stay out of my way."

He started down the far side of the hill, crouching over his Winchester and meandering around yucca plants and large rocks. A diamondback hissed to his right and struck, but Yakima held steady on his downhill course, only curling his upper lip at the rattling viper, which lifted its head again, tightly coiled and seemingly confounded by its miss.

As Yakima gained the bottom of the hill and approached the cabin's rear, a thud sounded straight ahead. He dove behind an overturned hay cart. Then, gaining a knee but keeping his head low, he peered around the cart toward the cabin's back wall as the rear door opened with a raspy bark.

A man stepped out. Tall, and wearing a curly beard the same dark red as his hair, a sombrero hanging down his back from a thong around his neck, he stopped outside the open door, from which the louder strains of the guitar and women's laughter emanated. So did the smell of roasting meat and tortillas fried in liberal amounts of lard.

Yakima's mouth watered and his stomach contracted at the aromas. He watched the curly-haired man stagger slightly as he turned to one side, looked straight down his chest, bent his knees a bit, and began fumbling with his fly buttons. He wore silver-trimmed, red-stitched charro slacks that fit him tightly across the thighs but whose billowing cuffs all but hid his silver-toed black boots. The slacks were dusty with several good hours of trail riding, and his hair was dusty, seed-peppered, and sweaty.

The man wore three pistols, two in a stylish cross-draw rig, the other—an attractive pearl-gripped piece—in a shoulder holster adorned with a large gold medallion.

A well-packed trail snaked out to a roofless privy on Yakima's right, but judging by the lime green galleta grass growing in a single oval-shaped patch among the rocks near where the Mexican stood, the privy saw little use.

Yakima had doffed his hat. Now he looked around the hay cart's left side. The man had his dong out, and he was loosing an arc of dark yellow urine into the grass. He whistled softly, drunkenly, and swiveled his head slowly.

When he'd turned his head toward the hill down which Yakima had come, he froze. Still peeing, he frowned, his single auburn brow forming a V over his freckled nose.

Yakima turned to look at the hill, and he winced. Apparently O'Shannon had started to follow him down the hill. When the Mexican had come out of the roadhouse, the gambler was trapped with no near cover. He crouched there now, on one knee, his revolver in his hand, chapped lips stretched back from his white teeth in chagrin.

Yakima turned back to the Mexican, whose piss stream was dying and whose expression had grown even more severe. Suddenly, before he'd stopped pissing, he shuffled around and squared his shoulders at the hill. His right hand began sliding across his belly toward the walnut-gripped revolver in the holster on his left hip.

Yakima rose from behind the hay cart and snapped the Yellowboy to his shoulder as he cocked it. Dust puffed from the man's leather vest as the Winchester's whip crack drowned his exclamation and punched a hole through his breastbone. He bounded straight back off his heels and slammed his head and shoulders against the wall of the roadhouse, to the left of the door.

Yakima winced as he heaved himself to his swollen feet and sprinted across the backyard toward the open back door from which the guitar strains and laughter suddenly died.

The Mexican continued to stand against the back wall, holding both hands over the hole in his chest, frothy blood bubbling up between his fingers. His jaw hung slack, and he turned his head to regard Yakima with wide red-brown eyes that owned an exasperated, horrified cast.

"So long, amigo," Yakima rasped as he ran past the dying man through the back door.

He stopped just inside the door and took a quick look around at the rickety wooden tables scattered before him in smoky morning shadows relieved by buttery light emanating from the dusty front windows. A bar stretched across the room to his right, with a stairway flanking it. An open second-floor balcony ran around the room.

A beefy Mexican in a greasy apron stood behind the bar, his fists atop the ancient bar, scowling at Yakima. Three Mexicans stood with their bellies against the bar, heads turned toward the sudden intruder. Each wore several guns and at least one knife in various positions, and similar expressions as the aproned bartender.

Glowering, indignant leers.

There were about five men at the tables, and another man stood in the middle of the room with a guitar in his arms. The guitar player was frozen in place, frowning. Excluding the bartender, he looked like all the rest: banditos in dusty Mexican trail garb. Bearded or mustached, longhaired, sweaty, and savage, and with guns and knives bristling like cactus spines.

There were more banditos here than those who had stolen the horses and the mule, which meant they'd probably rendezvoused.

A young woman with coal black hair and vaguely Pima features sat on the lap of one of the men to Yakima's left, near a fire upon which a pot of beans bubbled. She wore a threadbare cotton shift down which the man's hand was stuffed, covering her small left breast. The *puta*'s jaw dropped as she ran her eyes slowly up and down Yakima's muscular, dusty, sweaty, sun-seared frame, and across the cocked Yellowboy in his big brown hands.

The corners of her mouth twitched with a building scream.

One of the five men sitting at the tables near the front, on both sides of the door, which had been propped open to the morning, muttered something in Spanish to the man sitting across from him—a bulky, round-faced Mexican with a steeple-crowned sombrero tipped back on his head. Bandoliers crisscrossed his chest.

He chuckled. The chuckle became a laugh, his heavy shoulders jerking, the cartridges on his chest winking in the light from the windows flanking him.

He glanced at the man who'd spoken to him then, and as he turned his head back to Yakima, his laughter died abruptly. Grimacing, he sprang from his chair, both hands reaching across his fat belly toward the big horse pistols sheathed on his hips.

He was faster than he looked, but Yakima shot him when he had both pistols half raised to his chest. Firing both pistols into the floor near the toes of his high-topped, mule-eared boots, he screamed and flew straight back through the open window, his sombrero-clad head disappearing first and then his knees and his boots.

His body hadn't yet thumped to the ground outside before all the other men in the room lurched to their own feet, grunting, screaming, or cursing while grabbing iron.

"NA-LOK-A!" Yakima heard the Pima girl scream to his

left a quarter second before he dropped to a knee, rammed his Yellowboy's brass butt plate against his shoulder, and started shooting.

The first three men went down like ducks on a millpond, one after another in a near-straight line, screaming, hats flying, blood spraying, one man shooting his toe off before he flew back through the unshuttered window to the right of the door. Spying the three men to his right bolt out of their own chairs, clawing iron, Yakima ran forward, dove onto the right side of a vacant table, and overturned it as he hit the floor.

Pistols roared. Bullets slammed into the table, one ripping through it and carving an icy line over Yakima's shoulder. Another bullet barked into the stone tile a foot in front of him, peppering his face with sharp shards.

He racked a fresh round into his Yellowboy's breech, rolled up onto his right shoulder, and, switching the rifle to his left hand, fired three quick rounds, the Winchester leaping and roaring in his hands, blowing up a thick, heavy cloud of fetid powder smoke. Through the smoke he watched the three banditos dance bizarrely around their table while the girl bounded away, shrieking, toward the far wall. Her top had slipped from her shoulders, and her bare brown breasts jostled and swayed, her thick black hair dancing about her shoulders.

The men screamed. Blood splashed like a tossed bucket of dark red paint. As one of the three twisted back toward the snapping fireplace, he drilled his own compadre in the mouth with his barking .44, instantly silencing his friend's shrill death shriek.

Yakima had seen a figure dash through the open front door now on his right, and he'd heard a pistol bark. Now he turned in that direction, swinging his Winchester around while ejecting a smoking brass cartridge onto the floor behind him.

"The balcony!" O'Shannon shouted, dropping to one knee just in front of the door and extending his pistol straight out and up.

The man fanned the .45's hammer, and he and the gun disappeared in a billowing cloud of smoke as the shots blasted the balcony. Yakima turned to look up at the second story, where four half-dressed men wielding pistols or rifles were dancing and spilling blood and screaming while the gambler's bullets slammed into their chests, bellies, heads.

A short, stocky man gave a grunt, bounced off the back wall near a curtained doorway, behind which a girl screamed, and slammed into the cottonwood rail at the balcony's edge. The force and weight of his body tore the rail out of its braces, and man and railing tumbled straight down through the smoky air. The stocky gent turned one complete somersault, and then the rail smashed against the floor in front of Yakima and the stocky gent hit the floor with a heavy thud and a loud groan on top of it.

His body convulsed. Blood gushed up from his beard-encircled mouth.

Meanwhile, two of the other wounded men on the balcony groaned and cursed in Spanish as they flopped around, dying. One tumbled toward the edge of the balcony screaming, "Jesus!" He reached for the rail that was no longer there and fell forward, turning one slow, limbs-akimbo somersault before he landed on his back atop the overturned table of the dead men beneath him.

His back broke across the edge of the table with an audible, sickening crack like that of a branch broken over a knee. He grunted, shook his shaggy head once, kicked his bare feet, and died.

Running footsteps and wheezing breath sounded from beyond the front door, growing louder as the runner approached the roadhouse. O'Shannon swung his head toward the door, cursed, and flipped his Colt's loading gate open. He was frantically plucking a bullet from his cartridge belt when the runner's long shadow angled across him.

Still down on his hip and shoulder, squinting through the powder smoke, Yakima tossed aside his own empty Winchester. He grabbed his staghorn .44, thumbed back the hammer, and raised the gun toward the front of the roadhouse as a tall figure burst through the door, eyes bright, two pistols raised in his gloved fists.

"Mierda!" he shouted, leveling both weapons at O'Shannon.

Yakima's Colt barked once, twice, three times. The tall man screamed, tossed both pistols over his head, and staggered back out the door and hit the porch with a wooden *thump*.

O'Shannon knelt where he'd been when the tall man had run in. The gambler's hands quickly, expertly continued filling his revolver with fresh loads. He flicked the loading gate closed, spun the cylinder, and rose, aiming his revolver out the open door. Webs of powder smoke glowed in the sunlight.

The gambler turned his head this way and that, inspecting the tall man, whom Yakima could hear groaning outside. Then O'Shannon turned to Yakima, who pushed to his feet and looked around warily, thumbing cartridges through his Yellowboy's loading gate.

Yakima remembered the bulky bartender and swung around, levering a shell and pressing the rifle's butt against his right hip. The bartender winced and stepped back. He held his left hand to his bloody right upper arm. A sawed-off shotgun lay at an angle on the scarred surface of the bar.

"When I came in, he was about to use that boulder vaporizer to dissuade you from bothering his clientele." O'Shannon turned toward Yakima, then continued looking around warily, cocked pistol before him, in case one of the dead men came back to life.

"Obliged."

"Don't mention it."

The bartender winced as blood streamed down his hand. "They were good customers," he said. "Always paid their bills, were easier than most on my *putas*."

"Probably paid their bills with horses and mules, huh?" Yakima kicked a pistol away from a still-twitching hand. "Like those in your corral?"

The man winced again, wheezed a sigh, and clamped his hand more tightly over the wound.

Someone groaned behind Yakima. He turned to see the Pima whore climb out from beneath a dead man, grunting disgustedly and getting heavily to her feet. She looked at Yakima, her face and dress blood-splattered, then shook her black hair away from her face.

She pulled the straps of her dress up, covering her blood-speckled breasts, and looked around. She moved to her left, jerked an overturned chair to one side, and dropped to her hands and knees, quickly gathering the coins and green-backs that had spilled from the table, upon which three of the dead banditos had been playing poker.

The bartender leaned over the bar and ordered her in Spanish to leave the money, but the girl continued gathering the loot as though she hadn't heard him, raking the coins into one neat pile, the paper money into another.

On the balcony, three other girls in various stages of undress—one wearing only a pair of men's oversized boots, several beaded necklaces, and a steeple-crowned sombrero, peered down in shock at the bloody saloon below.

Yakima raked a chair out from an upright table and eased his aching body down. He kicked out another chair and set his burning feet atop it with a weary sigh.

In his cow-pen Spanish he ordered the bartender to leave the *puta* alone and to dish him up a bowl of beans.

"What are we doing?" O'Shannon said. He'd found his new Henry repeater among the ruins and was holding it up to inspect it.

"Lunchtime," Yakima growled.

Chapter 10

In a dream, Faith screamed.

Calling for her, he ran toward the scream. But the night was as dark as the bottom of a deep mine, with only occasional flickers of milky moonlight glowing on the walls of a stony corridor.

"Ya-ki-ma!"

Her sobbing, desperate plea echoed around him.

He stumbled forward, tripping over sharp upthrusts of hard rock.

"Faith!"

The night exploded with mocking laughter. It was the laughter of the roadhouse pimp, Bill Thornton. It was like the laughter he'd heard as the light had faded from Faith's eyes as he'd held her in his arms, the roadhouse in flames behind him. It was the laughter of a malevolent God.

"Don't kill her!" Yakima heard himself bellow, his voice cracking on the high notes. *"She's all I have!"*

He stumbled forward, feeling his way in the stygian blackness, as Faith's sobs dwindled into the distance along with the maniacal laughter of the man who'd killed her.

Yakima jerked his head up from his saddle. Sunlight blasting under the cover of the mesquite shrub nearly blinded him. As he lifted his hand to shield his eyes, a rattle sounded. At first he thought it was the whine of a near cicada.

His breath caught in his throat as he saw the diamondback coiled tight as a wheel hub about five feet from his right hip. Yakima froze. His heart thumped. He stared into the snake's eyes—penny-colored, tiny and flat as spent BBs.

The viper had no doubt been seeking the mesquite's shade. Now its rattling tail lifted, and its forked tongue protruded from its flat mouth to lick the air in front of its face, taking Yakima's measure by his scent on the hot breeze.

Yakima glanced up the stone scarp rising before him. O'Shannon was sitting up there, legs before him, knees bent slightly out to both sides. He held his rifle straight up and down in front of him, the butt snugged against his crotch. Shaded slightly by a single gnarled cedar pushing up from a crack in the rock, he was looking off to Yakima's left.

The man had proven himself a good shot in the Mexican roadhouse three days ago, but he wasn't good enough to shoot the snake from that distance even if he'd been facing in Yakima's direction.

The half-breed turned his attention to his sheathed pistol hanging from a branch of mesquite about three feet to his left and another three feet above the ground. As the breeze moved it gently, the sun shone on the horn handle, the oiled hammer, and the brush scars of the soft leather holster.

Too far away. He'd never make it.

Sliding his gaze in the other direction, he saw the knife sheath he normally wore behind his neck. He'd removed it to sleep and set it down near his right knee, the sweat-stained, hide-wrapped handle of the Arkansas toothpick angled toward his hip.

If the snake didn't deem the place occupied and slither off to find other shade nearby, the razor-edged blade was Yakima's best bet.

He held still, his head slightly lifted from his saddle. He suppressed his anxiety, breathing shallowly through slightly parted lips.

"Easy . . ." he silently urged the snake.

It worked. The rattling softened slightly, and the rattle itself dropped back down to the burnt orange caliche.

"There . . . that's it."

The snake pulled its head back slightly but remained coiled, and its forked tongue continued to test the air warily.

Slowly Yakima slid his right hand down along his body toward the toothpick's handle. He eased it down slowly, barely raking the coarse sand and fallen mesquite beans. Something moved in front of him, and he lifted his eyes to see a kangaroo rat poke its head out from a hole at the base of the stone scarp.

It wiggled its round ears, twitched its nose and its tail. No doubt grateful that Yakima was the one confronting the snake, it gave a little squeak and retreated back into its burrow.

The sound distracted the snake slightly, and it lifted and turned its head. Yakima took the opportunity to move his hand down past his hip a little faster. He wrapped his hand around the toothpick's slender handle. Biting the inside of his lower lip and holding his gaze steady on the snake, he eased the blade from its well-oiled sheath.

He had the knife as far as his hip when the diamondback turned its head back toward Yakima. The tiny eyes blazed fury and the rattling rose suddenly, drowning out the other desultory afternoon desert sounds.

The rattle rose in a blur, and then the head darted toward Yakima with the speed of an Apache arrow.

Yakima held the knife out two feet from his side. The snake slammed against it. The head, cleanly sliced from the neck by the razor-edged blade and propelled by its own momentum, sailed across Yakima's belly to lie snapping its jaws furiously beneath the half-breed's hanging holster while the rest of the long body flopped, writhed, and whipped against Yakima's hip, flinging sand and rocks every which way.

Yakima pushed to his feet and, holding the bloody toothpick in one hand, stretched down to try to grab the wildly writhing, headless body. It was like grasping for a landed fish that was madly seeking water. He reached for it twice, missing both times before holding it down with his boot and then grabbing it around the bloody stump and holding up the scaly, stone-colored body for inspection.

It was like holding a beating heart in his hands.

"That's a hog there," he said, relieved and satisfied as his green, flashing eyes sized up the five-foot snake that fought desperately to free itself from his grip.

It was nearly as big around as Yakima's own bulging forearm.

Still holding the snake in his hand, he walked over to his saddlebags on the ground near a small, crackling fire upon which his teapot steamed and chugged slowly. From the bags he produced his secondary knife. It was an old toothpick that would no longer keep its edge and whose handle was so dry and cracked that not even soaked rawhide could hold it together.

It was the first knife he'd acquired when he'd fled the boardinghouse he'd been sent to by a Denver City constable after his mother had died, leaving him orphaned, and he'd tried stowing away on the back of a prospector's wagon. He'd intended to light out for the Front Range of the Rockies to make his fortune panning for gold, which his German father had tried to do for years without luck.

Before sneaking under the wagon's tarp to ride among the prospector's freshly purchased possibles, the half-breed boy—caught between worlds, belonging to no one and no one belonging to him—found the knife on a dead man lying facedown in a bloody mud puddle between two whorehouses on Sixteenth Street in Denver, only a few blocks from Union Station.

Now he set the snake down beside the fire. It was still twitching as though trying to bite him without a head. The head itself had chomped down on an exposed root of the mesquite bush and had fallen still while pumping its noxious poison into the shrub.

Yakima held the body down with one knee while he used the newer knife to slice a slit lengthwise down the thick, coarse skin—a six-inch cut starting at the bloody nub from which several fishlike bones and ragged skin protruded. Then he took the older knife, pinned the loose flap of skin to a flat, bleached chunk of cottonwood, and continued lengthwise down the body, until he'd reached the tail.

He removed the rattle with a single quick slice.

Setting the good knife aside, he used his bare hands to peel the skin away from the smooth white meat. When he had the entire tube of flesh free of the skin, he draped the skin over a rock and set his stewpot of soaking pinto beans nearby. He sliced the meat crosswise into two-inch chunks, tossing every three or so chunks into the pot with the beans.

He was halfway down the snake's still improbably writhing body when he heard O'Shannon scramble down from the scarp behind him. His boots crunched gravel and his spurs trilled softly as he approached the fire.

"What do you have there?"

"Supper."

"Christ." The gambler, whose face looked as rosy as an Arizona sunset from the searing sun and blasting wind they'd encountered over their nearly two-week journey so far, sat down on a rock on the shady side of the fire ring. "How'd you land that thing?"

"With the help of a kangaroo rat and a lot of luck," Yakima said, tossing another handful of the delicate meat, which he knew from having eaten rattler on many occasions had little taste but plenty of nutrition, into the bean pot.

O'Shannon set his rifle down and leaned forward to pour himself a cup of coffee. "Haven't seen hide nor hair of anything—man or animal—in three hours. I do believe we're alone here."

"If there were Apaches around, you wouldn't know it till they came calling."

"Yeah, well, I never fought Apaches. My war was with the Sioux and Cheyenne." O'Shannon sipped the piping-hot brew as he regarded Yakima curiously. "By the way, what are you?"

"Mongrel."

O'Shannon smirked and sipped his coffee. "Where'd you learn to kill like that?"

"Like what?"

"Like . . ." O'Shannon chuckled nervously as he tipped his cup to his lips once more and stared at Yakima over the steaming rim. "Without hesitation. You even seem to enjoy it."

Thornton, Yakima thought. But that wasn't entirely true. His Chinese friend, George, had taught him to kill efficiently, but he'd never killed with such an utter lack of regret until recently. And he'd never feared being killed less, either.

He tossed the last of the meat into the bean pot, picked the pot up by its wire handle, and set it on a flat rock in the fire.

"I reckon I just learned that I'd have to kill or be killed, and the easiest way to go about killin', when you have to, is without mercy. And then I suppose you get used to it." He set a couple of knotty piñon branches on the dancing flames beside the pot. "Where'd you learn to shoot a revolver like you did at the roadhouse? West Point?"

"Barrooms," O'Shannon said. "After I figured out I had a knack for gambling and didn't have to rely on my father's monthly allowances that kept me living just above the level of a grub-line rider."

Yakima looked around, making sure the smoke from the fire hadn't drawn unwanted visitors, his eyes probing every nook and cranny among the rocks and boulders, and brush clump and shade wedge.

O'Shannon must have taken his silence for indignation, for the gambler said around his coffee cup, "I didn't mean to offend you with the question. A merciless man is what I need. A man not bound by the usual bonds of civilization is the only man who'll be able to organize and command Jason's roughnecks and lead them against the hooligans running loose down here."

Yakima was staring up the faint horse trail they'd been following southeast, his attention holding on a couple of hawks swirling low in large, lazy circles. "No offense taken." Yakima rose and grabbed his Yellowboy. "I'm gonna walk around, then go on up the scarp and keep watch. Sun's on the wane. We'll pull out as soón as we eat."

He started walking up the trail.

"Sometime tomorrow morning we should reach Don Ungaro's rancho on the Rio Sombra," O'Shannon said.

Yakima glanced back again.

"We'll spend a day there, let the horses rest. With any luck we'll be able to talk the old man out of a Gatling gun and some dynamite. He's accumulated plenty for holding off revolutionaries and Apaches over the years. That kind of firepower should up our odds a little."

"Don Sergio Ungaro?"

"You know him?"

"Nope." Yakima had only heard of him—one of the wealthiest of the Sonoran land barons, who, it was said, had acquired his hundred thousand square acres in a shady land grant deal with Spain, squeezing out its rightful owner, who had somehow offended the king.

The hacendado lived like a hidalgo in a small castle in a verdant river valley, with a veritable army at his beck and call. He ruled his kingdom with an iron fist, and it was said that his peons spoke his name in halting, fearful cadences.

So Yakima would meet the old son of a bitch. That should be interesting, anyway. As much as anything interested him these days except the constant, always challenging game of staying alive when he really didn't care if he won or lost.

"Keep an eye on the stock," he said, and continued walking up the trail through the catclaw and ironwood.

Feeling uneasy, he kept his eyes on the hawks, which had recently been joined by three large, shaggy *zopilates*—Mexican buzzards that always shadowed death.

Chapter 11

Three bodies, impeccably dressed in the attire of the Mexican landed gentry, twisted and swayed in the hot, dry breeze.

The ropes stretching their necks from a stout branch of the lone sycamore creaked and snarled beneath the barks and mewls and bizarre, frenzied chortling of the half dozen buzzards that had found the carrion and driven the hawks off to a branch of a nearby dead cottonwood, where they sat and waited in stony silence.

The buzzards had fled to higher branches of the sycamore when Yakima and Cleve O'Shannon rode up, and they quarreled and growled now, lowering their wretched bald heads to scold the interlopers with sharp disdain.

Two men and a young woman. One of the men, wearing a thin, impeccably trimmed gray beard, appeared to be in his mid- to late forties. His cheeks already bore the buzzards' gashes, and one eye was half out of its socket.

The other man was younger, early twenties. The woman was even younger—a girl still teenaged. She was fully clothed, but her crimson basque and white ruffled shirtwaist had been torn down the front, half exposing small, pale breasts, and her velvet skirts were torn and soiled.

Raped and beaten.

The men had both been beaten before all three had been hanged on the low sycamore branch, their polished black boots and the girl's calf-high patent leather shoes nearly brushing the spindly dry brush below. A weed clung to the cracked sole of her left shoe, dangling against the ground and swaying this way and that with her slack, lifeless body.

The girl stared at Yakima from beneath drooping lids. The eyes were pale yellow, not blue like Faith's. Still, a cold, invisible hand caught his innards in a clawlike grip, and he turned away to inspect the ground around the tree, which was turning purple as the sun sank behind the western peaks.

Beside him, O'Shannon held his roan's reins taut as the horse skitter-stepped and nickered, repelled by the smell of recent death.

"Merciless bastards." The gambler glanced at the red-wheeled carriage overturned in the brush about fifty yards from the hanging tree, resting against a cactus-sheathed rock, the splintered tongue angled up in the air. The pull horse had likely been taken by the murdering *revolutionarios*. "Ran down their buggy and did . . . this. Poor girl. She can't be much over seventeen."

Yakima gigged Wolf in a broad circle around the buggy, holding the apple with one hand as he leaned out from his stirrup, closely inspecting the ground. "There were a dozen of them." He sat up straight and looked around, wariness etching his dark brows. "Those bodies and these tracks are fresh. They can't be far."

O'Shannon continued staring up at the three corpses, both repelled and fascinated. "You think this man's her father?"

"Likely the *segundo*. They left 'em hanging here for her father—and the boy's father—to find them and get the message his rancho's under siege."

"We're close to Don Ungaro's spread, but I don't recognize these people."

"Come on." Yakima reined Wolf around and gigged him southward toward the green and blue hills rolling up toward shelving mesas and towering precipices of the Sierra Madre. "Let's get some miles under us."

"Like I said," O'Shannon growled behind him, gigging

his roan into a trot and taking a wary gander eastward, the direction the killers had ridden, "this is no country to trifle with."

"Who's trifling?"

"Makes me wonder if we shouldn't have brought more men," O'Shannon said as he loped his roan off Yakima's right stirrup.

"More men make more tracks and lift more dust."

"Yeah, but, Christ . . ." O'Shannon looked behind him, his blond hair lifting under his slouch hat. "A full dozen of those kill-crazy lobos ran that buggy down . . ."

"What's the matter, amigo?" Yakima curled his lip wolfishly at the man as his own long black hair blew behind him in the sage-peppered wind of early dusk. "You getting cold feet? Starting to wonder if your pa's allowance wasn't enough after all?"

A thunderous chortle sounded behind the riders—a sound as loud as the din of a Friday-night carnival crowd—and they both turned to see a ragged flock of *zopilates* swoop down over the sycamore to join the first three buzzards in a swirling, fighting, quarreling feeding frenzy.

"Yeah," O'Shannon said, turning forward, a befuddled frown on his face. "I guess you could say that. Does that make me a coward in your eyes?"

"No." Yakima shook his head. "Makes you sane."

O'Shannon glanced at him, the befuddled frown remaining. "I get the feeling you wouldn't turn back even if I did."

Yakima kept his head forward and shaped a grim smile as he urged Wolf into a ground-eating lope. They cut over a low saddle and into the broad valley beyond.

When they'd ridden hard for nearly a mile, they slowed their pace to a trot and watched the night close down over the low, rocky walls of the valley and the last dying rays of the sun paint the distant mesas in shades of rose, pink, and salmon.

Wolves howled as the stars kindled, and quail and chaparral cocks called from the sage and creosote—their last mournful cries before relinquishing the day to the desert bats and owls of the night.

"We should be on Ungaro land now," O'Shannon said around midnight, as they mounted after resting their horses for twenty minutes near a clear, cool, star-dappled stream sheathed in oaks and sycamores. "Still a long ride ahead, though."

An hour later they saw that the two men and the girl they'd come upon earlier were not the only ones to have met a grisly end in this part of Sonora. As they crossed another, narrower stream, they came upon four men in peasant garb, two wearing empty bandoliers on their chests, hung from two cottonwoods, their hands tied behind their backs, their tongues protruding and swollen. Their holsters and knife sheaths were empty.

Their clothes hung in rags from their spindly bodies, and dried blood was crusted over the deep whip slashes.

"Revolutionaries," O'Shannon said. "Probably run down by Ungaro's men."

Yakima spat to one side and reined Wolf up the stream's opposite bank and into the dark, columnar pines, where he spied a grave mounded with rocks and marked with a crude wooden cross. A small crucifix hanging from the cross glinted dully in the starlight.

Since they were within a few hours of Don Ungaro's hacienda by dawn, they continued riding, and the rising sun revealed even more carnage—five bullet-riddled peons lying dead by a hay cart, four more, including a baby and a woman, in the yard of a burned-out thatch-roofed house and barn. In addition to having been shot, the men had been beheaded, and their own bloody scythes were cast around the manure- and straw-littered yard as though dropped from the sky.

Chickens pecked at the eyes of one of the severed skulls. O'Shannon made a retching sound as he dismounted to throw a rock at the birds.

In a narrow, sun-splashed valley later that morning they found a dozen gnarled fir trees scattered across a brushy slope, each bedecked with a hanging cadaver so badly bruised and disfigured it was impossible to tell if the dead men had been revolutionaries, innocent peons caught up in the war, or the don's vaqueros. It was obviously vaqueros, however, that they came upon around noon, lying dead before the walls of an ancient, crumbling church flanked by an overgrown cemetery.

All five men wore the traditional deerskin charro trousers, red sashes, white or pin-striped shirts, and low-cut, fancily embroidered vests of the Mexican range rider. Their steeple-crowned sombreros lay around the dead men, who'd been gutted by predators and left where they'd fallen after being executed against the bullet-pocked, bloodsplashed walls of the church.

Their guns were gone, their holsters empty. The boots of two of them had been taken as well.

In the heat of midday, the sickly sweet smell of wellseasoned viscera burned even Yakima's eyes.

An hour later they picked up a well-traveled wagon road and started following it due south through a broad valley carpeted in green grass and blooming wildflowers and cactus, with a stream running along a low mesa on their right. The sun shone through high, purple, rain-swollen clouds, and the air smelled like rain.

Distant thunder rumbled, adding an even more ominous air to an already ominous, majestic, savage land.

"So far, so good," O'Shannon said as he and Yakima trotted their horses. "The hacienda is just on the other side of that rise."

"I do believe you just jinxed us," Yakima said.

O'Shannon glanced at him. "Huh?"

"Take a look."

A hundred yards ahead, four riders were moving their horses up out of a ravine perpendicular to the wagon trail—riding slowly, taking their time, all glancing over their shoulders toward Yakima and the gambler, their highstepping Arabians swishing their tails. They spread out across the trail, turned their Arabs—three duns and a cream—toward Yakima and O'Shannon, and stopped.

Sunlight shafting through the purple clouds hit them directly, winking off one man's silver-trimmed bridle, off another man's spur, off another's ivory-gripped six-gun sitting up high on his right hip.

O'Shannon muttered a curse as he and Yakima continued jogging their horses forward, the half-breed feeling a caterpillar of apprehension roll over in his gut. He held his gaze on the four men before him, sliding it around occasionally, looking for more possibly lurking in the brush along both sides of the trail.

To his right, the stream trickled through its stony bed. Wolf's and the roan's hooves clomped. Thunder rumbled. The men before him grew larger as he and O'Shannon approached, slowing their horses to a walk when they were within fifty yards and closing.

With any luck, the four would be Don Ungaro's riders, as they were on the Ungaro hacienda. But something in the malignant stares of the four—three Mexicans and one who looked Americano, though he wore the stylish garb of the Mexican vaquero—told him otherwise.

Clomp, clomp, clomp.

Tack squawked. Wolf lifted his head and loosed a whinny, rattling his bit chain. The cream Arab answered with a shrill whinny of its own, and its rider, the American-looking gent, checked him down hard.

The four men grew close enough now that Yakima could see that the one on the far right, leaning toward the others, had a chipped front tooth. His sombrero was too big for him, and the pistol he wore wedged behind his chocolate brown cartridge belt was old and rusty—in stark contrast to the matched pair of Bisleys that were thonged low on his thighs.

The Bisleys and the hat were likely hand-me-downs— from dead men.

"Amigos," he said as Yakima and O'Shannon checked their horses down in front of the quartet and Yakima quickly dallied the rope of his pack mule around his saddle horn. "Welcome to the range of Don Jesus Obrégon Alvarez y Ungaro!"

O'Shannon glanced uneasily at Yakima, then returned his gaze to the four. "You're Don Ungaro's men?"

"*Sí*, Senor," said the one who with his cobalt blue eyes and wavy sandy hair looked American. Tooth and claw talismans had been sewn into the low crown of his felt sombrero—a much more ragged affair than that of the first man who'd spoken. "Like I say, we welcome you. You are friends of the don?"

"*Sí*," Yakima said. Canting his head toward the gambler, he added, "I mean, he is."

"Is he expecting you, Senor?" asked the blue-eyed gent, who had a thick Mexican accent. A border mongrel. When he spoke, he puffed his cheeks out slightly, and Yakima didn't trust those blue eyes farther than he could throw the man's cream, bullet-scarred Arab into a stiff wind.

Yakima and O'Shannon both said, "Yes" and "No," respectively, at the same time.

The four men before them, holding their reins taut in their gloved fists, regarded them blandly. Suddenly the mongrel's blue eyes flashed, the corners of his wide mouth rose, and he threw his head back, laughing heartily.

The other three looked at him. They looked puzzled at first, and then, one at a time, they began laughing as well. The one on the far right didn't laugh as hard as the others, however, and his light brown eyes rolled sideways in their sockets, nervously glancing into the scrub on the south side of the trail.

O'Shannon smiled uneasily as he held his reins in his fist up close to his dusty pinto vest. Dust streaked the sweat runneling down through the thin blond beard that covered his cheeks.

He glanced at Yakima, who didn't return the look but kept his hard-eyed gaze on the four laughing men in front of him, holding his right hand, fingers spread, flat against his thigh. In the corner of his right eye, he spied movement on a low sandstone dike about fifty yards to the right of the trail.

He'd only just registered the line of riders moseying

along the dike when the mongrel on the cream Arab stopped laughing suddenly. He jerked his hand toward the Colt Navy on his thigh.

Yakima slapped iron and drilled a neat round .44-caliber hole through the middle of his broad sunburned forehead.

Chapter 12

As the single crack from Yakima's smoking revolver flitted out across the valley, the blond mongrel's Colt Navy dropped from his fingers and thudded against the ground, startling his horse.

The man's eyes rolled back in his head as he sagged straight back in his saddle, then lolled to one side. Blood bubbled up from the hole in his forehead. With a weary sigh, he rolled down over his stirrup and hit the ground between his horse and the stocky, bearded rider to his right with a solid *smack* and a faint ring of his spurs.

Yakima held his cocked Colt half out in front of him.

The other three men—banditos or revolutionaries or whatever they called themselves—stopped laughing abruptly and acquired indignant looks as they checked their startled, prancing Arabians down. They shuttled their glances between the dead man and Yakima, rage building in their swarthy, ragged features.

Yakima glanced quickly toward the right of the trail. The other riders—six, he counted now—were following a cattle trail angling down the dike, heading toward him and O'Shannon. All six had their weapons drawn.

The gent with the Bisleys and the oversized sombrero regarded Yakima with blue fury and snapped through gritted teeth, "You feelthy, smelly Indio *dawg*!"

With that, still holding his reins in one bulging fist, he grabbed one of his Bisleys, whereupon Yakima calmly shot

him out of his saddle. As the man screamed, Yakima turned
his Colt on the Mex to the far left of the pitching line of
frightened horses, and the Colt roared once more.

At the same time, O'Shannon fired two quick rounds
with his own Colt, and the man in the middle of the group
clutched his throat with the hand holding his reins and the
hand holding his gun, inadvertently triggering the cocked
weapon and blowing his chin off.

While the nub of the man's chin flew through the air in a
vaporous red spray, Yakima whipped his gaze to the right.
The riders were all off the scarp now and shouting and
shooting as they galloped toward the trail. O'Shannon regarded them in horror, holding his smoking Colt straight up
and down in his right hand and trying to keep his horse
checked down with his left.

The other, now-riderless horses were dancing and prancing around him and Yakima, lifting a thick cloud of adobe-
colored dust.

Yakima whipped a shot toward the oncoming riders.

"Don't think we wanna wait around and palaver with
those fellas!" he shouted, ripping the pack mule's rope from
his horn. The mule would have to fend for itself.

A bullet whistled between him and O'Shannon, who
triggered two shots over his roan's twitching ears, and one
of the Mexicans screamed and clutched his chest. "No, I
don't think it would do us any good at all!"

Yakima rammed his heels into Wolf's flanks, and the
black lurched off his rear hooves with a bugling whinny as
more bullets sliced the air around his and Yakima's heads.
As Yakima shot up the trail, Wolf stretching his muscular
legs out broadly, O'Shannon and the roan were holding
their own off Wolf's right hip.

Behind them, pistols and rifles popped and cracked and
hooves drummed as the Mexican border roughs gave chase.

Climbing a long, gradual rise that followed the curving,
powdery trail, Yakima heard new thudding hooves on his
left. He turned, and more frigid snowmelt injected itself
into his veins when he saw at least ten more riders in som-

breros and bandolier-draped serapes galloping toward him through the chaparral on the trail's right side.

Smoke puffed amid the creosote and pipestem cactus. Pistols cracked and tack chains clattered. Bullets raised dust to the right of the trail and chewed shards from a boulder on the other side.

There was a loud, shrill bray, and Yakima glanced behind to see the pack mule keeping pace, long legs scissoring, big ears stretched back against its head, rope bouncing along the ground beside it.

Yakima triggered two shots into the brush on the right of the trail and heard a loud yelp; then he put his head down and slapped Wolf's rear, urging more speed. Glancing over his right shoulder, he was mildly surprised to see O'Shannon's roan losing only a little ground to the hammering, broad-barreled black stallion.

O'Shannon crouched low in his saddle, lips stretched back from his white teeth, hat brim bent against the crown. He turned a quick look behind and triggered a shot over his shoulder, then faced forward again, bouncing up and down in his saddle, muttering something Yakima couldn't hear above the guns and the thundering hooves, coaxing more speed from the roan.

As he and Yakima approached the crest of the rise, bullets plunking into the ground around and behind them and spanging wickedly off stones, Yakima turned to see one rider approaching at a breakneck pace on his left. The man, who wore an eye patch and whose sombrero had blown off to hang from a thong down his back, extended a pistol and fired.

The bullet sliced a hairbreadth beyond Yakima's nose. Yakima emptied his own Colt at the man. The man flinched as the half-breed's shots were thrown wide by the rough ride, and kept coming, batting his large Chihuahua spurs against his paint mustang's already-bleeding flanks.

The bearded, broad-faced Mexican grinned cunningly. He lifted his right hand over his head and pulled a sawed-off double-barreled shotgun over his shoulder. As he thumbed back both triggers, Yakima quickly holstered his pistol and shucked his Yellowboy from the sheath under his right thigh.

He cocked the rifle one-handed and angled it back behind him, resting the barrel against his side under his left arm. As the Mexican aimed his sawed-off gut-shredder one-handed over his pinto's sweat-lathered shoulder and continued grinning, Yakima squeezed the Winchester's trigger.

The Mexican's head jerked up as the slug plowed through the center of his upper chest, through the V formed by the jouncing thong from which a tobacco sack hung around his neck. The gut-shredder rose as well, booming loudly, fire and smoke bursting from the large twin maws and sending two loads of deadly buckshot into the air over Yakima's head.

With a scream that was audible even above the noise of the thundering hooves, the man sagged forward over the pinto's shoulder and dropped the shotgun, which bounced away along the sage- and bluestem-carpeted ground. The man fell after it and rolled wildly, his sombrero whipping in a blur about his shoulders.

One of his compatriots' horses kicked the man, tripped, and turned a forward somersault with a shrieking whinny and a scream from its rider, who quickly disappeared in a dun gray cloud of plummeting horse and wafting dust.

"There's the hacienda!" O'Shannon shouted as he and Yakima continued tearing down the trail.

Yakima stared into the broad valley bordered by towering red sandstone ridges and scarps and gentle slopes tufted with grama grass, junipers, and cedars—all painted several shades of green, purple, and gold by sunlight and cloud shadows.

Roughly a half mile away, what looked like a toy town from this distance shone on a low, shrub-bristled hill near a towering precipice looming in the north. The hacienda was surrounded by a high wall that shimmered white in the sunlight. The wall—constructed of both stone and adobe, it appeared, and patched in many places—must have covered at least half a square mile as it jogged over and across the gentle chaparral- and boulder-strewn hills.

Here and there about the hills inside the wall, the red-tiled roofs of adobe outbuildings rose amid the trees. But the centerpiece of the enclosed area was a massive red-tiled, cream-adobe barrack sitting well above the other buildings and the wall itself. The casa, built in grand Spanish style, sprawled atop a low rise like a Moorish castle, or a series of smaller casas jammed together with a set of outside stairs and open galleries here and there, and with viga poles poking out from under the overhanging red roof. Trees and shrubs of different varieties obscured the place, and vines climbed the walls, appearing almost to overrun it.

From the Moorish tower over the front entrance the Mexican flag fluttered. Smoke lazed into the breezy air from three massive stone chimneys.

"If that's a Mexican cattle outfit," Yakima shouted, wincing as a bullet spanged off a rock ten feet to his left and another snapped a branch from a paloverde tree near O'Shannon's right shoulder, "I'm in the wrong business on the wrong side of the line!"

Keeping his head down, he turned to O'Shannon. "Does Ungaro know we're coming?"

"No!"

Yakima was eyeing the riflemen, whom he could now see peering over the top of the hacienda's adobe stockade, noting a couple of tripod-mounted Gatling guns in the wooden-roofed guard tower looming over the large wooden door in the wall of the stockade facing the trail.

"Might've been nice if you'd let him know. So we don't get shot an' all!"

"I was expecting to have time to ride in slow and announce myself!"

"This is Mexico," Yakima said with a wince as a bullet whistled over his head. He snaked his rifle around to fire into the galloping crowd fifty yards behind him.

O'Shannon, holding his reins high as he crouched low over his roan's outstretched neck, glanced at Yakima curiously. "What's that mean?"

"Don't expect anything to go like you expect!"

Just then something moved along the trail ahead and left. It was a shrub that at first Yakima thought was dancing in the wind. But the wind wasn't blowing that hard. Then, where the shrub had been a moment before, the brass maw of a stout-barreled Gatling gun appeared, as though sprouting from the side of a low, rocky, cedar-tufted hill.

Yakima's stomach dropped and his oysters tingled as he stared at the six barrels at the end of the plate-sized canister. Then he saw the man behind the gun—a shadowy, bearded figure with a long, gaunt face, in a low-crowned sombrero, and with bandoliers crossed on his red and black–striped serape.

The man's hand was on the crank, which stood straight up and down as he leaned low to squint down the barrel at Yakima and the gambler, moving the gun slightly from left to right to track them as they galloped down the trail.

Yakima's gut dropped farther, and bells tolled in his head. He'd just begun swinging his Winchester over the pommel of his saddle when the serape-clad man aimed the Gatling sharply back along the trail behind the half-breed and the gambler and showed his teeth as he began to fiercely turn the crank.

BLAM-BLAM-BLAM-BLAM-BLAM-BLAM!

The thundering *ratapan* of the .45-caliber repeater made Wolf bunch his muscles beneath the saddle. It drowned the thunder of not only Yakima's and O'Shannon's own hooves but the hooves of the riders galloping behind them. Their pursuers' guns were silenced just as suddenly, replaced by several wails and screaming whinnies thrown up by the bullet-riddled men and horses.

Yakima glanced over his shoulder to see a couple of horses turning somersaults into the scrub along the trail, unseating their riders, while others reared and pranced as bullets cut through them and the dying men threw up their arms, screaming and rolling off their horses' butts or sliding, cursing and groaning, down their stirrups.

Smoke wafted around the belching maw of the rotating Gatling gun. Dust rose around the pileup of wailing riders and screaming horses while one horse cut out of the broiling pack to take off west through the chaparral, its rider's boot hung up in the stirrup, his body bouncing along the ground behind the galloping horse, arms flung wide and flopping straight out behind his shoulders. He lifted his head to look down his legs, his scream quavering with each bounce.

Yakima turned forward and continued giving Wolf his head, hearing the mule bray above the thundering bursts of the Gatling gun, which dwindled gradually as he and O'Shannon outdistanced the gun and the carnage it was spilling into the trail behind them. Ahead, the front wall of the hacienda grew larger, and Yakima could see the adobe's pits and cracks in the brassy light shifting at angles between the clouds.

The air smelled more and more like rain, and a cool wind picked up, making his hat brim flutter and Wolf's mane rise.

Above the wall, several rifles cracked. The bullets whistled over Yakima's head.

As he drew Wolf to a skidding halt in front of the large oak door, O'Shannon pulling the roan to a stop beside him and the mule thudding up behind, the half-breed glanced back. A few of the pursuing riders had managed to survive the hail of lead from the Gatling gun only to be cut down from their saddles now by the riflemen, their horses screaming, one falling and rolling while its wounded rider cried out horrifically from beneath it.

The man was still screaming and rolling, holding his belly, his horse gaining its feet and shaking its head as though dazed, when two more small groups of riders rode out of the scrub along both sides of the trail. Several of the men were yelling and aiming their Winchesters or Sharps carbines at Yakima and O'Shannon.

Yakima wasn't sure what to make of this crew, for they were dressed much like the men who'd been pursing him and O'Shannon. But they didn't look quite as eager to turn him and the gambler into human sieves as the others had.

Three of the men rode boldly up to Yakima, waving their rifles at him and O'Shannon and shouting orders sharply in Spanish.

"All right, all right," Yakima growled, holding up one hand, palm out, and slowly returning his Winchester to its saddle sheath.

"Holster that hogleg," he told O'Shannon, who sat squinting into the dust, looking confused and spitting grit from his lips.

Quickly, realizing what the Mexicans were telling him, one riding up close enough to prod his chest with his Sharps barrel, he stuffed his Colt into its holster, then raised both hands to his shoulders.

"I'm a friend of Don Ungaro," he said. Then he tried it in Spanish, but it was drowned by the shouting and the thudding horses and the screams of the man still rolling around on the ground twenty yards up the trail.

One of the newcomers—a tall man dressed in far more ornate vaquero garb than the others, with a big black, silver-trimmed sombrero thonged taut beneath his chin—rode his steeldust Arabian stallion over to the screaming man. His long silver hair brushed his epaulette-stitched shoulders.

"Muerta, usted thieving, perro traidor!" Having called the man a traitorous dog, he extended a long-barreled, ivory-gripped, gold-chased Smith & Wesson toward the back of the man's head. The revolver popped.

The man's head bounced wildly before he slumped forward and buried his forehead, from which blood and brains oozed thickly, in the dust between his legs.

A wail rose from the still-swirling dust. Yakima extended his gaze along the trail to see another one of his pursuers flee into the brush. Screaming, begging for his life in Spanish, limping slightly on his bloody right leg, the man began climbing a low rise, angling away from the wall upon which several riflemen laughed mockingly.

The well-dressed silver-haired vaquero shouted, and one of his cohorts gigged his Arabian after the man, catching up to him as he crested the rise. The rider drew a long silver saber from an elaborately scrolled sheath on his hip and loosed a wicked-sounding whoop.

The silver flashed in the brassy light. The revolutionary's head toppled cleanly from his shoulders to hit the ground with a dull thud while his body continued shambling out of sight down the other side of the hill.

The head rolled back down the rise and came to rest faceup against a rock and a clump of grama grass, the eyes still blinking, lips moving as though it were muttering a silent last prayer.

Here I am, Yakima thought as he shuttled his gaze from the severed head to the men and horses prancing around him, once more in Mexico.

Chapter 13

The man who'd done the beheading trotted back toward the group milling around Yakima and O'Shannon, wiping off his bloody saber on the palm of his leather glove and sliding it back into its sheath with the ring of steel against steel. At the same time, the regal-looking gent with the long silver hair and shaggy silver beard moved his horse over to Yakima and O'Shannon, who sat with their hands raised as several rifles jutted toward them.

"Speak!" the silver-haired man ordered in near-perfect English. "Who are you and what are you doing on Ungaro land?"

"I'm a friend of the don's," O'Shannon said as his horse blew nervously. "I come in peace, wishing only to speak with the don of . . . uh . . . business matters. My name is Cleveland O'Shannon." He glanced at Yakima, who sat his saddle grimly nearby. "This is my scout, Yakima Henry."

"We were told to expect no visitors."

"He's not expecting me. But I assure you, the don and I are friends. And I wish to thank you for . . ." O'Shannon let his voice trail off ponderously as he glanced into the still-wafting dust up the trail, where several revolutionaries lay in bloody heaps. Wincing at the head resting against the grass clump at the base of the rise, he added grimly, ". . . the help."

The man with the silver hair regarded both the gambler and the half-breed skeptically, his crinkled, dark gray eyes hooded with bushy gray brows. His mouth was a wide slash inside his long, combed, dusty beard. He favored Yakima with an extralong stare, as though the half-breed were a problem that needed solving.

Finally, his eyes brushed the fine black stallion that the half-breed straddled, and then he glanced at Yakima once more before lifting his head toward several men now standing atop the wall. "Open the door. *Vamos!*"

He looked at O'Shannon. "If you are part of some ruse to do injury to the don, I must warn you, amigos, you are making a very grave mistake."

He glanced at one of the other men around him. While he put his fine steeldust stallion up close to O'Shannon's roan and leaned out to brusquely grab the Colt from the gambler's hip holster and the Henry rifle from his saddle boot, the other man confiscated Yakima's weapons, shoving the staghorn-gripped Colt behind his double cartridge belts and resting the Yellowboy repeater across his saddle bows.

The second man stared coldly into Yakima's eyes and curled his upper lip. "A green-eyed Apache." He pooched his lips out, making a wet sound, then spit to one side as though ridding a sour taste from his mouth.

The double doors squawked, and two men in the traditional white cotton slacks and threadbare serapes of the Mexican peasant stepped out from behind the wall, pushing the doors open in front of them, breathing hard and grunting with the effort. Each door must have weighed as much as a horse.

The Gatling gun in the tower over the doors was tilted nearly straight down at Yakima and O'Shannon, as were the three rifles on the wall. The riders kept their own guns bearing grimly down on the newcomers, as though waiting— expecting, yearning—for them to make a sudden, fatal move.

The hair along the back of Yakima's neck pricked. He felt as though he was standing before a firing squad. These men weren't messing around—he hoped none had a fever that made his finger twitch.

The silver-haired gent gigged his prancing stallion between Yakima and O'Shannon. Wolf eyed the steeldust darkly, arched his neck, nickered belligerently, and tossed his head.

"Not now, idiot," Yakima growled, holding the reins taut.

"Follow me," the silver-haired gent said and rode between the double open doors as a sudden burst of thunder pealed loudly and the sun faded as though a giant cloud had passed.

O'Shannon urged the roan between the doors, and Yakima followed. The other riders, still aiming their rifles, brought up the rear. Yakima glanced back uneasily, knowing that those stout doors would soon close and he'd be trapped here within these walls. The anxious feeling was not abated by his having seen how many acres the walls encompassed.

Turning his head forward again, he heard shouts and footsteps around him. A half dozen peons were running past him and O'Shannon and the trailing riders, dashing out the open doors. They sprinted back along the trail and descended on the dead men like vultures, instantly ripping at their clothes and their boots and hats.

Turning forward again as he followed O'Shannon, who in turn followed the silver-haired man, Yakima saw that they were climbing a low rise with makeshift peasants' shacks—built of stones and brush, mostly, sometimes with corrugated-tin roofs—nestled beside the trail here and there. There were occasional clusters of large brick-adobe stables and hay barns and hay wagons and other farm implements that were obviously a part of the rancho.

As the trail climbed gradually toward the massive main house partly obscured by the smoke of a dozen or so cook fires that filled the air with the smell of spicy Mexican cooking, two riders appeared on the trail ahead. The silver-haired man threw up his right hand, and Yakima halted his horse behind O'Shannon.

Thunder pealed, making the ground shake. The clouds had entirely closed off the sun now, and the women and children milling about the shacks scrambled inside, babies crying and the women berating their older children to *vamos!*

The eyes of a dead goat, hung from a low cedar branch for gutting, flashed redly as lightning forked in the sky behind Yakima.

Wolf whinnied and the men behind the half-breed began chattering anxiously about the weather.

"Don Ungaro, these two saddle tramps claim they know you," the gray-haired man said in Spanish as the two riders approached, one a short, goat-bearded, potbellied gent in his mid- to late sixties and wearing a short-crowned leather sombrero that had seen better days. The other was a massive mountain of a man with long, thick brown hair and a shaggy brown mustache curving down both corners of his thick-lipped mouth. "I hesitated to bring them to the house, but . . ."

The silver-haired man let his voice trail off as the don put his white-socked, fiery-eyed black barb up to O'Shannon's blue roan, his lower jaw dropping and his slanted eyes narrowing with shock and surprise as he thrust out his right hand eagerly. "O'Shannon! *Christo!* What brings you to this boil on the devil's ass of Old Mexico, huh? Are you crazy? We are at *war,* amigo!"

Rain started falling lightly, small drops peppering the dust of the wide trail between the shacks.

"I guess that's why I'm here."

The don's wily old almond-shaped eyes had found Yakima. He gestured at the half-breed with an age-spotted hand. "You ride with an Apache, amigo? Please explain."

"He's no Apache, Don. This is Yakima Henry. Half-gringo from north of the border. He's a fighting man. That's why I hired him to guide me down here."

A fighting man, Yakima thought with a wry inward chuckle.

The don inspected Yakima coldly, his old hands resting on his saddle horn. "Is he *civilized*? At the casa, I've women about . . ."

O'Shannon glanced at Yakima edgily. "I'll vouch for him."

Don Ungaro scowled at the half-breed once more, then glanced at Wolf. "Well, he's got fine taste in horseflesh. I'll give him that." He looked at the rider with long silver hair, who was apparently one of the hacendado's lieutenants. "Alberto, take your men to the bunkhouse. Chico and I will escort our visitors to the casa. I assume the shooting was . . ."

"The rebels, *Jefe,*" Alberto said in Spanish. Then, grinning wolfishly at Yakima and O'Shannon, he continued: "They were chasing your guests like foxes beating the brush for jackrabbits. It was a good opportunity to test the firepower of the new Gatling gun you posted outside the gate."

"It did well?"

"Ripped them to ribbons. The riflemen on the catwalk finished the others."

"Muy bueno," the don said as bullet-sized drops of rain began falling, thunder rumbled, and lightning flashed beyond the walls. "Come along, gentlemen!"

Don Ungaro and Chico reined their mounts around and headed up the trail, the rain falling in white sheets now and instantly turning the trail into a stream. O'Shannon held the roan back and turned to Yakima. "Don't mind the don. He was fighting Apaches long before the revolutionaries started swarming about this part of Mexico. Understandably, he's a little prejudiced. Better let me do most of the talking."

"You do that." Yakima grunted as Wolf splashed along the trail behind the don and Chico.

He and O'Shannon put their mounts into a jog. Yakima watched the shacks slide up along the trail. In more than one he saw wary glances from doorways and windows, and most of the fearful looks belonged to men, with several frightened children hovering around them. There were few women about. Those he had seen were either old or pregnant.

This vague, half-conscious observation was merely odd

to him, but that and the high walls guarded with riflemen and Gatling guns conspired to cause a dark bird of apprehension and claustrophobia to flutter around inside him. Automatically, his right hand hovered close to his holster. Then he remembered he'd been relieved of his guns. They were now headed off to another part of the massive, walled rancho.

As the rain slanted down, obscuring the big man and the small old man in front of him, rain sluicing off the flat brim of his black hat, he raked out a grim curse.

At the top of the rise, the hill flattened out and the casa loomed large and sprawling, like something the shifting plates of the earth might have graded up from deep below. Sheds and stables stood off to the side, nearly hidden amid the rocks, boulders, and pecan and Joshua trees.

All the buildings had a worn look and feel to them— cracked and patched, occasional shutters dangling from a casa window, with here and there a dead pecan tree standing stark against the stormy sky.

"Amigos, I love the rain!" the don said, slowly dismounting his fine barb, in no hurry despite the weather. He'd lit a cigar and it glowed softly beneath the overhanging brim of his leather sombrero. "It has been dry here, the hay burning up in my fields. We have needed a storm most badly. I hope it will last the rest of the day and all night!"

He held out a gnarled, arthritic hand to the large drops and clenched the paw as if to grab the rain, bunching his lips around his cigar.

"I'm glad for you, Don," O'Shannon shouted above the din. "But I don't think our horses appreciate the thunder and lightning quite as much as you do!"

"Hector!" the don shouted toward a broad stairway rising to two heavy doors of the casa, one of which stood open under a large arched pediment.

As though he'd been waiting there for orders, a stocky man in a serape ran out of the house and down the stairs, his rope-soled sandals clapping against his feet. A black cat bolted out the door behind him, then, the rain instantly pasting its fur against its back, wheeled, ran back up the steps three at a time, and disappeared inside the casa.

Hector wore a serape but no hat, and there was something about his black-bearded, heavy-browed, chinless face that seemed only half human.

"Take my guests' horses with mine to my own stable and treat them as well as you do my barbs!" the don ordered.

Hector muttered something unintelligible, then quickly gathered up the reins and began leading the three jittery mounts toward a stable on the east side of the sprawling casa. Wolf nickered and nipped at the don's barb, and Hector wheeled and whipped the black's reins against its neck.

"He better not stable those two together," Yakima warned the don as they all stood there in the rain, watching the horses. "And if he keeps whipping those reins at him, he's gonna lose a hand."

Ungaro casually plucked his stogie from between his teeth and sent a blue smoke plume into the driving rain. "That would be a hell of a fight, wouldn't it? El Diablo and your black?" He chuckled and extended his hand toward the cracked stone steps. "Gentlemen, shall we remove ourselves from the weather? I sense warm fires and succulent aromas beckoning."

As Yakima and O'Shannon began climbing the steps, raindrops splashing around them and the old don and the big ape following, O'Shannon tipped his head toward Yakima and said just loudly enough for the half-breed to hear above the rain, "Remember—I'll do most of the talking."

"So talk," Yakima muttered as he approached the top of the steps, that dark bird of dread flapping its wings in his lower belly. "And let's get the hell out of here."

Chapter 14

Yakima and O'Shannon stepped through the casa's open door. Stopping just over the threshold, the half-breed squinted into the room before him—a broad, sunken hall that appeared to have been a grand entrance at one time but that was now filled with long, rough-hewn tables, high-backed chairs, couches, and armchairs scattered willy-nilly around the room.

A fire burned in a broad hearth on the other side of the room, and from several large cast-iron pots emanated the smell of spicy frijoles and pork. A balcony ran along the far wall, above the fireplace, and beneath it, near a grand piano with a tattered flag of Mexico draped over it, hung half of a bloody pig carcass, its pink head remaining.

In the foreground, a dozen or so men in various styles of Mexican garb sat at the tables or on deep leather couches, playing cards, eating, and drinking, some with young Mexican women in skimpy dresses perched on their knees. Odors of tobacco and wood smoke hung thickly in the air.

One man at the far left end of the table had his head buried in his arms, his long black hair fanned out across the table around him. The din of the storm and voices and clattering dishes was loud, but Yakima could hear the man's regular, resonant snores.

"Come!" The don stepped around Yakima and O'Shannon, starting down the five stone steps toward the floor of what was obviously now a drinking, dining, and whoring hall. "Join me for a libation and food. My cooks are the best in all of Sonora!"

As the don crossed the room toward a round table amid the clutter of the mismatched furniture and the trash strewn about the floor, he stopped beside the sleeping gent. He cast an angry glance past Yakima and O'Shannon at Chico, then gritted his teeth and grabbed a fistful of the sleeping man's hair, jerked his head up, and slapped his cheeks—first with his palm, then with the back of his hand.

"Carlos, wake up, you miserable dog!" the don wailed, instantly casting a hush over the room. "How many times have I told you, I do not want you getting drunk in the middle of the day?" He slapped the wildly blinking man twice more and stepped back as Carlos regarded him, horrified. "What if we are attacked? What good would you be to me, then, uh?"

"I am sorry, Jefe!" Carlos yelled, looking as though he was about to cry, his tan cheeks showing crimson, his hair hanging in his dung brown eyes. "I did not mean to get drunk—it just happened!"

"Get out!" the don barked, his voice booming around the near-silent room, louder even than the thunder rumbling outside. "Go down to the stables and muck out the stalls, and stay there until I reinstate your casa privileges. It might be a while!"

When the long-haired man had slunk out of the casa, the don turned to O'Shannon, shrugged apologetically, and gestured for him and Yakima to sit in a couple of comfortable armchairs gathered with two others around a low table. The don sank into a high-backed, elaborately carved chair across from O'Shannon while the big man, Chico, made the more rustic chair beside the don creak dangerously beneath his considerable girth.

"I was just having a drink and a cigar," the don said, leaning forward to remove the lid from a cut-glass decanter on the table before him, "when I heard the Gatling fire. It's not as if I don't hear it enough to have gotten quite used to it, but I'm always curious. So I rode down to take a look."

His eyes sparkled as he splashed what appeared to be brandy into a glass and slid the glass to O'Shannon. "I am sure things have changed around here since your last visit, amigo. When you *and* your brother visited me last."

As there was only one other glass and a dirty coffee cup on the table, the don called across the room in Spanish for one more glass, then gave O'Shannon a wink and commented, "I don't allow Chico to drink. Ever," the don added emphatically with a wry snort and a furtive glance at the big man who sat with his long, heavy arms draped across the chair. Chico was regarding Yakima owlishly, moving his thick lips slightly as though muttering to himself, snarling.

Yakima watched the man blandly, but he wished like hell he had his weapons. Luckily, no one had frisked him and found the toothpick hanging down behind his neck. If the big Mexican ape sprang toward him, as seemed likely, he'd gut him like that pig hanging near the grand piano over yonder . . . and the devil take the hindmost.

O'Shannon was looking around the room. "It has changed somewhat," the gambler said haltingly. "And become more populated. With . . . uh . . . women as well as men."

The don chuckled and glanced at Yakima. "Do not mind him, Indio. He only bites if I tell him." He slid a freshly poured goblet of brandy across the table toward the half-breed, glancing at O'Shannon. "You allow him liquor in the middle of the day?"

Yakima kept his bland expression in place as he turned to the don. "Your lieutenant has our guns, and, unless we're prisoners here, I'd like mine back."

The don capped the decanter and sat back in his chair, which was so large it made him look pint-sized. He returned Yakima's bland expression but simmering menace shone in his washed-out brown eyes. "You'd like your guns."

"*Sí,*" Yakima said.

"Yakima," O'Shannon said, raising one hand, his cheeks

flushing beneath the burn that had turned to a leathery tan. "Like I said . . ."

The don raised both his gnarled hands from the broad arms of his chair and held his stare, turning more menacing by the second, on Yakima. "You would like your guns."

Yakima didn't say anything. He just stared back at the man.

The other drinkers and diners had resumed their drinking, eating, talking, and laughing while the storm flashed and thundered outside and rain washed over the viga poles and down the dim, deeply recessed windows. One of the men in rough trail garb took one of the young girls over his knee and, raising her cotton skirt above her waist, began beating her bare, tan bottom with a long leather quirt. He and the men around him laughed.

The squealing girl wasn't seeing the humor in it.

The don seemed not to hear the savage commotion. He continued staring at Yakima challengingly. When Yakima did not so much as blink, the don's nostrils flared with fury, and he suddenly heaved himself to his feet, walked around behind his chair and that of Chico and bent over Yakima, balling his fists at his sides.

"You come onto my hacienda without invitation. You come into my casa, accept my hospitality, and you expect me to let you strut around—big savage, green-eyed Indio— with *weapons*?"

"I'll take my weapons, and I'll take my leave."

The don's eyes blazed. He pursed his lips and flared his nostrils. In one sudden movement, he swept his hand back behind his left shoulder, then swung it forward, the back of his hand angling toward Yakima's face.

The half-breed's own right hand shot out and grabbed the don's right wrist eight inches from Yakima's left cheek.

"Oh, Jesus," O'Shannon muttered, running a hand down his face.

The don's eyes sparked like a freshly stoked blacksmith's forge. He looked at the big brown hand wrapped around his wrist and opened his mouth to speak, but it came out as a yowl as Yakima, his own rage stoked to a white-hot flame, applied more pressure.

With a savage grunt, Chico bolted straight up out of his chair. Yakima did the same, shoving the don back into the big Mexican. Reacting like a bear would react, all instinct and mindless aggression, Chico tossed his boss away with one hand.

The don yowled as he stumbled to Chico's left and hit the floor, rolling and shouting Spanish epithets. Chico bolted off his heels toward Yakima, lips bunched and eyes pinched down to slits, hands held as though to grab Yakima's neck and wring it.

At the last moment, Yakima stepped to one side. The big Mexican stumbled past him. Yakima brought a savage round-house up from his heels and delivered it resolutely against Chico's left ear.

Chico gave a high-pitched grunt and stumbled forward and back, eyes wide with surprise. Yakima stepped in and delivered two solid right jabs to the man's cheeks and jaw, then buried his left fist deep in his solar plexus—so deep that he thought he could feel his knuckles rake Chico's backbone.

Chico fairly exploded as the breath left his lungs, his long, stringy hair puffing out away from his face, and he folded like a jackknife. At the same time Yakima slammed his right knee into the man's face, hearing a soft crack.

"Rhoo-hawhhh!" the big man bellowed, lifting his head slightly, blood oozing from smashed lips. He staggered sideways, eyelids fluttering.

Yakima was on him again, grabbing his hair with one hand, the back of his tunic collar with the other. He ran him ten feet from the table at which O'Shannon sat, wide-eyed and hang-jawed, and slammed Chico's head into a four-foot-square concrete ceiling joist from which several dusty *ristras* hung, with a resolute smack and evoking an anguished groan.

Foot-long cracks appeared in the concrete around Chico's head.

Yakima released the man's hair and his collar, and Chico fell like three hundred pounds of firmly packed seed corn. As he hit the floor on his face and belly, dust wafted up around him. He wagged his head from side to side, placed his hands palm down on the floor, and tried to rise.

He didn't make it an inch before he collapsed with a loud *whoof* and then lay still.

The ratcheting of gun hammers broke the ensuing silence.

Yakima swung around to see several of the midday revelers standing near the end of the three long tables, staring at him and the comatose Chico in shock and fury. Two had their Colts aimed at him, while the man who'd been spanking the girl—who now sobbed on the floor by the man's chair, rubbing her bottom—came up behind one of the others. The girl spanker brusquely shoved the other man aside and began reaching for the old Colt Patterson residing in a silver-trimmed black leather holster mounted high and cross-draw on his left hip.

He curled his lips and widened his eyes as he shuttled his malignant stare from Chico to Yakima, who'd palmed his Arkansas toothpick, deciding that if he was going to die he'd gut a couple of these border roughs in the process.

"*¡Pare, usted los perros!*" the don wailed. Stop, you dogs!

Yakima glanced over his shoulder. The don sat on his butt on the stained and chipped flagstone floor, legs bent before him, low-heeled brown boots with gaudy Chihuahua spurs resting on their sides. His short, unadorned doeskin jacket was thrown open to reveal javelina-skin suspenders and a pocketful of long Spanish cigars.

He was staring at Yakima with both anger and—what was that tempering cast? Admiration?

O'Shannon stood near his chair, swinging his head around in all directions, eyes incredulous, wary, scared shitless. He didn't seem to be breathing.

The don turned his head slightly to regard the men near the tables and snarled, *"¡Ponga sus armas en el suelo!"* Put down your guns!

The men looked at the don as though they'd hadn't understood what he'd said. The don shouted the order once more, told them to sit back down at their tables or find some work to do.

The men, truckling like scolded dogs, holstered their weapons and slumped back down in their chairs. One of the half-dressed young women, her thick black hair hanging to the small of her naked back, ran across the room to help the don to his feet, muttering anxiously.

When the don stood smoothing his thin gray hair back from his high forehead with both hands, he jerked his arm free of the girl's grip and ordered her away with an annoyed, impatient air. Continuing to stare with a puzzled, incredulous expression at Yakima, he brushed off his coat with the backs of his hands and moved toward Chico, limping slightly on his right ankle.

The room was still so quiet that Yakima could hear not only the hammering rain and intermittent barks of thunder but the beans bubbling and sizzling on the fire and the water dripping over the eaves in shimmering waves down the windows.

His heart beat insistently. He thought he could even hear O'Shannon's pounding ticker as the gambler continued to stand near a chair, wearing an expression like that of a condemned man awaiting a firing squad.

The don dropped to a knee beside Chico's unmoving bulk. He lowered his right ear toward the man's back, then touched a finger to Chico's stout neck.

"Christos!" the don rasped, looking up at Yakima in awe, his brows forking. "You killed this hombre."

Chapter 15

Yakima stood his ground near Chico and Don Ungaro. He rubbed his thumb and index finger across the blade of his Arkansas toothpick, just down from the thin brass hilt, waiting, wondering what would happen next.

Without his guns there was no way he could fight his way out of the room. But he could do some damage before Don Ungaro ordered his wick blown.

"I told you, Don," O'Shannon said with a slow, nervous chuckle, sweat beading his forehead. "He's a fighting man."

"*Sí.*" The don straightened, wincing slightly as he put weight on his bum right ankle. He was half a head shorter than Yakima, and he looked up at the half-breed with a wistful expression on his haggard face, strands of gray hair sprouting on his upper lip and his chin.

Slowly, he began to laugh, shoulders twitching. As his laughter grew amid the thunder and pelting rain outside, the others in the room turned toward him, whispering skeptically among themselves. The don, lifting his shoulders and laughing heartily now, raised his hands and looked down at the motionless body of Chico, shook his head fatefully, as though at a hilarious cosmic joke, and continued laughing until, snorting and regaining control of himself, he glanced at O'Shannon.

"Perhaps we need siesta, huh?" The don returned his smiling gaze to Yakima. "Let's sleep. Then you and the Indio will join me for dinner in my private dining room.

Alone. There"—the don narrowed an eye at the half-breed, pursed his lips, and nodded cunningly—"we will talk about what it is that brings you here, to Casa de Ungaro. And I will tell you what is rolling around in my thoughts as well."

The don looked beyond Yakima. "Pancho. *Rapido!* Take these men to the east wing and find rooms for them."

"*Sí, sí,*" muttered a voice behind Yakima.

He heard the scuff of soft-soled shoes on the flagstones, saw in the periphery of his vision a short man in a sombrero shuffle toward him among the tables.

"This way, Senores."

Pancho was a small, slope-shouldered, potbellied man with Indian-dark features, a ragged gray beard, and gray hair curling down from the ratty straw sombrero tipped back on his head. He wore a wool shirt under a weather-stained deerskin vest, duck trousers, and high-topped moccasin boots beaded in the Yaqui design. Pork grease and beans clung to the beard around his mouth.

His bulging molasses-colored eyes were rheumy from drink.

He lifted a wrinkled, nearly black hand to beckon haltingly, sucking his lower lip. Yakima and O'Shannon shared a glance, then Yakima, holding his knife down close to his side in his right hand in case he might still need it, canted his head toward the old mestizo.

O'Shannon looked at the don warily, then swallowed and began striding after the little Mexican half-breed, who shuffled off through the tables at which the others sat in hushed, awful silence. Sidling casually away from the don, the hacendado smiling back at him inscrutably, Yakima tramped between the tables, noting the dark sidelong glances lifted toward him. He followed the old mestizo and O'Shannon to the back of the room and up a narrow, winding staircase that smelled of mouse droppings and cold stone.

As they moved along a narrow hall, the old mestizo about fifteen feet ahead and not saying a word or even glancing behind him, O'Shannon nodded toward Yakima. "Nice work," he said with hushed sarcasm.

"Glad you liked it."

"I thought you'd been to Mexico before."

"I have. If you let a man slap you down here, you might as well give him a knife to cut your throat with."

O'Shannon sighed and continued walking, shaking his head slowly, darkly. "Chico's been the don's bodyguard for about ten years."

"He'll have to find another one."

As Yakima passed a half-open door on his right, he glanced inside, then stopped dead in his tracks. Beyond the stout door he saw a large, sunken, heavy-beamed room. Two sets of long, arched windows were open to the storm, and the wind and rain made the gauzy mauve curtains dance back from the frames.

There was a bed with a mauve canopy and a beaded curtain around it. The curtain was partly open on the side facing Yakima, and his heavy black brows furrowed when he saw the woman.

He could see only part of her, for she was lying on her side, facing the windblown curtains, her head resting on an arm. Completely nude, she was long-legged and cherry-skinned, and her finely turned thighs curved upward to full, round hips and a delectably fleshy bottom that led to a narrow, angular back with a willowy spine.

She must have sensed him standing there, openly ogling the masterpiece of her dusky-skinned body, because she lifted her head suddenly, thick black hair falling across her shoulder. She turned to look toward the half-open door.

Yakima's breath caught in his throat as he glimpsed the regal, well-chiseled face, dark brows, and brown eyes. He saw the heavy swell and side curve of a breast beneath her arm.

"Who's there?" she said raspily in Spanish, more annoyed than fearful.

"Senor . . . por favor!"

Pancho scuffed back toward Yakima and, keeping his head down, drew the door closed. There was a key in the door. He turned it and winced at the sound of the locking bolt.

Turning toward Yakima, the man held a finger to his lips, then brushed past O'Shannon and moved down the hall.

O'Shannon shook his head. "Can't take you anywhere."

Yakima shrugged as they followed Pancho along the hall and, apparently, to the far side of the sprawling casa. His mind lingered on the naked woman. He had a nettling, distracting sense that he knew her. But aside from a few whores and revolutionaries he'd run into on previous trips, he knew no one down here.

Unless . . . ?

Yakima shook his head.

Pancho finally stopped in a hallway on the casa's third story and threw a heavy oak door open. "Senor!" he said, gesturing O'Shannon into the room.

He shuffled down to the next door, threw it open, and extended his hand toward the room's dark, musty interior. "Senor!"

Yakima glanced at O'Shannon, who shrugged and said, "Sleep tight."

As Yakima stepped into the room he could hear Pancho shuffling back the way they'd come. He turned to the door, removed the key from the outside lock, and stuck it into the inside keyhole. Shutting the heavy door, he locked it, crossed the small room, which boasted a double bed and a few sticks of rough-hewn furniture, and opened the shutters of the single window.

Instantly, sprinkles of rain and a gust of cool, refreshing wind tinged with piñon and mesquite blew in, chasing out the stale tobacco smells and the mustiness. Beyond, he could see a line of pecan trees and shrubs and the red roofs of a couple of stables that shone briefly when lightning flashed.

Yakima absently touched his empty holster, wishing again that he had his guns. This was no place to go unarmed.

The woman . . .

Who the hell was she, and why was the door locked? Her dusky, pantherlike appearance was poignantly, sensuously alluring. Possibly a concubine. The don's own private whore.

From there, Yakima's mind strayed to the don's ominous words: "And I will tell you what is rolling around in my thoughts as well."

What thoughts?

Yakima no longer cared about the Gatling guns or the dynamite. He and O'Shannon would do very well just to get out of here with their skins. He didn't much care for dying weaponless, like a caged dog.

He looked at the bed. A nap would do him good. He sat down on the edge of the feather-stuffed mattress and wearily kicked his boots off. He stood to remove his dusty, sweaty tunic and denims and continued undressing until he was naked.

The breeze from the window felt silky on his trail-worn hide. He scratched his chest and belly luxuriously, ran his hands through his long, sweat-damp hair. He felt the dull ache in the knuckles of his right hand produced by his pummeling of Chico's thick head. His loins were tight from riding.

Crossing to the window, the flagstones cool against the soles of his aching feet, he stood looking down at the scrub and gravel and beyond the brick-red outbuilding roofs to the broad blue rain-shrouded valley over which snow-white clouds hung like cotton. Beyond the valley and above the clouds, several ridges rolled back against the horizon, barely visible among the low, brooding clouds.

The Sierra Madre.

He breathed deep, filling his chest with the aromatic smell of the desert rain—the smell of piñon, mesquite, greasewood, and vast canyons painted with cactus blossoms and wildflowers and roiling with tepid mountain streams.

There was the ubiquitous yet inexplicable scent of citrus

and aloe and the not altogether bad feeling of being hopelessly lost. As though you'd fallen off the edge of the world, and all its petty concerns and entanglements were far, far away, leaving only the keener and more significant but somehow less vexing problems of how to survive.

Mexico.

A knifepoint of haunting memories pierced him out of the blue. The last time he was down here he'd been with Faith, busting her brother out of a Mexican prison run by a psychopathic rurale.

Raw loneliness hammered him. His knees weakened, and the room shifted around him. He tightened his jaw against it and drove his clenched fists into both sides of the window frame.

A soft knock sounded on the door.

He wheeled, his rain-damp hair blowing about his shoulders. Reflexively, he looked for his cartridge belt, forgetting it was empty. The Yellowboy was gone as well.

A soft female voice said through the heavy oak panel: "Senor? May I enter?"

Again reflexively, he thought of the naked girl on the bed in the room that was far more opulent than the one he found himself in now, and he registered a warm stirring in his loins.

He crossed to the door and tipped his head toward it. "Who is it?"

Silence.

Then: "Senor? May I come in, please?"

Yakima turned the key and opened the door six inches, peering into the hall. A girl stood alone before him. Not the girl from the canopied bed. This one was shorter, plumper. Her hair was cropped at the neck, and her eyes were wide, her nose short and broad, her lips long and full.

She wore a dress so gauzy that Yakima could see her entire body through it—the heavy, large-nippled breasts, the slightly distended belly, and the broad, rounded hips. On her stubby feet she wore rope-soled sandals.

Barely audibly, she said, glancing up at him demurely, her full lips parted sensuously, "Por favor . . . ? Don Ungaro sent me."

"No joke?" Yakima looked at her suspiciously, but there weren't too many places to a hide a weapon in a getup like hers. Just the same, he didn't trust any "gifts" from Don Ungaro. He started to close the door. "Well, tell him to go . . ."

He let his voice trail off, thinking about it, scrutinizing the girl once more. He needed a nap, but a tumble couldn't hurt. He stepped back, drawing the door open. As she stepped into the room, her eyes touched him like a warm hand, and he instantly felt a pull below his belly.

He threw the door shut. She stood before him, smiling shyly, letting her eyes furtively stray up and down his broad, hard-muscled, naked frame. Yakima stepped toward her and, staring down at her—her head came only to his chest—grabbed the flimsy dress at her waist. As he began pulling it up, she gave a slight gasp of surprise and raised her hands above her head.

Yakima lifted the dress, which weighed less than one of his socks, over her outstretched arms and tossed it onto the floor. She lowered her arms. Wisps of her short dark hair hung in her eyes. Yakima placed his hands on her cheeks, swept the hair from her eyes with his thumbs.

Her ripe breasts swelled, the pink nipples jutting from the large aureoles that darkly covered most of the bottoms of the full orbs. Despite the size of her bosom and the womanly sensuality in her mouth and eyes, he didn't think she was much over seventeen, if that.

He asked how old she was.

"Eighteen this month," she said in Spanish.

"Does the don force you to do this?" Yakima asked her in his cow-pen version of her native tongue.

She shook her head slightly. "The others, perhaps. Me . . . I . . ." Her eyes dropped to his swollen dong that was gently caressing her fleshy, sensuous belly. "I like."

Yakima leaned toward her, grabbed her under the arms.

She gave a small shriek as he lifted her off the floor. Expertly, she wrapped her legs around his back, hooking her ankles behind him. She laughed with unabashed delight, brown eyes flashing in the stormy light from the window.

She threw her head back and groaned as he gentled her down on him before backing her onto the bed and mounting her slowly as he spread her legs wide with his arms.

She threw her head back on the pillow and squeezed her eyes closed. *"Sí . . ."*

Chapter 16

After Yakima and the girl, whose name he saw no point in learning, finished making love amid the fresh breeze and the thunder of the storm—a satisfying, tension-relieving coupling despite the circumstances—they languished for a while in the bed, entangled in each other's limbs.

When, stroking her hair, he asked her about the naked woman he'd seen earlier, she climbed out of bed quickly, frowning angrily. She threw her dress on over her head, glanced at him once, miffed, and left.

Her sandals clapped sharply in the outside hall until they were drowned by the storm's last grumblings.

"Well, I'll be damned. A jealous *puta*."

Yakima was too tired and sated to dwell on the naked beauty. The bed rose up to engulf him.

Someone tapped on the door. A man's voice called, "Senor? *Por favor*."

Yakima jerked his head up out of a deep sleep, for several groggy seconds trying to wrap his mind around where he was. At the same time, he reached instinctively for the revolver he normally would have hung from a bedpost. Of course, neither the gun nor the holster was there.

He looked around. The tap sounded again at the door, and the voice, louder this time: "Senor? Queekly, *por favor*. Don Ungaro is waiting."

The name braced Yakima like a cold slap, and he re-

membered the wall and the grand casa populated with
Mexican misfits, including the don.

"Comin'."

He swung his legs out of bed, brushed his hair back, and
dressed. Stepping out of the room, he set his black hat on
his head and drew the door closed behind him. Against the
far wall leaned another Mexican—not Pancho but a man
of similar age and stature who had a large neck goiter—
smoking a cornhusk cigarette.

The next door up from Yakima's opened and laughter
spilled out, followed by O'Shannon and a comely Mexican
girl, about the same age as Yakima's whore and with a
round, smiling face and pigtails. She wore a burlap dress
and sandals. A beaded blue necklace hung across her breasts,
and a wilting pink flower was pinned to her hair. O'Shannon had one arm draped around the girl's shoulders and a
cigar in his teeth.

He rolled the cigar to the side of his mouth and glanced
at Yakima. "You get one of these?"

"Yeah, but I scared her off."

"Don't doubt it a bit, amigo." O'Shannon placed a hand
under the smiling *puta*'s chin and turned her face to Yakima. "Look at that there. You ever see a girl with friendlier
eyes? And I'll tell you, her eyes aren't the only thing that's
friendly."

The gambler winked as he puffed smoke from the side
of his mouth. The man's wife would be happy to hear that,
Yakima thought. But he figured he had no room to judge,
since he'd bedded the man's wife himself and felt a contin-
ual rake of chagrin over it. The *puta* continued smiling, but
Yakima could tell she didn't understand a word the gambler
was saying.

"Amigos, *por favor*," said the man with the cornhusk
cigarette, beckoning as he trotted off down the hall. "The
don awaits your company!"

"Damn," O'Shannon muttered as he, the girl, and Yakima started following Ungaro's messenger boy. "For a few
hours there I'd forgotten about our plight."

"How 'bout we don't linger?" Yakima said. "Let's get the guns and the dynamite and vamoose."

"I hear you, pardner," O'Shannon said, walking arm in arm with the girl. "But please—I'm begging you now—let me do the talking?"

The Mexican messenger led them up a narrow flight of stairs and through a broad room that was smoky from the fire in the large hearth, over which several hanging pots bubbled. Judging by its size and shape, the room might have been a dining room, though most of the furniture, except for a cluttered food preparation table, was now gone. A chubby, round-faced man clad in a ratty undershirt stood over the table, stirring tortilla batter in a large wooden bowl that he held close to his chest as he regarded the gringos grimly.

The messenger led Yakima and O'Shannon past the table and through an arched doorway onto a broad balcony that looked southward toward a maze of cook fires flickering in the twilight. The balcony floor was still damp from the rain, and the viga poles dripped. The cooling air was fresh and aromatic with the smell of the recent storm, which, judging from the distant lightning flashes, had rolled on toward the purple peaks of the Sierra Madre.

"Por favor," the Mexican whispered, and gestured for the men to enter the balcony, where the don stood, elegantly attired and gazing out over his domain, a drink in one hand, a cigar in the other.

As O'Shannon stepped forward, the girl ducked out from under his arm and wheeled, whispering in Spanish, "I go now!"

"Senorita!" O'Shannon called as she retraced her steps through the cavelike room behind him.

The don turned from the low wall and spread his hands to indicate the long table before him set with plates, silverware, goblets, and two demijohns of wine. "Gentlemen. Please. Come. Join me. Forget the *puta*, my friend O'Shannon. They are—how you say?—a dime a dozen around here."

Yakima glanced to his left, where three big men in serapes lounged around a small table, drinking from a demijohn and playing poker. Rifles leaned against their table or against the adobe wall of the balcony. The black cat Yakima had seen before in the rain now sat atop the wall, scrubbing its face with a paw.

On their knees beneath the cat, a silver-haired old woman and two children shucked corn, setting the glistening yellow cobs in a large wooden bowl. Neither the woman nor the children—a little boy and a little girl—looked up from their work. The cardplayers, however, all stole quick, glowering glances at the two gringo newcomers over their pasteboards and smoidering cigarillos.

No doubt word had spread quickly of Yakima's cleaning of Chico's clock. The half-breed would have to watch his back with an especially sharp eye from now on, as a hard challenge glowed dimly in the three big hombres' sneering, measuring stares.

The table was set for four. As the don took the seat at the end, he gestured O'Shannon into the seat facing the wall to his right and Yakima into the seat beside O'Shannon. That left the seat to the don's right, with the high-backed chair facing the wall.

"Yes, I see you have many fine-looking senoritas fluttering about," O'Shannon said as he doffed his hat and dragged out his chair. "Peon girls, I assume?"

"Sí," said the don as Yakima doffed his own hat, dropped it to the floor, and sagged into the chair beside O'Shannon, eyeing the unclaimed table setting across from the gambler. "In the wake of the countless skirmishes with revolutionaries and banditos that have quite literally taken over this corner of Sonora, I have had to give refuge to the peons and their families who work for me in the fields. It is always the poorest and least able to defend themselves who suffer the most in barbaric times."

The don filled O'Shannon's wine goblet from the demijohn and glanced at the man sharply. "And these are *barbaric* times, my friend. Make no mistake."

The don walked around behind O'Shannon and leaned between them to fill Yakima's wineglass. As he did so, he placed his hand on Yakima's right shoulder and squeezed. "They are times that require barbaric actions from barbaric men." He glanced down, smiling inscrutably at Yakima while continuing to squeeze the half-breed's thick shoulder, then wheeled and, limping only slightly now on the ankle he'd twisted, strode back to the end of the table.

"But more about that later." The old hacendado set the demijohn on the table and eased himself down into his chair, smoothing his glistening hair back from his temples. "The girls, uh?" He grinned at both men. "You like?"

O'Shannon snorted and glanced at Yakima. "What's not to like? Henry and I appreciate the, uh, visitations."

"Restful, were they not?"

"Well, I don't know that I got all that much *rest*," O'Shannon said with a wry arch of his sun-bleached blond brows, holding his wineglass high above the table, "but after Rosaria tapped on my door, I discovered I wasn't all that sleepy after all. *¡Salud!*"

The two men clinked their glasses together, laughing. "There are more where those two came from," the don said, sliding his gaze between the gambler and the half-breed. "I allow only the ripest beauties into my casa"—he canted his head toward the old woman who, finished with the corn, was now hauling herself to her feet and heading toward another set of arched doors, the children quickly gathering up the stray corn shucks on the floor behind her—"except, of course, for those women adept at the more practical pursuits such as cooking and cleaning. They provide sport and much-needed . . . uh . . . comfort for my men who work so hard defending my property from those barbarians I mentioned earlier."

The don raised his glass toward Yakima, who had not taken part in the previous toast. "*¡Salud!*" He threw back a fair mouthful of the wine while Yakima only glowered at him, fingering the bottom of his glass and not liking the predictable but subtly menacing undertone of the conversation so far.

The don was little more than a half-crazed pimp who exploited those who worked for him. Now Yakima realized why he'd seen so many angry, wary-looking men alone with the children on the ride up to the casa. All the comely women, even those married with children, were here in the casa to service the don's army.

Ungaro was not unlike Bill Thornton, who'd sent the bounty hunters after Faith. Yakima wished O'Shannon would get down to brass tacks so they could prepare to pull their picket pines come first light tomorrow morning, and fog the sage and greasewood out of here. He hoped the gambler got down to business before Yakima's temper got the better of him and he wiped the ubiquitous mad leer off the hacendado's face with a quick slash of his toothpick across the man's stringy throat.

The gambler had been about to open the discussion, clearing his throat and beginning tensely with, "Well, then, Don, if you'll forgive me, but I'd like to tell you why I'm here . . ."

O'Shannon let his voice trail off. The don had lifted his gaze over the gambler's head to stare toward the smoky, candlelit doorway behind them, his eyes fairly glistening as his mustached lips spread back from his small white teeth in a faintly truckling, unashamedly adoring grin. "I'm afraid you'll have to forgive me, amigo. I wish to introduce you and Senor Henry to a very special guest."

Yakima glanced over his shoulder at the radiant female figure silhouetted in the doorway behind him, and his breath caught in his throat.

Chapter 17

The young woman standing tall and high-busted in the arched doorway, curly black hair glistening in the flickering candlelight, appeared to be the singularly dusky, sensual conjuring of some ancient Spanish legend involving heroic knights, beautiful Spanish princesses, and bloody wars in far mountains.

She wore a strapless purple gown that clung to her every curve and that was cut low enough to reveal all but the tips of her heavy breasts, between which nestled a jeweled silver crucifix hanging by a silver chain with diamond-shaped links. The girl thrust her shoulders back, breasts out, and the proud pose shone in her face as well. It was sharp-lined, classically hewn, and dark enough to suggest some Aztec blood. She had broad, flat cheekbones, a straight nose lifted slightly at the tip, and a dark mole at the left corner of her full-lipped mouth.

She was a striking figure. The kind of woman whose presence was like a dull knife in a man's belly and a constant tug in his loins. But as she stood there, a lacy mantilla draped over her head, silver hoop rings dangling from her ears, a wild, perpetually defiant light shimmering in those wide black eyes, Yakima turned his head quickly away from her.

Maybe too quickly, he realized when in the periphery of his vision he saw O'Shannon frown at him.

Yakima didn't want the woman—whose given name, he

had learned on his last trip to Mexico, was Leonora Domingo but who was known throughout northern Mexico by her outlaw name, Gato Salvaje de Sonorato—to recognize him suddenly and perhaps give herself away. For the Wildcat of Sonora, feared and hated by the hacendados as well as the rurales and federales, couldn't possibly be in the don's casa under anything but false pretenses . . . and with duplicitous intentions.

"Ah . . ." the don said, rising slowly from his chair and beaming up at the wild, erotically charged beauty as though at the coming of Mother Mary herself, "a very special guest, indeed."

O'Shannon shoved his chair back too quickly and nearly stumbled over it as he rose and turned toward Leonora Domingo with his blue eyes wide and a self-conscious flush turning his tanned cheeks the color of chili peppers. Reluctantly, Yakima slid his chair out, stood, and turned slowly to face the young woman, keeping his chin as low as he could without looking ridiculous—although the don's eyes were riveted on the Spanish vision before him.

"Gentlemen, I give you the inimitable Senorita Leonora Domingo."

Yakima raised his eyes to the girl's face. His gut clenched when her lustrous gaze met his, furtively probing his own for about one second before secret recognition shone in her eyes. It was like a tiny dark sheen, there and then gone in an instant, when she blinked.

Expertly maintaining a casual expression, giving nothing away, she turned her head toward O'Shannon. The gambler fairly lurched toward her like a love-struck schoolboy, wiping his hands on his pinto vest, then reaching out to take the girl's offered hand in his own.

"Senorita Domingo," he said, lowering his head to kiss her hand as though it were the hand of the princess of Spain. "I'm Cleve O'Shannon, friend and business associate of the don's. And I can't tell you, milady, how wonderful it is to meet a woman of such exquisite charm and captivating beauty."

"The pleasure's mine, Mr. O'Shannon," the senorita said with a throaty sensuality in her only slightly accented English, which she'd picked up running roughshod with her band of *desperado/revolutionarios* along the border. She cut her cool, dark-eyed gaze toward Yakima, arching her lovely brow with only a hint of irony. "And who is this big . . . uh . . . what is he, anyway—Apache?"

Yakima had to fight to keep his expression implacable. The Wildcat of Sonora knew very well he was half-Cheyenne.

Before O'Shannon could introduce him, Yakima said his name without inflection and held the girl's half-incredulous, half-mocking gaze with his own. "And the pleasure's mine, Senorita."

"She is known as the Wildcat of Sonora," said the don proudly, still smiling broadly. "But I like to think that I—a man old enough to be her grandfather—have come the closest of any man to taking the sting from her bite and the sharpness from her claws."

"Oh, come now, Don Ungaro," the girl said, casting one more fleeting, faintly questioning gaze at Yakima as she moved out from the doorway. "You wouldn't want me to lose *all* of my feline qualities now, would you? What is a tame woman, anyway, but one of those guileless little whores you have running around half dressed and slathering after your desperadoes like mongrel bitches in heat?"

The mantilla sweeping out behind her silver earrings, she strode around behind the table to the empty chair beside the still-beaming don. "*¿Usted sabe lo que significo, no usted?*" she added with a lusty gleam in her eye, sitting down as the don held her chair for her. You know what I mean, don't you?

The don snorted in boyish delight as he eased the girl's chair toward the table and limped over to his own.

"Wine, *mi amore*?" the don asked, holding up the bottle.

"If it's too late for tequila," the senorita rasped, brushing her flirty gaze from O'Shannon to Yakima and holding the half-breed's stare for another meaningful second before returning her eyes to the don, at whom she smiled with exaggerated affection.

The girl wore her disdain for the old man like a silk cape woven with burrs and cactus thorns. Fortunately for her sake, the don had deluded himself into believing the senorita's affection was genuine.

The don laughed and shook his finger at the girl—every bit the wildcat that Yakima had known last year when she'd helped him and Faith and his ragtag team of Americanos bust Faith's brother out of the Mexican prison in the Sierra Olivadas—the Forgotten Mountains. "Now, now, *mi amore*," he chuckled. "We know how salty-tongued you can be when you've had the tequila."

"Only as salty-tongued as your desperadoes."

"Ah, *sí*. But my desperadoes are men. They are expected to be salty-tongued." The old hacendado held out his hand to indicate her delectable body nearly spilling in all its naturally tan, ripe exoticness out of the low-cut frock. "You . . . you are a beautiful young woman—the loveliest in all of Mejico and perhaps even in Spain—and far more pleasing to the eye than to the ear."

The Wildcat of Sonora rested her chin on her fist as she smiled at the don, her lips spread in a straight line across her face—a smile so frigid that Yakima felt his shoulders tighten with dread. O'Shannon must have had the same reaction, because he glanced at Yakima as if to say, "Oh, boy . . ."

But just as the don's own smile began to jell on his ragged face, the senorita raised the corners of her mouth, leaned toward the old man, placed a hand on the back of his neck, and drew his head to hers. She kissed him softly, her steely smile in place—the way a snake kisses a paralyzed rabbit just before it devours it.

The senorita did not strike, however.

Instead, holding his head near hers, she said, "You and you alone, Don Ungaro, know how to make a woman feel like a woman!" She pulled his head toward her again, jerking it down rather harshly, planted another quick, aggressive kiss on his lips, and let him go.

"Now, then, Senores," she said, turning to O'Shannon and Yakima, "what is it that brings two such gallant wayfarers to Mejico? The don's war with the savage *revolutionarios* or"—she smiled and narrowed her eyes slightly, smokily—"his many voluptuous women?"

O'Shannon grinned over his wineglass at the girl, smitten. "I have to confess, Miss Domingo, I didn't realize how many voluptuous women—"

"A Gatling gun and a few sticks of dynamite," Yakima cut in, impatient despite the unexpected appearance of one of the most beguiling women he'd ever met.

The don turned away from the senorita for the first time since she'd sat down. Staring at Yakima, he arched his brows in surprise, then switched his questioning glance to the gambler.

O'Shannon chuckled and put his hand on Yakima's back. "You'll have to forgive my friend. He's forgotten after the long ride with the sun beating down that in Mejico business is not discussed until after the meal."

"Ah, *sí*," the don said, his eyes glistening from drink as he narrowed them shrewdly, nodding his understanding.

"As I was saying," the gambler continued to the girl, "I didn't realize the don had adorned his palace with so many lovely furnishings. If I had, I would have slipped down here much sooner and more frequently."

"And how do you know the don?" she asked, closing her rich upper lip over her wineglass.

"My father and Don Ungaro were business partners. They owned a mine together not far from here. My brother, Jason, and I came here often when we were boys, riding horses, hunting, and fishing in the don's amazing trout streams."

"How is your father, Cleve?" the don asked.

"Wealthy and befuddled," O'Shannon said. "Especially after the passing of my mother last year. Heart stroke, I'm afraid."

"I am sorry to hear that. I am sorry, too, that I have been so long out of touch with Brian. After the mine closed"—

the don shrugged sadly, then gave the senorita a pointed glance beneath his brows—"and with all the trouble I've been having with *revolutionarios* and *revolutionarias* of late, I haven't had time to keep up my friendships."

"Except those you have made with *revolutionarias, mi amore*," said Senorita Domingo huskily, giving him a craven look, which he obviously found mesmerizing, judging by the way his eyes seemed nearly to roll back in his head.

As the old don leaned toward her, pooching out his lips for a kiss, she straightened suddenly, brushing him off. She cast another quick, furtive glance at Yakima, who was fully appreciating her performance while wondering what her motives were, and threw back a liberal slug of the wine. A thin red stream dribbled down the corner of her mouth, and she brushed it away with the back of her hand.

"Perhaps we'd better eat," the don said with a sigh, regarding the girl warily as she splashed more wine into her glass. "Too much blood of the saints on an empty stomach makes her"—he chuckled wryly—"frighteningly full of piss and vinegar!"

Don't I know? Yakima thought as he held his glass across the table for the Wildcat of Sonora to fill. She gave him an oblique stare from beneath dark brows that made him wonder all the more what she was up to.

The don had to bark only once, and not loudly, before the meal was delivered by the old woman and the children who'd been shucking the corn and the pudgy gent who'd been stirring the tortilla batter.

There was roasted corn, peppers, refried frijoles, warm tortillas, and large portions of chicken and goat meat roasted in sage and garlic. Two more bottles of wine were brought to the table and, as per the senorita's request of the don, a crock of tequila.

The meal was as good as Yakima had ever eaten in Mexico, but he had trouble enjoying it with Leonora Domingo leveling occasional wistful glances at him from over her tequila glass or corncob. And with the three well-armed hombres at the far end of the balcony laughing and glancing at him frequently with dark menace while they drank tequila, smoked foul-smelling tobacco, ate burritos and beans, and cleaned their guns.

The night was dark and hushed in the aftermath of the storm, the air cool and clean and rife with the smell of the cook fires flickering around the don's massive, crumbling casa. Occasionally there rose the sound of a baby crying or a goat bleating or a coyote yammering in the distant hills.

When Yakima and the others at his table had finished their plates, the somnolent strumming of a guitar sounded out among the lonely fires around which sat the sad men and children of the women held hostage in the house to service the don's pistoleros. Occasional victorious or drunken whoops or embittered female shrieks sounded from one of the bunkhouses or from the casa itself, setting Yakima's nerves on edge.

As they dined, the don and O'Shannon spoke casually of earlier times when the gambler's wealthy Eastern father had joined the don in a Mexican mining venture that apparently had soured shortly after its initiation. During the conversation, in which Yakima took no part, the don held an eye on the senorita beside him—kept a hand on her forearm, in fact—like a father making sure his somewhat rebellious young daughter was behaving as befitted a lady.

When the table had been cleared, the don dismissed the Wildcat of Sonora in formal Spanish. It was time now for the men to speak of serious matters.

"Take a hot bath, Senorita," the don told her as she made her way—a little unsteadily, Yakima noticed—around the table. "Brush your hair. Put on some of that fragrance that smells like lemon blossoms." He grinned and held up his glass of cognac in salute to her. "I will be along very soon, *mi amore.*"

"I will be waiting," the senorita said, blowing the don a kiss over her shoulder with a seductive pooch of her ripe lips and hooded eyes, "with much anticipation."

She let her hot, dark glance fall on Yakima once more in

passing, then disappeared through the arched doorway behind him and O'Shannon.

"An amazing woman," the gambler told the don after all three men had watched her disappear into the kitchen's smoky, candlelit shadows.

"There are few more amazing than she," the don said, holding a long cheroot between his lips as he puffed, his gaze lingering after the girl. "She is a wild filly who has been haunting the canyons and cordilleras of my hacienda for years. Now, finally, she is mine. The queen of my remuda."

"Congratulations." O'Shannon glanced at Yakima and chuckled as he returned his gaze to the don. "How'd you finally run her down?"

Silence, as the don stared into the kitchen, where the old people and the children were bustling about in hushed quiet, washing pots and scrubbing tables. Strains of guitar music wafted softly in the fire-punctuated dark below the casa, and the men to Yakima's far left continued chuckling among themselves, clinking glasses, firing matches, and tossing pasteboards.

When Yakima returned his gaze to the don, he found the man staring at him wistfully through the cigar smoke. Yakima felt a hitch in his chest. His right cheek twitched apprehensively.

The don rolled his drink-rheumy eyes toward the gambler. "The story of my corralling that high-blooded filly is one for another time, amigo. Now perhaps it is time for you to tell me what has brought you to my hacienda . . . since it is obvious you are not here merely to hunt the puma or to fish for red-throated trout in my streams." The don pursed his lips and shook his head slowly, darkly. "Sadly, those times have passed."

Chapter 18

Prompted by the don's bold, menacing stare, O'Shannon quickly sketched out his and Yakima's mission here in Mexico and his need for at least one Gatling gun and as much dynamite as the don could spare.

"I believe that the dynamite will afford us enough of a distraction to get us to the top of the mesa where Jason is holed up with the silver," he said, holding one of the don's cigars in one hand and a shot glass of tequila in the other. "And the Gatling gun will get us down off the mesa with the silver. Hell, with that kind of firepower, we'll be able to blast our way all the way to El Paso."

O'Shannon chuckled and shuttled his glance to Yakima on his left and to the don on his right.

"A silver mine . . . so near to my hacienda," the don said, regarding O'Shannon with hooded eyes. "I had no idea."

The gambler frowned. "Well, how could you have had an idea?"

"*Sí*, how could I?" The hacendado smiled frigidly. "When neither you nor Jason told me?"

O'Shannon stared back at the don, smoke from his cigar curling up across his cheek. "On our initial assays of the property, we came down through Texas and Chihuahua. We didn't come through Arizona. If we had, we certainly would have stopped—"

"And would you have told me, Cleve?"

O'Shannon hesitated. "Of course."

The frigid smile again, broader this time, colder. "And would you have cut me in . . . after all I did for your family when you came to Mexico all those years ago?"

O'Shannon's brows furrowed. Even in the shadows thrown up by the flickering candles and lanterns, Yakima could see the man's face darkening. "I guess we didn't give it much thought, Don Ungaro. My father wasn't involved . . . and we hadn't seen you in years."

"So you come down to my country uninvited, you discover a cache of silver ore, and you don't give me the simple, civilized courtesy of asking me"—the don tapped his chest and raised his voice—"me, the one who made it possible for you to come down here the first time; me, who taught you and your brother to hunt the puma; me, the largest landowner in all of northern Chihuahua *and* Sonora!—if I would like to be involved in the venture?"

With that last, he lowered his voice and sank back in his chair with such a menacing, deeply offended expression that Yakima found his hand once more edging toward his Colt revolver that wasn't there.

The man at the table on the far side of the balcony had fallen eerily silent. There was only the distant guitar and the sound of a baby crying, the occasional sputter of a guttering candle.

O'Shannon sat frozen in his chair, holding the don's stare with a shocked one of his own.

"No," the don said finally, shaking his head as he continued to sag back in his seat. "It is out of the question. Even if I wanted to help such an ingrate, it would not be possible."

"I fully intended to pay you, Don. It wasn't like I—"

"No, no," the don said, frowning and shaking his head. "You have said enough. Even if I wanted to help you, amigo, I could not. With the mangy yellow dogs who call themselves *revolutionarios* attacking me at all corners of my rancho and making such frequent assaults on my wall, I cannot spare a single gun or a single stick of dynamite."

The don glanced at Yakima and blew a smoke ring over

the table. "Now, I have a request of you, Senor O'Shannon. One that you, unlike myself, will not be able to turn down. You will leave the *norteamericano* Indio, Henry, here with me."

O'Shannon leaned slowly back in his chair. He glanced at Yakima, frowning incredulously, then turned to the don. "Surely you're joking."

"I do not joke in these trying times, amigo."

"What do you want with Yakima?"

"To replace Chico, the man he killed. A life for a life, eh? It is only fitting."

Yakima's hand closed so tightly around his chair arms that the wood cracked audibly. "Go to hell, old man. Find another gun slave. I'll be out of here tonight, and if you try to stop me, I'll . . ."

Yakima let his voice trail off as the thud of dropping feet and the rake of sliding chairs sounded from the far side of the balcony. He turned to see the cardplayers getting heavily to their feet—three big men pulling their sombreros onto their heads, two of them hefting Winchester rifles while the third snagged a pepperbox revolver off the table and took a last drag from a half-smoked cigarette.

Yakima jerked back in his chair and started to heave himself to his feet while raising his hand toward the sheath at the back of his neck.

The angry rasp of two cocking levers froze him. A third one followed as the three bearded bruins drew up to the end of the table, spreading out in a half circle around him, self-satisfied expressions drawing their mustached lips taut and slitting their eyes. The two with Winchesters aimed their cocked rifles from their waists while the third held his pepperbox trained on Yakima.

"You see, senores," the don said lazily, self-satisfied, "it is not possible to refuse my request."

"Don, please," O'Shannon said. "You have no right to enslave the man I've hired—"

"On my own rancho, in a time of war, I have the right to do anything I wish. You might as well stay, too, Senor

Cleve. Without help, you will not get through to your brother's mine. *Revolutionarios* of every stripe stitch this land. Along with Indios and common thieves. Your brother is likely dead, his silver plundered." The don's shoulders jerked as he laughed. "It is likely halfway to Monterrey by now."

He glanced at the three armed apes and canted his head toward the door. "Take them to the cellar. Keep them there until they are convinced that they must fight for me—swear their loyalty to me—or die." He narrowed an eye at both Yakima and O'Shannon. "Until they realize that if they betray me, they will be hunted down like dogs and tortured slowly in the fashion of the Lipan Apache."

Yakima lurched automatically toward the rifle-wielding hombre nearest him.

"Yakima!" O'Shannon shouted.

The half-breed stopped halfway out of his chair. All three rifles were aimed at his heart. He didn't have a chance. The idea of being locked in that cellar was worse than death.

He had to wait, however. Bide his time for a chance to spring himself. Fighting now would be certain suicide. Maybe, in the don's drunken state, he wouldn't remember the—

"Don't forget the pigsticker he has tucked down the back of his shirt," Ungaro told the trio behind Yakima, giving the half-breed a knowing grin.

While two kept their rifles aimed at him, the third side-stepped around him, planted his pepperbox hard against Yakima's lower back, and removed the Arkansas toothpick from the deerhide sheath hanging down his collar.

"Off with them both!" the don ordered, throwing up a dismissive hand and turning to look out over the balcony. "No food or water until they've agreed to declare their loyalty to Hacienda de Ungaro!"

"Don, please!" O'Shannon pleaded. "You can't do this. You're a friend of my father's. You're a friend of mine. Are you *mad*?"

Puffing his cigar, the don flicked a hand up near his ear as though brushing away a fly.

"Up!" ordered the man who'd relieved Yakima of his pigsticker.

He nudged O'Shannon with his rifle butt. The gambler turned around in his chair and glared up at the man. It was a look Yakima hadn't seen before in the normally mild-mannered gambler's features. His eyes were sharp, his jaw hard. The man with the rifle backed up a bit but leveled his Winchester at O'Shannon's nose.

The gambler, keeping his jaw clenched, muttered several Spanish curses as he stood up from the chair. The man with Yakima's pigsticker backed away, and the gambler, glancing at Yakima incredulously, stepped through the arched doorway and into the kitchen, where the two old people and the children stood in hushed silence near the snapping fire. The woman had her arms loosely—protectively—draped over the little girl's shoulders. All four stood as tense as soldiers awaiting inspection.

Walking side by side, Yakima and O'Shannon made their way past them. The three riflemen followed ten feet back, just out of reach of Yakima's nimble hands and feet. As he approached the hall door, Yakima saw in the corner of his eye the old woman cross herself quickly and whisper what sounded like a prayer.

A large wooden door was thrown open, and there was the unmistakable squeak of a sizable rat. The door hinges screeched as well, but Yakima knew the squeak of a rat when he heard one, and the scuttle of tiny clawed feet and the raking of a leathery little tail. Unfortunately, he also recognized the smell of rat shit and the mushroom-like odor of scorpions and snakes.

As he and O'Shannon descended the broad stone stairs that curved like a horseshoe, one of the riflemen prodded them mockingly with his Winchester.

"You do that one more time," O'Shannon said, "and I'm

going to relieve you of that weapon and shove it up your hairy ass and pull the friggin' trigger."

He said it in English, and Yakima didn't think the three Mexicans spoke or understood English, but the man apparently got the gist of the threat. He rammed the barrel once more against the small of each prisoner's back and chuckled. As the gambler and Yakima approached the bottom of the stairs, O'Shannon grunted and wheeled.

He nudged the Mexican's rifle aside with one arm. The man, caught glancing back and laughing with the other two men who were flanking him, tripped the Winchester's trigger. The explosion was deafening. The bullet blasted the mortared stone wall with a crashing roar, sending shards flying in all directions.

"Hold on!" Yakima shouted.

Too late.

The gambler bulled straight into the man behind him, who was three steps farther up the stairs. The man with the rifle screamed and fell backward against the steps. Cursing and grunting and panting like a rabid dog, the gambler smashed his right fist against the Mexican's jaw and lunged for the rifle.

He'd barely gotten his hand around the receiver when one of the Mexicans behind him sprang forward and laid the butt of his Winchester against the top of the gambler's head, smashing the man's dusty hat flat against his skull.

O'Shannon grunted, jerking his head up and down. Then his eyes closed, and he sagged sideways. Yakima lurched forward and caught the gambler around the shoulders, keeping him from tumbling the last four stone steps to the bottom.

"You carry that big-mouthed son of a bitch, huh, amigo?" snarled the man who'd brained O'Shannon while the man O'Shannon had leveled blinked and shook his head as he slowly heaved himself to his feet without any help from his friends.

His English was so lousy that Yakima could have understood him better in Spanish.

The third Mexican held a burning torch high above his head and grinned down at the two unfortunate prisoners.

"Yeah, yeah," Yakima growled, lifting the unconscious gambler over his shoulder. "I carry the big-mouthed son of a bitch."

Chapter 19

A scream sounded at the periphery of Yakima's unconsciousness.

He opened his eyes and lifted his head from the scrap of smelly gunnysack he'd found amid the storeroom's boxes, barrels, crates, sundry goods, and trash. O'Shannon gave another soft cry as, dropping both legs off the two barrels Yakima had laid him on after the three Mexicans had closed the storeroom's heavy double doors and locked them, he brushed his hand across his thigh and grunted with revulsion.

Something crawled away on the cracked stone floor. It was pale and crablike and about the size of a pocket pistol.

"Scorpion!" the gambler rasped, running the heel of his hand across his chest. "Christ. A sting from one of those . . ."

"Almost as bad as a bite from your friend Agundo."

The scorpion crabbed along the edge of three long stone steps that rose to a platform upon which a frame containing several wine casks hulked, heading toward a ragged crack in the cellar's stone wall, from which a thin thread of milky daylight washed.

Dawn. Yakima hadn't realized he'd slept all night. But there wasn't much else to do in the cellar's stygian darkness. Outside, he could hear the desultory voices of his and O'Shannon's three jailers and the faint clink of tin cups.

O'Shannon clutched his head, groaned, and lay slowly down on the barrels again. "What the hell happened to my head?"

"You don't remember?"

The gambler shook his head slightly, sucking a sharp breath through gritted teeth.

Yakima sat up and leaned back against an empty crate that had once held a Gatling gun. "You took a page out of my book. They weren't merciful."

The gambler breathed heavily. "He's gone mad. The man I knew as a boy didn't live like this. I knew he'd run off his three sons and his daughter had been killed in an Apache raid, but he'd run his ranch like a true hidalgo."

"What about a wife?"

"If I remember right, the first one died before he took over the Spanish land grant. The second died in childbirth."

"And then the revolutionaries started giving him hell." Yakima scratched his forearm and stared up through a long, narrow window against the ceiling, where a strip of pearl sky shone. "Well, he means to keep us here. Right here. And those doors yonder are stout. I tested 'em last night when I heard our three turnkeys snoring on the other side."

There was a muffled gun crack somewhere out on the valley floor beyond the casa. Then another. Faintly, a man yelled. One of the men outside the storeroom's stout oak doors said something with a start in Spanish, reacting to the distant gunfire.

O'Shannon lifted his head and cocked an ear. "Is that . . . ?"

"Gunfire."

There were several more cracks and pops, faint as distant small branches broken for kindling. The gunfire continued sporadically, as did the faint drumming of hooves.

"Sounds like our friends the *revolutionarios* are at it again," O'Shannon said, lying back down with a groan. "Maybe," he added with an ironic chuckle, "they'll come break us outta here."

"Wouldn't count on it," Yakima said, chewing his cheek and looking around like a caged panther. "That stockade wall is right thick, and it appeared he has it well protected with those belching cannons, as the Injuns call 'em."

He heaved himself to his feet and walked over to stare

up at the window. It was too narrow for anyone but a small child to crawl through.

"Christ," the gambler said. "I knew getting through to Jason wasn't going to be a Sunday walk in Central Park, but I didn't know I'd get trouble from the very man I expected to help me the most. Aside from you, I mean."

"No offense taken. But I do think you oughta reconsider your friends."

O'Shannon sat up again, dropped his legs down the side of the barrels and, rubbing the crown of his skull with one hand and wincing, regarded Yakima apologetically. "Sorry I got you into this."

Yakima hiked a shoulder. "I'm usually in a fix of one kind or another." He'd walked over to the crack in the stone wall and was running a hand along both sides of it, trying to judge how firm the stones were.

Damn firm. He cursed.

A shout rose from outside the storeroom—a Spanish bellow uttered too quickly for Yakima to follow. It was punctuated with a high-pitched, *"Vamos!"*

The men directly behind the doors uttered excited exclamations. There was the stomp of boots and the clatter of weapons, and then spurs rang on stone steps, fading quickly as the three jailers ran up the stairs.

Yakima glanced at O'Shannon and frowned. "Somebody must be calling for reinforcements."

"Sounds like the *revolutionarios* are giving the don quite a time."

As Yakima strode to the doors, he stopped suddenly. In the distance sounded the *rat-tat-tat* of a Gatling gun.

"There's your belching cannon," O'Shannon said, still sitting atop the barrels and staring straight ahead as he listened to the growing commotion outside and the creaks in the adobe ceiling as boots clomped around in the casa.

Yakima pushed against the heavy double doors. They bent inward slightly where they latched together, but he could see through the slight crack between them that they were solidly barred on the outside. From the creaking sound the bar made when he rammed his shoulder against the doors, he could tell it was a wooden locking bar, not metal.

Wood would give if you put enough force against it.

He backed up and clenched his fists together.

What seemed to be a loud thunderclap sounded outside. Only it wasn't thunder. Dynamite. In its echoing wake, the Gatling gun was silent.

More shouts sounded around the casa. They were growing more vehement.

"Damn," O'Shannon said, clambering down off the barrels and moving toward the small window. "There was some black powder behind that blast. Sounds like they might've taken out a Gatling gun."

Yakima felt a tingle of optimism. The likelihood of the revolutionaries busting through the wall and overtaking the casa was slim at best. They'd probably been trying to do it for months. Still, if he and O'Shannon could break out of the storeroom while the don's soldiers were distracted . . .

He lurched forward and rammed his shoulder against the doors. They creaked and groaned.

He backed up and rammed them again, feeling the aching blow through his chest.

"Forget it," O'Shannon said, walking up behind him. "They're locked from the outside. A brahma bull couldn't . . ."

He let his voice trail off as Yakima rammed the doors again, making them creak and groan louder this time, ancient dust puffing out from between the grains of the old oak.

"It's your shoulder," the gambler drawled. "If you dislocate it, don't . . ."

Again he let his voice trail off. Yakima froze. A keening wail sounded from somewhere inside the casa. At first, Yakima thought it was a baby's cry, high-pitched and broken. Then it came again, slightly lower pitched.

A man's shriek of unbearable pain and agony.

The shriek rose and died again, rose and died again, almost like the howls of a distant, wounded wolf. The dirge broke and became garbled, then fell into what sounded like panting mixed with sobbing. And then the gunfire—rifles and pistols and at least one more Gatling gun—picked up outside, drowning out the keening, hair-raising wails.

"What the hell's that?" O'Shannon asked.

"Sounds like someone needs their breakfast." Yakima bunched his lips, squeezed his fists together, and rammed his shoulder once again against the doors. His shoulder barked painfully, but he stepped back to try again.

"I'll be damned!" O'Shannon said. "Think I heard the bar crack that time."

More hoofbeats sounded around the casa. Jostling shadows passed the window. In the far distance, the Gatling gun was rattling out a near steady stream of bullets above the angry barks of the rifles and pistols and the occasional whinny of a horse.

Yakima rammed his left shoulder against the doors once more, then switched shoulders and continued pummeling the center of the doors until the locking board complained with an audible crack. It didn't break, but it was cracking.

"By George, you're getting there!" O'Shannon ex-claimed. "Once or twice more and you'll have it!"

Yakima gave the gambler a wry glance. "Thanks for the help."

"You're built for it. I'd snap like a twig."

Yakima stepped back and set his feet. Both of his shoulders and his chest ached from the pummeling he was giving himself as well as the door. He hoped the locking board gave way before his own bones did.

He drew a deep breath, steeled himself against the next blow, and bolted off his heels, the doors growing quickly before him as his feet propelled him forward. His shoulder had just brushed the splintered oak panels before the crack between the doors grew suddenly.

He grimaced. The doors were opening.

He caught a glimpse of a dark-haired figure and heard a shocked female screech as he rammed both doors wide with a sound like a thunderclap and, unable to put the brakes on his own momentum, bulled straight into the ante-room. He crossed the room's ten-foot width in a blink, flew over a small wooden table cluttered with cards and tin coffee cups, and smashed his right shoulder against the stone wall on the other side of it.

He heard a crunching sound in his shoulders and rib cage, and the table flew apart around his hips like split kindling.

Yakima piled up against the wall, turning his back to it, wincing and clutching his battered shoulder, and followed the table's splintered remains to the floor.

"Christos!" the woman's raspy voice shouted. "What the hell are you doing, you crazy bastard?"

Seated among the scattered cards and cups, Yakima shook the cobwebs from his eyes and, still clutching his throbbing shoulder, looked up to see Senorita Leonora Domingo scowling down at him, fists on her hips.

She wore a black sombrero, a doeskin vest with nothing beneath it but her deep, alluring cleavage, and form-hugging leather slacks split on the insides from mid-calf down to her silver-tipped, fancy-stitched red boots. Over the slacks she wore cracked bullhide chaps adorned with large silver conchos.

"I told you I was going to open it," she scolded, beetling her thin black brows above her lustrous chocolate eyes.

Yakima blinked again to quell the fireworks blossoming behind his retinas and drew a deep breath. "I reckon I didn't hear you."

Leonora grinned down at him coquettishly. "Or maybe you were just showing off for me, uh?"

O'Shannon stood in the open door, lower jaw hanging as he looked the delectable *bandita/revolucionaria* up and down. "What . . . the . . . hell . . . ?"

She wheeled toward him, her thick hair flying about her shoulders. On her hips she wore two pistols, bone-gripped silver-plated Remington in the cross-draw position high on her hip and a pearl-gripped Colt thonged low on her leather-clad thigh. "If you want to get out of here, grab your hat and come with me!"

As O'Shannon dashed back into the storeroom for his hat, the senorita glared down at Yakima. "Are you going to sit there all day, you big Indio bull? The Jesus Cristobal boys have given us a diversion, but it might not last until Christmas!"

With that, she strode quickly toward the broad staircase, spurs ringing, chaps flapping against her legs. Yakima grunted as he heaved himself to his feet, grabbed his hat from the table wreckage on the floor, and started up the stairs with O'Shannon hurrying along behind him.

"Who was wailing?" Yakima asked the girl, noting even in their dire predicament that her round hips had one of the loveliest sways he'd ever seen.

The senorita stopped at the top of the stairs and, grabbing her Colt and cocking it, poked her head through the gap in the open door, looking cautiously around. Then she moved up into the hall, where the morning light was brighter, and glanced back at Yakima.

Curling her upper lip, she growled, "Let's just say that in his delicate condition the don won't be pestering any more senoritas." She threw her head back slightly and chuckled, thoroughly satisfied with herself. "But he'll be able to sing in the boys' choir on All Saints Day just *muy bueno!*"

She peered around again, holding her revolver out in front of her. She looked as comfortable with that big pistol in her hand as most girls looked holding a hairbrush.

The distant gunfire and the incessant cackling of the Gatling gun were in stark contrast to the tomblike silence of the misty morning casa.

"Come on," the senorita ordered. "Hurry!"

She started running.

Yakima glanced back at O'Shannon, then took off after her.

Chapter 20

An enraged Spanish scream filled the corridor down which Yakima, Senorita Domingo, and O'Shannon were creeping, heading for a back door so they could avoid the turmoil roiling around the front of the house and in the south yard.

Judging by the pounding boots and excited yells echoing down the honeycomblike corridors, some men were rushing toward the battle that was raging at the east wall while others were hurrying to tend the don, whose wails could still be heard echoing throughout the halls, punctuated by his bellowed Spanish epithets, most of which were variations on "*Puta* bitch! Bring me her traitorous head!"

From the shadows down the broad hall behind Yakima, Leonora, and O'Shannon, boots pounded and spurs rang raucously, growing louder as the runners approached.

"Hide!" the senorita hissed.

She bolted into an intersecting corridor on one side of the hall while Yakima and O'Shannon ran into a hallway on the other side. Her back to the wall, she edged a look around the corner. Yakima did the same, his heart thudding.

He was weaponless. Not even his toothpick.

Up the hall, the runners appeared, first their scissoring legs as they descended a handful of steps from a higher level. One of the men yelled too wildly, angrily in Spanish for Yakima to decipher exactly, but he was sure they were looking for the senorita, whom someone had seen heading toward the back of the house.

He glanced across the dingy corridor at the girl. She returned the look. She pressed the silver-plated barrel of her Remington revolver against her wide mouth, spreading her lips with a cunning grin.

Yakima pulled his head back against the wall and glanced at O'Shannon. "We need weapons," the gambler whispered, blue eyes wide with desperation.

The boot thuds and spur jangling grew louder, as did the rasp of labored breathing.

Yakima glanced across the corridor as Senorita Domingo lurched toward him into the hall, raking the Remy's hammer back while smoothly, quickly unsheathing the Colt. Dropping to one knee in the middle of the hall, she extended both pistols straight out from her shoulders, aiming toward the runners, and screamed in Spanish, "Dic, vermin-infested coyotes!"

The thuds faded, replaced with surprised grunts, shrieks, and bellows.

"Tell *el diablo* that the Wildcat of Sonora sent you!"

The senorita's guns roared, stabbing smoke and flames, leaping in her small, feminine brown hands. She laughed madly and loudly, her hair dancing across her forehead, as the men's bellows turned to shrieks and wails of agony. The thumps of dropping bodies and the clatter of rifles followed.

The explosive din died for a moment, the pistols' reports echoing in the cavelike quiet. The senorita stared out over her still-extended smoking guns.

A man wailed. Leonora's Colt leapt and roared. The wounded man grunted, and there was the smack of a body hitting the floor.

Yakima glanced around the corner. Up the hall, five bodies were lumped across the floor, strewn as they'd fallen. Blood shone dark red and oily as it pooled around the still-quivering corpses. Pistols and rifles shone in the morning light that angled through a side window.

Yakima turned to O'Shannon, whose lower jaw hung slack with awe. "I believe we're heeled."

Yakima ran out from around the corner as the senorita, remaining on one knee, flicked open her Colt's loading gate and began dumping spent shells onto the floor.

"Don't tell me I never did you any favors," she said as the brass cartridges clattered around her.

Yakima plucked a Schofield off one man's bloody chest and spun the cylinder. "Leave it to you to remind me!"

O'Shannon shoved a Colt Navy behind the waistband of his whipcord trousers and stooped to grab a Winchester. "You two know each other, I take it."

"Mere acquaintances," Yakima said, sliding a second pistol from a dead man's holster—a side-hammer Smith & Wesson modified with the British-style grips of the Bisley.

Senorita Domingo laughed heartily as she thumbed fresh cartridges from her belt into her Remington. "That isn't how I remember it!" She threw an arm around Yakima's neck, kissed him violently, then flicked the Colt's loading gate closed and began jogging down the hall, the small silver spurs adorning her worn red boots ringing like sleigh bells. "Let's get out of here while we can. I was beginning to think I'd live to be an old lady in this madman's hell."

"If she did what she claimed to Don Ungaro," O'Shannon said, jogging abreast of Yakima as they both followed the senorita's fleet form down the broad, stone-tiled hall, "the don's gonna have men nipping at our heels like the hounds of the devil himself."

Yakima shoved his second pistol into his waistband, took his stolen Winchester in both hands, and racked a shell into the chamber. "Let's hope his hounds are kept busy at the east wall."

A minute later they were running down narrow stone stairs at the rear of the casa, past a crumbling patio stippled with dead pecan trees and across the open yard, heading downslope toward brush and rocks.

"You know where we're going?" Yakima called to Senorita Domingo, who was sprinting ahead of them while casting a cautious glance up along the casa's south side.

"I've been here for three long weeks, lover," the senorita

called over her shoulder. "And I wasn't just milling around looking sexy!"

Yakima wondered what she had been doing. He would learn in due course and whatever it was, it wouldn't surprise him. No sexier border bandit had ever existed. She was as wild and crazy as any Mexican mustang filly addicted to locoweed, fight-scarred stallions, and the intoxicating thrill of revolution.

She, Yakima, and O'Shannon sprinted along a path down the scrub and boulder-strewn knoll, heading for several tile-roofed stables, a peak-roofed hay barn, a blacksmith hovel, and a rattling windmill on the other side. A riderless horse ran toward them up the hill, trailing its reins, shaking its head and snorting wildly—apparently incensed by the savage gunfire and billowing black smoke rising in the west.

As the horse approached, Leonora grabbed its reins. The horse bolted sideways, ripping the reins from her grasp, then switched direction as it galloped up the hill, whinnying.

"Bastardo!" the girl shouted, then wheeled and continued running toward the stables.

Leonora ducked down behind a springhouse in which water trickled tinnily and edged a peek around it toward the stables. Yakima did likewise on the other side, while O'Shannon knelt on one knee behind them, doffing his slouch hat and rubbing the back of his neck, his face etched with pain from last night's clubbing.

"You see anyone around?" the girl asked.

Yakima peered through the dust wafting in the morning's golden sunlight. The only movement was the dust and a couple of breeze-jostled, dew-dappled tumbleweeds. "Looks like they grabbed their mounts and vamoosed. You got any idea which barn our horses are stabled in?"

"How would I know that?" the girl said, her voice pitched with excitement. "You two go look. Saddle me one while you're at it. A stallion. I'll stay here and keep watch."

She glanced at Yakima as she held both her big pistols up around her shoulders. "And for God's sakes, hurry. I left a bloody mess in there, and if the crazy bastard is still alive, he's going to make me pay and keep paying. Slow . . . if you get my drift!"

This last she nearly shouted when she was only halfway through her tirade. Yakima and O'Shannon had run out from behind the springhouse and were sprinting toward one of the stables.

They found not only their horses and the mule but their revolvers and rifles as well, in the second barn they checked. The horses had been fed and well cared for, and the men's gun belts hung from ceiling joists with Spanish tack, their rifles resting across saddle trees.

There were no stallions in the barn, so Yakima rigged a handsome steeldust barb gelding for the senorita. The emasculated horse seemed a fitting gift under the circumstances.

Leaving all but one of the pistols he'd confiscated from the dead men—he didn't want to overburden himself and Wolf with gun iron—he and O'Shannon mounted up and headed for the broad open doors, Yakima trailing the senorita's gelding by its bridle ribbons.

A sudden blast of gunfire brought him up just short of the door. He drew back on Wolf's reins as the stallion pranced uneasily beneath him. Outside, a man grunted and a horse whinnied. Hooves pounded.

Yakima unsheathed his staghorn Colt and was cocking it when a dun mustang galloped furiously past the stable. Its rider trailed along the ground behind it, the man's high-heeled boot caught in the stirrup. His sombrero was ripped off his head, and his arms were flung straight up above his shoulders. As the horse passed, Yakima caught a glimpse of blood streaking the man's forehead.

Yakima gigged Wolf through the doors and into the yard, looking cautiously around. Two more men were lying in the dust to his left, one of their horses galloping up the hill to the north and the other running in wild circles in front of the blacksmith shop, lowering its head and loosing angry whinnies.

Beyond, over a low hill, more black smoke rose in the west. No doubt the result of another dynamite explosion Yakima had heard while he'd been saddling Wolf in the barn. The shooting continued, as did the screams of men and horses.

Leonora Domingo was running toward Yakima and O'Shannon, her smoking Colt in her hand. "Three more dead dogs!" She glanced at the horse that Yakima trailed, lowering her head to peer beneath its belly. "I told you a stallion, you bastard. I have no use for geldings!"

"Fresh out of stallions!" Yakima said. "Stop crabbing and climb into that hurricane deck! There a door in the south wall?"

"*Sí!*" Leonora ripped the gelding's reins from Yakima's hands and vaulted into the saddle. "You owe me *big*, amigo! I may not be riding a stallion today, but I'll bet you all the gold in El Dorado I'll be riding one tonight!"

With a flashing wink, she raked her spurs against the gelding's flanks and tore off along the trail, heading west of the barns.

"Be careful," she said when the west wall appeared before them, a brush-roofed guard tower rising above the broad wooden doors. "There's a Gatling gun in that tower. It's probably manned in case Cristobal's army swings around to this side of the hacienda!"

"If it's manned," O'Shannon said, riding on the other side of the girl from Yakima, "how in the hell are we going to get through those doors?"

"You leave that to me, amigo. I've been to this dance before!"

A small brick guardhouse sat beside a large boulder near the double doors beneath the tower. Another, lower roof jutted out from the wall to the left of the doors. Under the roof three saddled horses stood facing a long stock trough and hay crib. The horses' belly straps sagged toward the ground.

With their horses tied to a rock spur behind them,

Yakima, O'Shannon, and the senorita peered out from behind the guardhouse, which an unshuttered window had
told them was empty. The three guards belonging to the
three horses were in the tower, manning the Gatling gun,
the brass canister of which was burnished by the angling
morning sun.

A quick look told Yakima that the three men in the tower
were looking eastward, one smoking, the other two nervously conversing. All three mustached men wore filled bandoliers crossed on their chests. Two held rifles in their
hands.

When one of the men started turning his head toward the
guardhouse, Yakima jerked his head back behind the thatch-
roofed hovel. O'Shannon and Leonora did the same from
the other side, turning toward him.

The gambler looked worried as well as gaunt from the
braining he had sustained. "It's only open ground between
here and those doors. They'll see us if we try to run for it.
The way they're barricaded in there, I don't think we can
shoot them without at least one cutting us to pieces with
that Gatling."

"Amigo," Leonora said, frowning, "why so violent and
noisy?"

"Huh?"

"I told you, I've been to this dance before."

The girl smiled wolfishly and shuttled her glance from
the gambler to Yakima. Both men frowned at her, puzzled.
As she began loosening the leather tie strings holding her
doeskin vest closed, she rose from her knees and moved
toward the corner of the guardhouse.

"Where you going?" O'Shannon hissed.

Too late. She had stepped out from behind the guardhouse and was strolling toward the tower, both hands raised
before her.

"That woman is crazy," the gambler told Yakima.

"Uh-huh."

Yakima edged a look around the side of the guardhouse,
watching the girl dwindle into the distance, swinging her

hips and rolling her shoulders seductively as she raised her chin toward the tower, her curly black hair tumbling down the small of her slender back. The men had spotted her, and all three had shuffled toward this end of the tower, frowning down at her warily beneath the broad brims of their sombreros.

"Amigos!" she called. "I would like to take my horse out for a little ride. What are my chances of getting you to open the doors for me?"

The men glanced at each other skeptically, frowning. All three were keeping an eye on the smoke billowing in the west.

"Forget it!" replied one of the men in the tower, planting his fists on the rail and staring down at her. "Go back to the house before the don finds you missing!" He pointed. "Haven't you heard the gunfire?"

Yakima watched with one eye from behind the rear of the guardhouse as the girl slid her hands out to her sides, shoulder high, her knuckles facing Yakima. She clutched a flap of her doeskin vest in each hand, the leather tie strings dangling.

She cocked one leg and shook her hair back from her supple tan shoulders coquettishly.

The man with his fists on the rail opened his mouth slightly and widened his eyes. The other two shuffled up to stare over his shoulders, the muscles in their faces falling slack.

"Christos!" one of them muttered.

The man beside him swallowed so violently that Yakima could see his Adam's apple bobbing.

"How about we do a little bartering?" suggested the senorita. "You three and me in the shrubs for two open doors?"

The man closest to the edge of the guardhouse dug his fingers into the weathered wood. The other two looked at each other and grinned.

"*Sí*, why not?" said one.

"Hold on!" ordered the man nearest the edge.

The other two were already scrambling toward the ladder.

The third man raised his fist toward the other two and barked, "Stop! Our orders are to man the gun!"

"It doesn't take three to man the gun!" yelled one of the others as they both descended the ladder beneath the tower, grinning over their shoulders at the senorita still holding her vest open.

"*Sí*, you man it, Tío!" shouted the other man as he and his cohort leapt the last few feet to the ground and faced Leonora, hitching up their pants, grinning, and sauntering up to her like cardsharps to a high-stakes poker match.

"This way, amigos," Leonora said, dropping her hands.

Glancing casually back toward Yakima, she strolled toward a low, brushy knoll. The two Mexicans, one short, the other tall and with a shaggy, gray-streaked beard, turned to follow her. The short man was chuckling softly.

The man in the guard tower swore and rammed his fist against the railing. "Damn you both to hell!" he cried.

Then he swung around, dropped through the hole in the tower floor, and started down the ladder, grunting and panting and peering over his shoulder at the other two men following the senorita up the knoll toward a stone spur at the top.

The senorita swung around to face the men as she walked backward, her large tan breasts jostling slightly between the open flaps of her vest. Yakima heard her laugh, saw her crook a finger at the men, then step behind the spur. The two men followed her, the short one still chuckling and rubbing his hands eagerly on the thighs of his deerskin breeches.

"That woman's a devil," O'Shannon chuckled softly with disbelief, peering over Yakima's shoulder.

"Uh-huh."

As the third man began tramping after the girl and the other two men, all of whom now disappeared behind the stone spur, a man screamed suddenly. A gun popped, clipping the yell. Halfway up the knoll, the third man stopped suddenly, bent slightly forward at the waist, holding his hands over his holstered pistols.

"Mierda!" cried the other man behind the spur.

The short man staggered out from behind the rock, clutching his bloody belly while the toes of his boots dragged in the dirt. He twisted around toward the rock, threw his head back, and screamed for mercy. The senorita stepped out from behind the rock, her vest still open. Her extended revolvers popped and flashed at the same time.

Blood and brains blew out the back of the short man's head. The force of the bullets lifted him two feet in the air and threw him four feet straight back in the brush.

The third man stood frozen halfway up the knoll. He'd placed his hands on the butts of his revolvers but kept the guns in their holsters, as though they were cemented there.

As the senorita strolled down the knoll toward him, smiling, her full breasts jiggling, he shook his head back and forth wildly. *"Por favor,* no!"

He'd barely gotten the "no" out before the senorita's guns flashed once more.

When the third man had rolled to the bottom of the knoll, half his head missing, Senorita Domingo twirled her smoking guns on her fingers. She began tying her vest closed over those magnificent breasts and jogged toward the now-empty guard tower.

"Come on, amigos! I think I have just supplied you with a Gatling gun!"

"Did I already say I think she's crazy?" O'Shannon asked Yakima, still peering out in disbelief from behind the guardhouse.

"Yep."

Chapter 21

If you were a bird riding the midafternoon thermals a thousand feet above the broken desert floor—and there was a bird, a golden eagle that had just finished dining on a lobo-killed javelina and was looking for more to eat before nightfall—the three riders would have appeared little larger than kangaroo rats against the vast, sprawling backdrop of sun-seared desert sparsely dotted with tufts of brittlebrush and barrel cactus, and savagely scarred by deep, dry arroyos where snakes hid from the sun under cracked boulders.

Spying no other movement, the eagle decided to drop lower and inspect the three riders and the mule trailing one man and a black horse by a lead line. It did so merely because it had nothing else to do at the moment, and it was enjoying the swoop and lift of the air current. Besides, horseback riders carried meat occasionally, the scraps of which they sometimes tossed into the scrub around them. But these riders, unlike the stocky, dark-skinned nomads—always riding, always in a hurry—with long black hair and clad in spare swatches of deerhide, were not feeding as they rode.

The eagle swooped a hundred feet over the heads of the three humans, close enough to see the white-socked black stallion lift its head curiously, the sunlight glowing like pennies in its black eyes, and give a nearly inaudible whinny. The bird loosed an inquiring cry in response, then banked sharply again.

It picked up another air current and lofted high toward a distant pedestal rock jutting ten miles to the southwest, where it knew the chances for snagging a jackrabbit or a young coyote would increase in an hour or two, when the sun angled westward.

"He is hungry," the senorita said, shading her eyes to follow the lone bird's long arc southward, its shrill, ratcheting cry dwindling gradually as it was leisurely swallowed by the brassy, bowl-like sky that dominated everything out here— terrible in its indifference to man or beast. "And so am I."

"No doubt," O'Shannon said. "You already put in a day's work, Miss Domingo."

"Do I frighten you, Senor O'Shannon?" Leonora rode ten feet off the gambler's right stirrup, swaying gracefully with her steeldust's movements, holding her reins in one hand up high beneath her chin.

"On the contrary, Miss Domingo," O'Shannon said, squinting an eye at her, letting it roam rakishly across her delightful form. "I'm quite impressed."

"Is it my body you're impressed with or my savagery?"

O'Shannon chuckled. "I have to say, I've never known a woman quite as ... uh ... *frank* as you, Miss Domingo. But now that the question has been put to me, I'd have to say both."

He let his eyes drop to her cleavage, the breasts jostling behind her doeskin vest and all but freeing themselves with every bounce.

The senorita laughed. "Keep it in your pants, amigo. I am more taken with the wild, free men of the frontier." Glancing at Yakima, she lounged back in her saddle, resting her gloved hand on her horse's dusty, lathered rump. "You, Senor, have the heeled, constipated look of a married man. Probably a woman with money or breeding. Maybe both, huh?"

"Christ!" O'Shannon blinked at Yakima's back. The half-breed rode fifteen yards ahead, trailing the mule that was now packing the Gatling gun they'd horsed down from the guard tower. "Is she one of those Mexican witches?"

Yakima pulled his horse up to the edge of a hundred-foot-deep canyon—a sheer slash in the desert floor, around thirty feet wide at this point, that couldn't be seen until you rode right up to it.

"We'll camp in a bit. Likely find water down there."

"That's probably what he said." Sitting his horse beside Yakima's, O'Shannon looked down at the horse and human bones strewn along the base of the canyon's far bank.

Bits of cloth still clung to several of the human bones. A Stetson hat and saddlebags moldered between two chunks of driftwood.

A Texas-style saddle, caked with sand and dirt from several spring floods, lay on its side, propped by the horse's bleached rib cage, to which a few remnants of colorless hide clung. Nearby, the hot breeze fluttered a rice-paper-thin strip of snakeskin.

"Rode up on it at night, I'd guess," Yakima muttered as he reined Wolf down a narrow path stamped into the side of the canyon wall by mustangs, deer, and bobcats.

He and the others tossed their gear down on the shaded side of the canyon, semiprotected by a sharp bend in the dry watercourse and a deep alcove in the sandstone wall that was spotted with flashing mica bits and shards of dinosaur bones. When they'd tended their horses, they built a small fire and set coffee to brewing, then filled their canteens and picketed their mounts and the mule near a spring dribbling down from the canyon's northeast wall and around which short grass tufts grew and old bobcat and coyote tracks were etched in the mud.

Yakima's group wouldn't stay here for more than a few hours, as the spring would likely draw night visitors—possibly another bobcat and/or the Jicarilla Apaches that roamed this ancient land, or the equally merciless Mexican Indios, the Yaqui. They'd remain only long enough to catch a couple hours' rest and to fill their bellies with food and coffee.

Then, after the sun had died, they would continue along

the canyon floor, following O'Shannon's map toward the mesa where the silver was cached.

"If you want to take the first watch, I'll spell you later." O'Shannon finished dabbing water to his bruised head and, corking his canteen and knotting the wet neckerchief beneath his collar, lay back against his saddle. "I think I'll see if I can't shake this headache."

Chewing jerky, Yakima grabbed his rifle and tramped off down the canyon. He followed another wild-horse path up the side and after checking for snakes and spiders, snuggled down amid the boulders of a high stone scarp, facing the way they'd ridden.

They'd seen no sign of the don's men shading them, but that didn't mean they wouldn't. It was unlikely, given the size of the attack the *revolutionarios* had effected on the hacienda, that Ungaro's men would follow, but the senorita had given the old man a parting gift he wouldn't soon forget. Unless he was dead.

If he lived, he'd likely put a high bounty on her head, and probably sweeten the pot to have her brought back kicking and screaming so he could finish her himself slowly.

The whole mess reminded Yakima of Faith. That dark claw of relentless memories grabbed his belly again. He brushed dust from his Yellowboy's receiver and fought back the bleak feeling that continued to haunt him like a heel-nipping, yellow-toothed cur.

When would the memories stop stabbing him so savagely?

"When you're dead," he muttered, then dug in his tunic pocket for his makings sack.

Keeping an eye on the saffron desert he'd just traversed, watching for dust, he rolled the cigarette, fired it, and smoked it down to a nub. Nearby, a spur rang on rock. He reached for the Yellowboy resting across his thighs.

"Don't shoot me, hombre," Leonora said, her boots clattering on the rocks below. "I am being a good woman for you."

Her black-hatted head appeared down from and to the right of his niche, rising as she climbed, the thong swinging beneath her chin, dusty chaps flapping. She held a smoking tin coffee cup in her left hand. Yakima smiled. Her other hand was closed over her holstered Remy's grips.

She gave him an oblique smile, then bent forward, extending the cup. "*Café* for the big man I am so happy to see again."

"Oh?" Yakima took the cup. "Why are you so happy?"

"Because you make a woman feel like a woman, stupid." Leonora squirmed down into the niche beside him, nudging him aside with her leg, grunting. "And I have no one else."

"What happened to Arvada?"

"Dead. The don's men. Specifically, the one with the long silver hair—Alberto Espinoza—backshot the legendary Christos Arvada. I meant to kill that yellow pig before I left the casa." Leonora shrugged, plucked the stub of Yakima's quirley from between his fingers, and took a drag, sucking the smoke deep into her lungs, lifting her bosomy chest. "There'll be another time."

"How in the hell did you ever get into the don's casa?"

"When he killed my men, I let him take me prisoner. I endured his beatings until he *forced* me to declare my loyalty to him." The senorita took another drag from the quirley, then gave it back to Yakima. "Forced." She spat with revulsion. "*Javelina* shit!

"I let the fool *believe* he'd whipped me to the edge of my endurance. He played right into my hands. I truckled and begged his forgiveness. I hugged his ankles and kissed his boots. I swore I'd be his woman for as long as he wanted, just as long as he didn't beat me anymore. And he is so deluded that he thought I was serious.

"I became his whore and his arm ornament, huh? He paraded me around his peons to boast that he had tamed the legendary Wildcat of Sonora, had her eating scraps from his table and amusing him in his bed."

She smiled icily, hardening her long, fine jaw and dimpling her smooth, darkly tanned cheeks. "But I was only biding my time. The pretense was not difficult with an old man who only *thinks* he is a bull. I've known corpses with more prowess in bed. I let him become more and more secure with the illusion, until I was ready to cut him with his own stiletto and leave him howling in his own blood. Your appearance and the *revolutionarios'* attack this morning were the diversions I'd been waiting for."

Yakima sipped his coffee and stared out from the niche at the washed-out, yellow land. He and Faith had literally run into Leonora's ragtag bunch of *banditos/revolutionarios*— in a hidden canyon in the Sierra Olivadas.

Christos Arvada had been Leonora's first lieutenant and lover. A legendary outlaw, whipcord thin, ominously silent, and fast as lightning, he'd been as despised as Leonora herself by hacendados throughout northern Chihuahua and Sonora, and by many American ranchers in Arizona, New Mexico, and Texas as well. The two were notorious for stealing cattle and running smuggling trains back and forth across the border to fund their revolution with the intention of freeing the campesinos and peons from the slavelike employ of the Mexican landed gentry, like Don Agundo himself.

As with most of the so-called revolutionaries in Mexico, her noble cause was often lost amid her wild-assed banditry.

Yakima took the last drag from the quirley and stamped it out against a rock with his boot toe. "Your whole gang is gone?"

Leonora nodded. "They ran us into a box canyon, pinned us down, and cut us to ribbons with Gatling guns." She chuckled and probed a crack in the rock before her with a silver-tipped boot toe. "I guess we rustled one longhorn too many, huh?"

She turned to Yakima and blinked a sheen of tears from her eyes. "Where is your woman? The blonde?"

"Dead."

Leonora turned her head forward again. "We all die. Some are lucky and go sooner. We others are left with the memories and the difficulty of staying alive."

"Hell of a job out here."

"But what else are we going to do?" Leonora rested her head against Yakima's shoulder, rubbed her cheek against his arm, catlike. "I am glad you are alive, my *grande* Indio. I missed you."

"Best keep missing me. This job with O'Shannon is likely my last fandango. You want no part of it."

"What else am I going to do?"

"Take some time off. Even wild-ass *revolutionarias* need a break now and then. Head to Monterrey and walk on the beach for a few days. Maybe you'll find a respectable, well-heeled man with money."

"One way or another, I'd only kill him." She lifted her head and raised her brows alluringly. "You need dynamite. And I have dynamite. Only a few miles farther and a little south. Do you think your well-groomed friend would cut me in for a few pounds of magic powder?"

Yakima glanced at her cleavage. "He'd be crazy not to."

She tipped his hat over his eyes playfully, then slid her face up under the brim and kissed his cheek. "I will tend the horses and clean my guns."

Yakima poked his hat brim back off his forehead and allowed himself the manly pleasure of watching her retreat from the niche, her charro slacks stretched taut across her round, womanly bottom. She stopped on a boulder just below, turned sideways to him, staring off into the distance, and placed her fists on her hips.

"You will forget her, Yakima. As I will forget Christos." Her voice was wistful, sad. Turning back toward him, she added, wrinkling the skin at the bridge of her nose, "But that is part of the sadness, no?"

She dropped down out of sight, her spurs chinging softly, boot heels grinding gravel.

Yakima dug his makings pouch from his pocket again and began rolling another quirley.

Chapter 22

They rode all night through the seemingly endless, winding defile, their only company the clomps of their horses' hooves on the rocky ground, the eerie rustle of the chill breeze scented with cedar from the higher altitudes, and the occasional whine of a hunting bobcat or jaguar.

At nine o'clock the next morning the Wildcat of Sonora led Yakima and O'Shannon into a broad box canyon at the end of which sat an old shepherd's stone hovel that had long since lost its roof, its windows, and its doors. It was flanked by three rock-mounded graves and bent, bleached wooden crosses.

"Home sweet home, amigos."

The senorita dropped smoothly out of her saddle and after ground-hitching the gelding strolled toward the dilapidated hovel's doorless front entrance. Yakima watched through the gap as she kicked dirt from a small area at the cabin's rear, then reached down and pulled up a trapdoor with a grunted Spanish epithet.

She dropped the door with a boom. Dust wafted. She cursed again and waved a hand in front of her face, coughing. Spitting grit from her lips, she turned toward the front of the cabin, where Yakima and O'Shannon sat their horses, regarding her skeptically.

"How much you need, Irish?"

O'Shannon shrugged. "How much you got?"

"Maybe you better come take a look."

O'Shannon glanced at Yakima, then swung down from his saddle. Dropping his reins, the gambler stepped through the cabin door. Yakima dismounted as well and followed the man inside, where O'Shannon knelt beside the six-by-four-foot hole in the ground.

It appeared to be about six feet deep and about twice as large as the door, the sides showing the pits and gouges made by tools probably a century ago. It was now being used by the senorita to store at least twenty wooden crates marked MAGIC BLACK POWDER CO., LAS CRUCES, NEW MEX. TERR.

"Jesus Christ!" O'Shannon exclaimed. "Where did you get all this dynamite?"

"Never mind that, amigo. How much you need? And then we discuss my compensation."

"Compensation?"

"Do I look like a girl who works for free?"

O'Shannon glanced at Yakima again. The half-breed smiled.

O'Shannon looked into the hole. "You have enough magic powder here to blow the entire Mesa of Lost Souls off the face of the desert. But considering we have only the one mule to carry it, ten or twenty sticks oughta do it."

"Which is it?" the senorita said with a haughty air. "Ten or twenty?"

O'Shannon scowled at her. "Fifteen."

She gestured into the hole. "Have at it. Those crates hold twenty sticks each, packed in straw. There are caps and fuses in there somewhere. Go ahead. Rummage around."

"You want me to dig them out? It's your hole."

"Sorry, amigo," the senorita said, plucking a black cigar from O'Shannon's shirt pocket. "I'm afraid of spiders."

After O'Shannon agreed to the senorita's demand of a thousand dollars in exchange for her badly needed dynamite and her guiding the men on a shorter route to the Mesa of Lost Souls than the one shown on the gambler's map, they immediately resumed the trek.

As Leonora had promised, her route was shorter and faster. Two days sooner than they'd originally planned and in spite of having to skirt two roaming bands of desperadoes and one small but well-armed rurale contingent, the trio hunkered on the slope of a broad, sandy bluff facing the Mesa of Lost Souls in the east.

Yakima adjusted his binoculars' focus as he glassed the mesa's western slope.

Tufted with straw-colored brush, cacti, and cedars, the incline rose gradually from a broad, rocky wash at its base. Three hundred yards from the wash, a sandstone wall vaulted another fifty yards straight up to the mesa's crest. The wall was a fluted, palisaded, cracked, and wind-weathered mess of ancient rock around the pits and hollows of which raptors quarreled and from which occasional tufts of spidery brush or cedars sprouted.

"Jason said there was a trail of sorts on the west side," O'Shannon said, crouching with Leonora in the brush to Yakima's left. "You don't see it?"

"I see it," Yakima said, raking his thumb lightly over the focus wheel, clarifying what appeared to be little more than a goat path climbing the steep sandstone wall at a dangerous angle. "But I sure as hell don't like it."

"Let me take a look."

Yakima handed the glasses to the gambler.

"She's pretty steep," Leonora said.

The senorita lay belly down on the ground, resting her chin between two tufts of Spanish bayonet as she stared over the lip of the hump of earth they were on, trying to keep well out of sight of the *revolutionarios* likely hidden among the shrubs and boulders of the mesa's apron slope.

"She's steep, all right," O'Shannon said, spreading his chapped lips as he stared through the binoculars. "Jason said it was the only relatively easy way up, aside from the main wagon trail to the north. But the desperadoes have every inch of that covered."

"They probably have this one covered, too," Leonora said. "To keep anyone from sneaking down."

Yakima continued to eye the steep trail up through the rocks. It switchbacked once about halfway to the top. Likely it had been blasted out of the rock face by the Jesuit monks who'd built the mission at the mesa's crest, to be used as an escape route in the event of an Apache or Yaqui attack.

"They probably don't have this one as well covered." Yakima brushed an ant from his chin. "Five or six men, maybe. But I'm still not convinced we can lead the horses up that trail."

"Can't leave 'em down here," O'Shannon said. "We need them for the supplies, and we need the mule for the Gatling gun."

Leonora grabbed the glasses from O'Shannon's hands. "Let me look."

Staring through the binoculars, the girl whistled softly. "*Sí.* Very steep. Very narrow. But it probably looks narrower from here."

"You see anything of the desperadoes at the bottom?" Yakima asked her.

She slid the binoculars from side to side slowly, then up and down. "No. But there appears to be a hollow near the base of the trail, surrounded by spurs. If they are covering it, they will be there."

"We have to take them out," Yakima said.

O'Shannon glanced at him over Leonora's back. "How?"

"We have a Gatling gun, don't we?" Yakima took the glasses from Leonora and scrutinized the mesa once more. "If we need to, we'll use the dynamite."

"I'd prefer we save the gun and the dynamite for when we get to the top," O'Shannon said. "We're going to need both for the trip down the trail."

"There ain't gonna be a trip down," Yakima said, sliding the glasses into their felt-lined box, "if we don't get up there first."

Leonora turned to him, grinning with her eyes, and placed a gloved hand along his cheek. "You think like a Mejicano, amigo. That's a compliment."

Behind her, O'Shannon chewed his lip as he squinted across the dry wash toward the slope rising to the base of the sandstone wall. "When do we do it?"

Yakima grabbed his Winchester and began crabbing back down toward the ravine where they'd tethered their horses and the mule. "Midnight."

Fifteen minutes after midnight, after spending most of the evening dozing in the arroyo's soothing shade or playing three-handed poker for matchsticks—neither Yakima nor Leonora had more than a few coins to their names—Yakima stepped up to the edge of the broad wash running along the base of the Mesa of Lost Souls.

He had Wolf's reins in his left hand, his Yellowboy in his right. Leonora and O'Shannon flanked him, O'Shannon leading both his roan and the pack mule.

The half-breed peered out from between a couple of scraggly cedars, looking up and down the wash, the floor of which shone pale as chalk in the starlight. He neither heard nor saw any patrolling desperadoes. He glanced back at the gambler and the senorita, jerked his head forward, and stepped into the wash, heading quickly but as quietly as possible to the other side.

Wolf's hooves, which he'd wrapped in burlap taken from Leonora's dynamite cache, moved almost soundlessly through the leaf and needle-strewn dust of the arroyo, then up the low bank on the other side. The two men and the woman and the three horses and the mule continued up the gradual incline rising toward the base of the rocky wall showing velvet black ahead and above, capped with a million shimmering stars.

Except for crickets and the occasional mournful howl of a distant coyote, the night was as eerily silent as an ancient cemetery.

When they figured they were a quarter mile from the base of the stone wall, Yakima and O'Shannon continued ahead on foot while Leonora stayed back with the horses and the mule. Taking the animals any closer to where the

172 *Frank Leslie*

desperadoes were likely guarding the treacherous trail was too risky. The mounts' hooves were padded, but a sudden startled snort or nicker would give the group away.

One misstep now would be the last mistake they'd ever make.

Not long after leaving Leonora, Yakima, carrying the fifty-pound Gatling canister over his right shoulder and the tripod strapped to his back, began to feel the climb in his legs and arms. He raked air in and out, in and out, and shut the aches and pains from his mind as he watched the black stone wall loom larger with every lumbering step up the incline.

Meandering around a cabin-sized boulder, he caught the whiff of a piñon fire from ahead on the cool night air. The fire betrayed the presence of the desperadoes, who were in fact guarding the base of the treacherous trail. But how many were holed up in the hollow? Since it was an unlikely escape route for men with as much silver as O'Shannon's brother was packing, they'd probably posted only a small contingent as an extra precaution.

Well, he would see. No matter how many were there, the Gatling gun would come in handy in the dark. One thing in Yakima's favor, aside from the belching cannon, was that the desperadoes would be unlikely to suspect that anyone would try to gain access to the trail from the *bottom,* with the intention of climbing *up.*

When he figured he'd walked an eighth of a mile, breathing hard and with sweat pasting his buckskin tunic to his back, Yakima stopped near a fallen cedar for a blow. He glanced behind. There were only rocks and shrubs partly silvered by the starlight.

No O'Shannon. No footsteps or rasping breaths sounded either.

From forty yards back down the incline, voices rose—one louder than the other and speaking Spanish.

A sweat bead of anxiety dribbled down Yakima's cheek. Quickly but gently, he set the Gatling canister down and looped the tripod over the barrel. He'd left his Yellowboy with Wolf, so he had only his Colt, the spare Schofield he'd taken off the dead man in the casa, and his toothpick. Shucking the Colt from its holster, he began moving back the way he'd come, walking softly, holding one arm out for balance as he kept his weight on the balls of his booted feet from which he'd removed his spurs.

The voices grew louder. He recognized O'Shannon, speaking in placating tones.

Yakima darted right around a boulder, tramped down a steep incline, then worked back toward the voices rising on his left. They seemed to emanate from among the three cedars through which he'd passed just a minute ago.

He moved toward the cedars from downslope, saw the figures standing before him, one with his hands raised high above his head while the other, his back to Yakima, held a rifle on him. The Mexican was asking O'Shannon in Spanish what the hell he was doing out here and O'Shannon was replying in Spanish even worse than Yakima's that his horse had gone down several miles away and he was merely looking for water.

"*Agua*," the gambler repeated, jerking his shoulders. "I only look for *agua*!"

"Water, my ass," the Mexican said, glancing down at the saddlebags and the long belt of .45-caliber shells for the Gatling gun that lay at the gambler's boots. "What's with the cartridges? And what do you have in the saddlebags? Open them and show me before I blow a hole in you large enough to push a hay cart through!"

"Cooking supplies," O'Shannon said, fishing around for the words in Spanish.

"Show me, damn it, or . . . *heeeeee!*"

The Mexican threw his head back and stretched his lips over his teeth with the exclamation as the tip of Yakima's toothpick flicked off a rib and nipped the back of the man's heart. Clamping his left hand over the man's mouth and jerking him against his body, Yakima withdrew the toothpick quickly and thrust it forward once again, feeling the warm blood seep over his knuckles.

The man was musky with sweat, the smell of horses, sage, and campfire smoke.

He rasped and jerked in Yakima's savage embrace. His rifle clattered to the ground and his body began slackening, knees bending. Yakima released him and removed the bloody toothpick from his back. The man hit the ground on his knees, expelling his last breath, and dropped facefirst into a patch of curly red mesquite grass.

"I just stopped to take a breather," O'Shannon said. "And . . ."

He trailed off as Yakima gave a disapproving chuff, cleaned his blade in two quick swipes on the dead man's leather vest, and began tramping up the hill in the darkness.

Chapter 23

There were eight of them holed up in the bowl at the base of the steep trail, lounging around a small fire drinking coffee or tequila and sending up rancid-smelling puffs of tobacco smoke to mix with the area's general smell of shit, piss, and rotting trash.

They'd been here a while.

A couple of them played cards while others cleaned their weapons, growling and grunting their impatience. They were a scarred, bedraggled lot, probably the dregs of the group, given the assignment that carried the least likelihood of testing their minimal capabilities.

Aside from the man who'd stopped O'Shannon, they'd apparently posted no patrols or pickets.

Yakima quickly set up the Gatling gun on top of a scarp about forty yards north of the hollow and thirty feet above. Beside him, screened by cedar branches, O'Shannon prepared the ammunition belts, casting nervous glances into the hollow.

Yakima was almost ready, the machine gun's large clip in place on top of the stout brass canister, when one of the *revolutionarios* tossed down his cards, yawned, stood, and began fumbling with his fly buttons. He walked only a few steps from the fire, toward Yakima's position, before he began bending his knees and groaning as he evacuated his bladder on a yucca plant.

"Hurry," O'Shannon whispered.

The urinating man looked from side to side and then lifted his chin slowly toward the escarpment.

Yakima flipped the canister's locking mechanism open and raised the crank. "Okay."

"Ay caramba!" the Mexican screamed when his eyes discovered the brass canister poking out from among the cedars.

O'Shannon pulled the heaviest branch back from the barrel, and Yakima began turning the crank.

The raucous explosions tore the night wide open.

BLAM-BLAM-BLAM-BLAM-BLAM-BLAM-BLAM-BLAM!

A couple of Winchesters would have worked all right, but the Gatling gun cleaned up quickly and efficiently. The .45-caliber slugs rained down on the motley crew like a monsoon storm in the desert, and after the dust and smoke cleared and the screams left only their echoes chasing each other around the hillside, there was no question.

The men guarding the trailhead, twisted and piled here and there among the guns they hadn't been able to fully raise before the Gatling's blue whistlers cut through them, were dead. And not a significant amount of ammo had been spent.

"Jesus, I'd like one of those for Christmas!" O'Shannon whooped as he peered down the scarp through the wafting powder smoke, his rifle raised but with no reason to use it.

"Well, if you're real good . . ." Yakima grunted, moving quickly to lift the canister from its tripod.

At the same time, O'Shannon fired three quick rifle shots into the air over the scarp—the signal to Leonora that the path had been paved and to hustle along with the horses and the mule. When the Henry's echoes had died, O'Shannon scrambled down the scarp to inspect the bodies, making doubly sure that he and Yakima wouldn't buy a bullet in the back.

"They're deader'n beaver hats," he called up a minute later, his sun-darkened face showing in the fire's dancing flames as Yakima, shouldering the Gatling and the tripod, carefully made his way down the scarp.

At the bottom he rested the gun against a bleached cottonwood log.

"Listen," O'Shannon said, lifting his chin slightly and staring into the night. "You hear it?"

Faintly, men's shouts rose from the north. A horse whinnied. As Yakima knew it would, the Gatling had alerted the other *revolutionarios* involved in the siege on the mesa. Rifles would have alerted them, too. They were taking a chance, hoping that Leonora would get here well before the besiegers did and that the three of them and their mounts could get up the rock wall quickly enough to outdistance the gunfire that would come their way.

Hearing hooves pounding up the hill from the west and knowing that Leonora was approaching, Yakima moved to the base of the wall and inspected the trail that angled sharply up into the darkness. His gut tightened and his loins tingled with dread.

Leonora had been wrong. The path didn't look much wider up close than it had from far away. It was little wider than a goat path. And it was steep, nearly a forty-five-degree angle in places. Yakima couldn't imagine anyone using it as an escape route from the top of the mesa, let alone his party being able to keep from slipping off the wall like dice from a table and free-falling straight down through thin air.

"Don't shoot me, gringos!" Leonora called sharply as she and the horses and the mule thundered up through the brush, twisting among the strewn boulders. The beasts blew and snorted, and Wolf lifted an incredulous whinny at the smell of spilled blood.

Breathless, the Wildcat of Sonora dropped out of her saddle and raked her Colt from its holster, thumbing back the hammer and wheeling this way and that, wagging the gun around at the strewn dead men.

"These fellas won't be rising up anytime soon," Yakima assured her, grunting as he hauled the Gatling canister toward the big mule, which lifted its head against the lead rope that Leonora held taut in her free hand.

"You boys do good work," the senorita said, depressing her Colt's hammer. "But in case you hadn't heard, riders are galloping this way from the north and the south."

"That's why we're not sitting down for a meal," Yakima said as he and O'Shannon eased the Gatling into the make-shift rope harness hanging down the mule's left side. He cast a quick glance at Leonora. "What're you waiting for? Get climbing!"

Leonora went over to inspect the trail. "*Christo!* It doesn't look much wider than it did this afternoon!"

"Looks a little narrower to me," Yakima said, tightening the ropes around the Gatling gun. "But there's no use standing around talking about it. We have no other way out of here now, so move your ass, girl. Leave the mule and break a leg!"

"I love it when you order me around, Wild Man!" The senorita grabbed her reins and leapt into her saddle. "Last one to the top has to stand me a drink!"

She spurred her steeldust across the encampment to the base of the stone wall. She paused there to let the horse get a good look at the trail and to let what it was being ordered to do sink into its big head. Then she whipped her rein ends across its withers and started up.

"Easy, boy, easy," she cooed to the balking horse, loosing rocks down the side of the wall as they climbed, the steeldust lifting its hooves high and snorting. "It's not so steep. Just do what I'm going to do—pray to Madre Maria and don't look down!"

"Give me the dynamite," Yakima told O'Shannon when they'd both mounted their horses, the half-breed clutching the mule's lead line.

"What for?"

Yakima turned his head this way and that, listening. The hoof thuds were growing steadily louder from both directions along the wall.

"Don't ask fool questions!"

"All right, all right."

O'Shannon reached back to pull the saddlebags packed

with the dynamite from his roan's rump and eased them across to Yakima. The half-breed draped the bags over his left shoulder as O'Shannon spurred his roan to the wall and started up after several seconds of desperate urging and spurring.

Yakima put Wolf to the wall and raked him lightly with his heels, not giving the oft-stubborn stallion time to balk. Wolf was a mountain-bred mustang and shouldn't have much trouble with the trail, though Yakima doubted that many mustangs negotiated such perilous paths of their own accord.

The mule balked at first, but after a couple of hard tugs on the lead rope, it too began hoofing up the trail and was soon moving with more ease and confidence than Wolf.

Yakima leaned forward as the horse lumbered up the steep grade, quickly gaining enough altitude that he could see the jostling shapes of the riders galloping through the hillside's scrub from the south. It shouldn't be as easy for them to see him, O'Shannon, and Leonora against the velvet black mountain wall. But it was only a matter of time until they did or until they heard the occasional rocks and gravel the horses and mule were kicking down from the trail.

O'Shannon rode about fifteen yards ahead, the roan clomping haltingly, occasionally stopping to fidget. O'Shannon kicked it and hissed at it and whipped his rein ends across its withers until it tossed its head and resumed the trek.

Beyond O'Shannon, the senorita was having similar trouble. Yakima could hear her cursing the steeldust in Spanish, see the flash of her spurs as she raked them against the horse's flanks.

The shod hooves clomped and clanked, tack squawking and bridle chains rattling. They were making too much noise for Yakima's comfort, but the approaching desperadoes were making plenty of noise to cover it—at least until they stopped at the encampment and found their dead brethren.

Yakima looked straight up the wall at the stars shimmering beyond the crest. The men guarding the silver had cer-

tainly heard the Gatling fire. It should have been his group's
calling card. O'Shannon's brother's men would be waiting
at the top, but they were too far from the valley floor to
offer Yakima's party covering fire.

Wolf continued climbing, blowing and giving an occasional nicker. The mule followed doggedly, head bobbing,
digging its hooves into the trail and propelling itself forward. Occasionally it gave a mild bray or flapped its lips
with incredulity, likely wondering what in the hell they
were doing in such a place.

Yakima glanced to the right of Wolf's own bobbing
head, into the airy darkness over the valley. His belly shot
up into his chest, loins prickling, and he clutched the apple
with both gloved hands.

"Christ."

Heights had always bothered him, turned his knees soft
and his thighs hard. They made his head swirl. He resisted
the urge to leap from Wolf's back. It was an anxiety he'd
been born with, and he'd handled it by simply avoiding
high places.

No avoiding them now.

"Sit tight," he said to himself. "Breathe. Don't look
down."

Wolf's right front hoof slipped over the edge of the trail.
The horse lurched violently, nearly throwing Yakima into
the abyss. "Watch your footing, you clumsy cuss!"

Rocks spilled down the wall, clattering raucously.
Yakima gritted his teeth as the horse gave a shrill, panicked
nicker and fought his way back toward the wall, jerking
Yakima this way and that in the saddle. The half-breed
could feel the horse's heart pounding beneath the leather.

The horse overcompensated for the near-plunge, then,
even more flustered, reared angrily, and Yakima felt one of
his hands slip from the horn. His boots slid out of the stirrups as well, and he began to fall down the horse's left stirrup fender, checking the plunge suddenly as the horse set
its feet once more.

Yakima grabbed the apple, squeezed it in both hands.

Behind him, the mule brayed and backed up, loosing more rock down the mountain wall. Yakima was surprised to find that he was still holding the beast's lead rope.

"Easy," he told the mule, holding the rope steady.

Yakima's heart hammered and his stomach was tinny with nausea. This was no place, two hundred feet above the desert, to be wrestling a horse and a mule.

He took a deep breath and, against his better judgment, glanced to his right once more, into the dark gauze of the void billowing beside him, brushing his cheek with menacing tenderness. The valley was filled with the soft, hideous laughter of eternity in the form of men shouting excitedly in Spanish and hooves kicking stones.

The besiegers had discovered their shredded comrades.

"Come on," Yakima urged Wolf, raking the horse gently with his spurs. "Ahead, now . . . easy does it."

He heard the clatter of hooves on his left. Turning his head that way, he saw the large, pale form of the senorita's steeldust lumbering up the second switchback about fifty feet above him and rising as she moved up the wall toward the silent, looming crest that, at the moment, seemed as far away as the moon.

The senorita was hissing at the frightened mount. In the darkness, Yakima saw her holding her reins taut in both fists, her back tense. The horse nickered as one of its hooves got hung up in a talus slide. There was a tense moment as the anxious horse fought to keep its footing while rock slid down the wall beneath it, plunging just past the tail of Yakima's mule.

The senorita's nervous hissing grew louder.

Yakima heard the flat rocks clatter to the valley floor, snapping twigs and branches.

As the steeldust continued up the trail, O'Shannon's roan ambling tentatively along behind the senorita, an iron rod shot up Yakima's back, and his racing heart raced faster. Someone shouted hoarsely in Spanish, lifting his head to send his words careening toward the stars.

"There! On the wall! Kill them!"

Chapter 24

Something whistled over Yakima's shoulder, just missing the dynamite-stuffed saddlebags, and hammered the rock wall above and to his left.

From below, the whip crack of a rifle cleaved the silent night.

More shouting and two more shots, the slugs pounding the rocks around the three ascending riders. Somewhere above and behind him, the senorita's horse whinnied shrilly.

As Wolf gained the intersection of the two switchbacks, turning sharply left and climbing onto the next trail, Yakima yelled as two more shouts hammered from below, "Dismount and walk your horses! Hold on to 'em tight! I'm gonna make a little noise!"

"Ah, shit," he heard O'Shannon rake out—a blurred dark shadow before him and up against the mountain wall.

As guns flashed below, the slugs ricocheting off the rock wall around him with wicked whines, Yakima dallied the mule's rope around his horn, then slipped out of his saddle. Taking Wolf's reins in his teeth, he reached into his saddlebags and plucked out a dynamite stick. He fished around in the pouch again for a cap and a fuse.

He attached the cap and fuse to the stick, then flinched as a lead bee buzzed past his cheek to ricochet off a rock behind him with a wicked *spang* that dwindled quickly to a fading, echoing whine. His ears rang with tension, and he fought the dizziness that made the narrow, rocky trail pitch and roll beneath his boots, the dark stone wall pushing toward him, then falling away.

He stuffed the end of the prepared dynamite stick in his shirt pocket and reached into the pouch for another one. When he had the second one prepared, he raked a lucifer to life on his belt buckle, then touched it to the fuse.

Behind him, Wolf's hip clenched as the fuse sputtered and flared, sparking brightly in the darkness. Yakima gritted his teeth, knowing the light gave him away to the shooters, but he held the stick out from his shoulders, cocking his arm and waiting for the fuse to burn down a little.

Two more blue whistlers cut the air around him while a third smashed a rock scale three feet straight down from his boots. Wolf lurched and whinnied. Grinding his teeth into the leather ribbons, Yakima flung the flaring stick slightly out from the wall and watched it arc out into the darkness.

A gun popped and flashed below. The dynamite stick disappeared beneath a round knob in the belly of the rock wall.

Someone screamed shrilly.

KA-BOOOOMMMMMMMMM!

The blast sounded slightly louder than a cannon blast about one full second behind the umber burst of flame that flashed in the darkness at the foot of the mountain wall. Darkness even thicker than before trailed the blast. Then there was the rainlike patter of falling rocks and gravel.

Behind Yakima, Wolf and the mule fidgeted, prancing slightly, but held their ground. The horse pulled on the reins, making Yakima's molars ache. He bit down hard on the ribbons again as he fired the next stick and sent it careening down, down, down, arcing a fiery tracer through inky darkness.

A cry rose as though from the bottom of a deep well. *"Mierda!"*

KA-BOOOOMMMMMMMMM!

Quiet fell over the mountain. A silence so keen that Yakima imagined he could hear the stars burning in the vast universe beyond the crest, as black as a funeral shroud.

One brief, eerie scream from below was quickly swallowed.

Up the incline, hooves clomped and clattered as Leonora and O'Shannon continued up the trail. The gambler was chuckling bizarrely, betraying stretched and frayed nerves.

Yakima looked around above his position, glad the blasts hadn't loosed a rockslide. But he'd spied no loose boulders. Most of the wall of stone was solid.

Below, only blackness. No more gun pops and flashes. As he stepped back into his saddle, however, he heard the clatter of shod hooves below as the survivors of the two blasts rode to safety away from the mountain wall.

"Okay, fella," Yakima said, patting the black's sweat-slick neck. "Almost there."

Wolf blew and shook his head indignantly.

A few minutes later, as Yakima and the horse and mule rose along the steep trail, he saw a glow in the sky above the mesa's crest. Ahead, the senorita's silhouette drifted over the top of the ridge and out of sight. A few minutes later, O'Shannon's did the same.

Two up, one to go.

The crest grew before Yakima. The umber glow in the sky did as well.

When Wolf finally lunged up and over the crest, the mule clomping and snorting eagerly behind, Yakima felt as though a hundred-pound weight had been lifted suddenly from his shoulders. The mule ran up on his right, lifted his head, and shook his entire body with relief to be off the incline.

Yakima dropped the mule's lead rope and gigged Wolf over to where the senorita and O'Shannon sat before a semicircle of rifle-wielding figures. He heard O'Shannon introducing himself and the girl and asking about his brother. As Yakima rode up on the gambler's right, several of the hombres stepped cautiously back and sideways, negligently aiming their rifles at him.

"Who's this?" a bearded gent asked suspiciously, a quirley smoldering in the corner of his wide mouth.

All eight of the men in the group were bearded and gaunt, their clothes hanging on them. They were Mexicans as well as Americanos and one tall, bony-shouldered black man. Their sweat smells tanged the faint breeze brushing the scrub-and-rock-stippled top of the mesa.

Behind them, only forty yards away, a few humble adobe-brick hovels and a brush corral fronted a small church that boasted a stout wooden cross jutting over its front door. Around the church were several flickering fires.

"He's with me," O'Shannon said. "Where's my brother? I figured Jason would be here to meet us. He certainly had to *hear* us."

"Inside the church." This from one of the two figures striding up from the right, materializing slowly from the darkness. "Step down, fellas," he ordered the others. He was a broad-shouldered Americano in a shabby sombrero and a smoke-stained deerskin tunic with Indian beads decorating both breast pockets. "Who the hell else but O'Shannon's brother do you think would be coming up the suicide trail in the middle of the night?"

"That's what we've been waiting to find out," said the man who'd spoken before, narrowing one eye at O'Shannon warily. "How do we know he is who he says he is? The girl—she looks Meskin to me."

"You're very observant, amigo," the senorita rasped. "But if you wave that rifle at me one more time, I'm going to take it away from you and run it up from your ticklish end and scratch your throat with the barrel."

The others laughed. The man she'd threatened wrinkled his nose and glared at her.

"I told you her name," O'Shannon said with an air of strained patience, leaning forward in his saddle. "Did you think it sounded German?" He glanced at the man in the beaded tunic. "What's Jason doing inside?"

"Mending. Took a bullet the other day, but he'll be all right. You fellas—and lady—bring any supplies with you? We've been out of coffee for weeks and haven't had sugar for a month. Gotta say, I'm damn glad to see that Gatling gun on the mule. And was that dynamite I heard popping down below?"

"It wasn't firecrackers. Help yourselves to the supplies. There's not much." O'Shannon swung down from the roan's back, a concerned look on his face. "How did Jason get himself . . . ?"

"Cleve!" someone shouted from the direction of the church. "Dear God, you made it!"

Jason O'Shannon was a slender, stooped, hatless silhouette shuffling toward the group through the flickering fires with two crutches propped under his arms. A short-haired woman walked along beside him, half facing him and holding her hands toward him as though worried he would fall.

"Jason!"

The group parted as O'Shannon led the roan toward his brother and the woman while Yakima and Leonora shared a quick glance, then swung down from their mounts. While the two brothers shook hands and hugged, clapping each other on the back, the other men wandered over to the mule to inspect the Gatling gun.

Yakima kept the dynamite draped over his shoulder. Jason O'Shannon's roughnecks looked punch-drunk, and Yakima didn't want to risk losing the entire cache to a dropped cigarette.

"Yakima! Senorita!" O'Shannon beckoned broadly. "Come on over and meet my crazy brother."

Yakima loosened Wolf's cinch and slipped his bit from his mouth, then followed Leonora over to the trio. O'Shannon was now standing beside the woman, his arm around her shoulders. He and the other two were silhouetted against the fires behind them, but the gambler was grinning broadly.

"Leonora Domingo, Yakima Henry—my brother, Jason, and his lovely wife, Stella."

The senorita greeted the O'Shannons with a congenial bow, shaking hands.

"She's lovely," Stella O'Shannon told her brother-in-law with a significant grin that lit her soft gray eyes. A small young woman with a pretty, heart-shaped face, she leaned her head against her husband's arm. "Where did you find this one, Cleve?"

Leonora gave a snort and crossed her arms on her breasts.

"Stella!" O'Shannon said with a look of feigned horror. "Are you accusing me of stepping out on Ashley?"

Stella opened her mouth, but before she could speak, Senorita Domingo, tapping a boot toe in the dirt, said, "Senora, *por favor*—we have just met and already you insult me."

Stella laughed with delight. "Oh, she is a prize!"

With a loud clearing of his throat, Jason O'Shannon stepped awkwardly forward on his crutches hewn from forked cottonwood branches and padded with burlap, and extended his hand to Yakima. He wore a long, mountain-man beard that contrasted with the boyish features of his face. "Mr. Henry, I am pleased to meet you. Thanks for getting my brother through that hellish country in one piece. It wasn't long after I'd rather impetuously sent him my letter that I reconsidered. I was certain I'd be getting him killed."

"Not yet," Yakima said. "But we're not down the mountain yet."

"Yes, but soon, right?" Stella O'Shannon frowned anxiously. "We've been up here for two months, and even if we weren't about out of food . . ."

"That's what they're here for, honey," her husband told her.

Leonora nodded to indicate the bandage wrapped around the man's right thigh. "Who shot you, Senor? The desperadoes charged the main trail, uh?"

"They've tried charging the main trail, all right," Jason O'Shannon said grimly. "But this bullet I took from one of my own men. We had a mutiny attempt a few weeks ago."

He turned to his brother. "Five men decided they'd had enough of waiting around up here and decided they were going to make off with as much silver as they could carry on a packhorse."

"How'd they think they'd get off the mesa without being shot to ribbons?" Cleve asked.

"The same trail you came up." The younger, bearded O'Shannon shook his head. "The fools thought maybe Obrégon's men weren't covering its mouth. Anyway, they're all buried in the little cemetery behind the church."

Yakima frowned. "Who's Obrégon?"

Jason O'Shannon winced and shifted his weight on his crutches.

"Honey, you need to get off your feet," Stella said, leaning toward her husband and placing a hand on his belly.

"There's much to discuss." The younger O'Shannon glanced toward the far side of the little church, where a small stone hut sat, its windows wanly lit against the glove-like darkness. "Looks like the padre's up. Would you all care for a drink before you turn in? I'd imagine your nerves are shot from that climb."

The gambling O'Shannon raised an eyebrow at Yakima and the senorita, both of whom stood holding their horses' reins.

"*Sí*, amigo," Leonora said wearily.

Yakima shrugged. "I could use a snort." He grabbed the dangling reins of O'Shannon's roan. "We'll tend the horses, head over when we're done."

When the O'Shannons and Stella had headed off toward the little casa on the other side of the church, Yakima and Leonora began leading their horses toward the brush corral in which several horses milled darkly, their coats silvered with starlight. Two men had led the mule there and were unloading the Gatling gun and its ammunition in front of the gate, murmuring appreciatively.

Yakima was staring toward the north side of the mesa, where a small fire glowed—probably a coffee fire tended by the men guarding the main trail up the formation.

"I got a bad sense about this place, Wild Man," Leonora said.

"How's that?"

"I don't know." The senorita shrugged. Their boots scuffed in the silence. "I just have a feeling that coming up was a lot easier than going down will be."

Chapter 25

When they'd finished tending the horses and the mule and had turned them all into the corral, Yakima and Leonora tramped across the dusty yard to the little cabin.

In front of the church, three men lounged around a campfire. One was rolled up in his blankets, while a second played solitaire and the third, a middle-aged Mexican with the sweeping mustache of a caballero, strummed a guitar. A couple more men, patrolling the western edge of the mesa to Yakima's left, conversed in desultory tones, cradling rifles in their arms.

The half-breed and the senorita crossed the brush-roofed gallery, and Leonora knocked on the frame of the door that was propped open to the cool, high-altitude night.

"*Entre, por favor,*" said a raspy man's voice.

Yakima followed the senorita through the door and into the small room that boasted not much more than a straw sleeping mat, a crucifix on one wall, a few candles, and a table at which the two O'Shannons sat with a barefoot old man in a worn brown robe. A straw-basketed demijohn and three wooden cups sat on the table, while the three men were perched on stools, Jason O'Shannon with his bad leg extended and his crutches propped against the crumbling brick wall beside him.

The old man's eyes widened at the senorita, and his thin-bearded face bleached. He leapt to his feet, overturning his stool and stumbling straight back away from the table, crossing himself while his eyes remained riveted on the buxom *desperada* swathed in form-fitting leather and bristling with pistols and a bone-gripped bowie knife.

"Ahórreme, Jesús. ¡Es el Gato Salvaje del Sonora!"

His thin hair lay in curls about his pink head, and his robe was open to reveal a pale, spindly chest and part of one bony, mole-spotted shoulder.

"Take it easy, Padre," the senorita laughed. "I am here on a mission of peace. At least, for the time being . . ."

Jason O'Shannon shuttled a frown between the senorita and the priest. "You know this woman, Padre?"

"Sí," said the father, splaying his hands on the wall behind him, still staring at the Wildcat of Sonora as though expecting her to pounce at any moment. "Who in northern Mejico does not know this wildcat? She is as cunning and merciless as she is"—his old, drink-bleary eyes roamed the girl's delectable frame with horror and admiration—"lovely!"

"Stop it, Padre," the senorita said in Spanish. "You're making me blush." She gestured at the overturned chair. "Sit down. Take a load off. I have been tamed," she added, canting her head at Yakima standing beside her. "For the moment at least."

The father watched the girl warily as he picked up his stool and sat down gingerly. There was only one other stool at the table. Yakima gestured toward it, then sank onto the floor by the door and dug into his tunic pocket for his makings sack.

"I am sorry," the padre apologized, "but it is not every day a man shares his home with a legend. God, she is as beautiful as I have heard." He held up the demijohn. "Will you drink with me, Senorita? Perhaps later, then, I could hear your confession."

The senorita laughed even harder at that, throwing her lovely head back and thrusting her breasts up against her vest until they threatened to burst the doeskin's seams. "I don't think either one of us has the time a complete confession would take, Padre. But it is my honor to drink with you." She thrust out a cup. "Fill it to the brim, if you please. It's been a long, dusty ride."

When the padre had filled the senorita's cup, she held out the other unused cup on the table. The old man filled it, and the senorita leaned down to give the cup to Yakima, who took it as he fired his quirley with his other hand.

"*Gracias*, Padre," the half-breed said, puffing smoke and squinting. "A nice place you have here."

"*Muchas gracias*, amigo." The padre dipped his chin humbly and picked up his own cornhusk cigarette from where it smoldered at the edge of the table. He frowned as he drew a deep drag. "You are Indio? Apache? I detect no accent."

"My roots are farther north."

Jason O'Shannon sipped his wine, ran the back of his hand across his overgrown mustache and beard, then set his cup on the table. "Yakima Henry, meet Padre Ernesto Sandoval. Mr. Henry is the man whom Cleve brought to help us find a way out of this mess, Padre. With his help, and the help of a Gatling gun they brought, we should be out of your way soon."

"You are not in my way, my son. I rarely get visitors up here anymore, since the *revolutionarios* have been running wild about the land." Padre Sandoval glanced at Leonora anxiously. "No offense, my daughter."

"None taken, Padre. How long have you been up here, anyway?"

"I lose count. But I was a much younger man when I came. The church had been abandoned for nearly a hundred years, the cemetery untended. I tend it now, say Mass and hear confession for those who dare to come. Campesinos, mostly. A few pilgrims. Even banditos and"—he grinned slyly, his old eyes once more inspecting the girl's well-filled vest—"banditas."

"I'm afraid we made life a tad more exciting for the padre when we came barreling up here about nine weeks ago. He wasn't expecting us and our silver." Jason O'Shannon smiled, his blue eyes glinting with boyish chagrin at the old priest.

This O'Shannon seemed to have little of his older brother's guile and rakishness. There was a serious, quiet intelligence in his eyes, tinged with the naive adventurousness of a man who grew up sucking on a silver spoon but to whom the horizons always beckoned.

"And he wasn't expecting we'd stay this long, practically eating him out of house and home. If it wasn't for his well, his goats, his garden, not to mention the rattlesnakes he traps in the rocks at the south end of the mesa, we'd have starved weeks ago. And without the extra grain we'd packed and the padre's hay, we'd have damn few horses left, too. As it is, we've managed to keep our stock in good shape."

Cleve squeezed his younger brother's forearm. "I have to tell you, Jason, I was afraid I'd find only dead men up here. I couldn't imagine you surviving this long."

"You didn't tell Father, did you?"

Cleve shook his head. "It's our secret. He thinks the mine is still running smoothly and I'm running things from the Prescott office." He chuckled. "Well, I doubt he thinks I'd run *anything* smoothly, but doing the best I can, anyway."

"Everything was running smoothly," Jason said, scowling into his wineglass. "Until Obrégon stumbled on the mine. I think he must have followed the ore wagons back after the last run to El Paso."

He shook his head and gave his brother a desperate look. "With all the money we have invested—and most of Father's—if we don't get to El Paso with the silver, I'd just as soon I didn't make it, either. We'll be ruined, brother. We'll be swamping saloons in Juárez."

"You could do worse," the senorita said dryly. "A little poverty never hurt anyone."

Knowing the girl's animosity toward the monied classes, which was understandable given the hard life she'd lived,

Yakima blew out a long plume of quirley smoke and said, "We were talking about Obrégon. Who is he and how many men does he have waiting for us? How much firepower?"

Cleve O'Shannon tossed back a long drink of wine and glanced at his brother darkly before casting his weary, red-rimmed eyes at Yakima. The half-breed sat on the floor with one knee drawn up and an arm resting on it, quirley smoke curling about his deeply tanned face.

"Obrégon's a border outlaw, about Jason's age," he said. "Half-Mex. His father was a deputy sheriff in the Llano Estacado, and when he wasn't gunning outlaws, he himself was robbing stages and stealing cattle and gunning lawmen. Taught his boy right well.

"Anyway, Guy Obrégon's been running roughshod with a group of *banditos/revolutionarios* for the past five years, wreaking havoc and trying to establish control of the northern Sierra Madre. He got a fix on our mine about a year ago and tried running us out several times. We managed to hold him off with the help of the rurales, to whom we paid a hefty tax. But a couple months ago, the rurale contingent in this part of Chihuahua was cut to ribbons by Obrégon, who'd recruited a veritable army of Mexican and gringo cutthroats."

"As for Obrégon's firepower," the younger O'Shannon cut in, "I've seen no sign of cannons, Gatling guns, or dynamite. Only repeating rifles and revolvers. And he has plenty of men. Upwards of fifty. But I don't think they're all here. With field glasses, I've seen sizable bands coming and going, probably skirmishing with other bands of desperadoes between the mountains and the border."

Cleve said, "To have held the siege for this long, he's got to be desperate for the silver."

"What about the woman?"

Everyone in the room turned to Yakima. The senorita arched a black brow at him.

The half-breed rubbed out his quirley on the floor and glanced at the younger O'Shannon. "Your brother told me the man besieging the mesa had designs on your wife. As long as I'm gonna be fighting the man, I want to know everything that's firing his cylinders."

Jason glanced at his brother. "Told him about that, did you?"

Cleve hiked a shoulder. "Figured he had a right to know."

Jason sipped his wine and ran the back of his hand against his mustache and beard. "It's like this," he began, with a pained expression. "Stella grew up along the Texas/Mexico border. Came from a poor ranching family in San Pedro Canyon. She knew Obrégon when she was just a girl, and, after her father died, she . . . uh . . . became a little wayward."

"She ran with Obrégon," Yakima said.

Jason nodded grimly. "For a year. But when she saw the butchery the man was capable of, she quit him. A wealthy uncle sent her to school in Missouri and got her on the right track."

"Where did you meet her?" Yakima wanted to know. Since the girl had once run with the outlaw who was besieging the mesa, he thought he should know as much about her as possible.

"I met her on one of my first expeditions to Mexico. My father and Cleve and I stopped at her ranch for water. Her father was dead, and her mother and uncle were running the place, and Stella . . ."

The younger O'Shannon smiled vacantly, remembering. "Stella had come home to help her mother, who'd been crippled in a fall down a well. Stella had turned into a beautiful young woman, fulfilling all the promise of her younger years. She sat a horse beautifully." He entwined his hands and smiled down at his wineglass, a little bashful. "I fell in love."

"Any fence straddling on her part?"

Jason O'Shannon looked at Yakima, the sunburned nubs of his cheeks above his shaggy beard darkening. "What do you mean?"

"I mean, are you sure she's entirely devoted to you?

When we're heading down this mountain, we're gonna have enough people shooting at us from the front. I don't want to have to worry about my back."

The younger O'Shannon looked at his brother, frowning, his blue eyes having acquired an uncharacteristic hardness. "Where did you find this man?"

"We need him, Jason," Cleve said. "He's a hard fighter. What is it Father used to say? 'You're bound to get some gristle with a good cut of meat.'"

Jason glanced at Yakima, who sat waiting for an answer to his question. "You won't have to worry about your back, Mr. Henry."

"How far down the mountain are Obrégon's men holed up?"

"They stay about a hundred yards away, just out of effective rifle range. You can see them from the mouth of the trail, which I keep covered at all times, with at least three men patrolling the entire crest of the mesa, making sure none of the besiegers have found another way up."

Yakima thought it over. Yesterday, as they'd approached the mesa from the northwest, he'd gotten a fair look at the natural bridge that rose from a hill of the desert to the top of the mesa, though he hadn't been able to see the besiegers from that distance and in that light.

"I saw a freight wagon behind the corral," he said. "What kind of shape's it in?"

Jason raised a shoulder. "It's a Murphy, and it's in fine shape. I had it overhauled with new axles and wheels before we left the mine. It's what we used to haul the silver up here, what I intended to haul it out with."

Yakima nodded, a pensive cast to his gaze. He looked at Leonora, who sat with one boot hiked on a knee, her wine cup in one hand, a quirley in the other. She smiled at him as though with a secret only the two of them shared.

"All right," Yakima said. "We'll use the wagon to haul both the silver and the gun. I hope you have four fast horses that don't make a big to-do at the sound of gunfire . . . and dynamite."

Leonora's smile grew, her brown eyes dancing in the candlelight.

Jason said, "I have some fast, sure-footed mules, but I can't vouch for their spleen under fire."

Cleve O'Shannon stared at Yakima gravely, almost fearfully. "Should we wait till morning, after we've seen the trail, to decide how to play it?"

Yakima heaved himself to his feet. "I say we go tomorrow. Midmorning, after I've had time to scout the trail and there's good light to see all the shooters."

"Wouldn't it be wiser to wait a few more days, Senor?" the padre asked gravely. "They know of the Gatling gun and the dynamite. Tomorrow they will be ready for you to use them."

"They'll be ready for that *any* day from here out, but I doubt they'll be expecting us to ram them down their throats. We'll have that much surprise on our side." Yakima looked at Jason, who regarded him with an expression similar to his brother's. "Have a couple men up early preparing the wagon with your best hitch horses. I'll prepare the Gatling gun."

He pinched his hat brim at the padre. "*Gracias* for the wine, Father."

"Go in peace, my son." The old padre offered an apologetic smile. "It is just an expression, of course."

Chapter 26

Yakima checked on the horses and the mule, glad to find that Wolf was too tired to stir up trouble with the other mounts. He retrieved his saddlebags and his saddle from the stable, tramped around behind the corral and the stable, and found an isolated place to camp at the edge of the mesa, well away from the others.

He needed some peace and quiet, time to organize his thoughts. He felt strangely indifferent about tomorrow, in spite of the fact that he would be making war with the Obrégon bunch. In fact, he had a feeling he was going to sleep like a dead man.

He wasn't worried about death—a profoundly liberating feeling. And he found little interest in life when it wasn't threatened.

Once he'd arranged his gear, propping his Yellowboy within reach of his saddle and blanket roll, he built a cigarette and sat on a flat rock at the very edge of the mesa, staring out at the stars that hung down from the stygian sky like Christmas ornaments from a universe-sized tree. The breeze smelled like stone and sage with occasional whiffs of juniper and piñon.

There was only the sound of the breeze pushing against the rocks, scratching leaves of the Spanish bayonet together, and the occasional yammer of a distant coyote or the screech of a cougar or mountain lion. From the direction of the church and the cabin, only silence.

Then there rose the faint, familiar ring of approaching spurs.

"Wild man, you back here?" Leonora called softly.

"Yep."

Blowing smoke through his nostrils, he turned to see her approaching from the far corner of the corral. She had her saddle and saddlebags hooked over her shoulder, and she strolled toward him with her hair bouncing on her shoulders, her doeskin vest looking like damp clay in the darkness.

He'd have preferred being alone, but he could smell her now on the breeze—a faint feminine smell sheathed in the odor of leather and horses—and he felt a stirring deep inside.

"You can't hide from me, Yakima," she said, throwing her saddle down beside his. "It's been a long time since I've been with a man. A real man."

She doffed her hat and strode slowly toward him, removing her cartridge belt and letting it drop at her feet. She shook her hair back from her shoulders and lifted her hands to her chest. Her fingers began slipping the leather ties of her vest from their small silver stays, the vest inching away from her deep, dark cleavage.

Yakima dropped the quirley at his feet and mashed it out in the gravel.

Rising from the boulder, he took off his hat and began removing his shirt. Before him, the senorita pulled her vest back to her shoulders, revealing the large, heavy breasts, and dropped the vest on the ground with her guns. She followed them up with her chaps. Then her hands went to the buttons on her leather pants, and she leaned forward, bending her legs gracefully, to slide them down her legs.

Yakima kicked out of his boots and then shucked out of his jeans, and a minute later, naked and aroused, he stepped toward the Wildcat of Sonora, waiting for him with her clothes, guns, and bowie knife piled around her bare feet.

Her legs were long and tightly muscled, the thick brown thighs sculpted by a lifetime of riding. Her hips were full, her belly flat. She was firm and ripe and perfectly curved and angled, and he could smell the primal lust emanating from her like the musk of a bitch in season.

Leonora said nothing, but Yakima could hear her breathing through her parted lips. Her breasts rose and fell slowly, heavily. Her hair fluttered out slightly in the cool, refreshing breeze that, in the moonlight, Yakima could see lifting gooseflesh across her shoulders and down her arms.

He placed his hands on her breasts, cupping them gently at first, caressing the jutting nipples with his thumbs. His heart hammered at the feel of the heavy, smooth, firm globes in his hands. They were warm and growing warmer. After a time, touching her with only his hands, he slid them behind her breasts to her sides and ran them slowly down her back. He placed them flat across her full, fleshy bottom and squeezed, lifting.

She groaned, her chin coming up and her head falling back.

Suddenly, he removed his hands from her bottom, stooped down, and holding one arm at the small of her back and the other behind her knees, swept her up in his arms.

Laughing with surprise and delight, she wrapped her arms around his neck, relaxing her body and surrendering herself completely.

While he kissed her, she dropped one of her hands down his belly, and massaged him, working him into a lather of frenzied passion. When he could take no more, he carried her to his saddle, knelt down and laid her on his blanket roll. He continued kissing her, hungrily nuzzling her neck and her breasts as he crawled between her knees, raising her legs with his arms, wrestling her into position.

They rasped, groaned, and grunted.

Finding her ready, he plunged into her.

"Oh, Wild Man!" she cried as he thrust, throwing her head back on his blanket. "What are you trying to do—*kill* me?"

But she didn't let him stop. She rocked as he thrust, his bulging arms propped on either side of her shoulders, her hands clutching his muscular buttocks desperately, squeezing and pulling him toward her, her legs flapping like wings, as they toiled together beneath the blazing stars.

"You are in your element, gringo Indio, uh?" she said huskily later, under the crackling stars, as she rested her head on his belly and massaged him languidly with her hand beneath the blanket that partly covered them both. "I don't just mean with me, though I must say you certainly filed down a lot of rough edges. I mean out here, on the run in Mexico, with guns blasting and dynamite exploding."

He hadn't thought much about what had caused his even mood and this sense of well-being. But she must be right. When you're dodging desperado bullets in Mexico, you don't have time to think about such things as a pretty woman you buried in Colorado. No time for dwelling on the past or the future when you're toiling between the spread legs of a wild *bandita*.

He put his hand in her hair, closed his fingers around it. His loins tingled beneath her caress, the warmth of her cheek on his belly, one of her legs hooked over his.

"I like it down here just fine," he said, pressing his head luxuriously against his saddle, feeling beneath his stirring desire the fatigue of the day fall over him like a warm, welcoming blanket. "Yep, I like this just fine . . ."

"When we are finished with the Irishmen," she said, "you will stay with me, huh? We will have a grand time—you and me, Wild Man. There are many wars to fight in Old Mejico!"

"All right."

She looked up at him, frowning. "Huh?"

A faint, relaxed smile lifting the corners of his mouth, Yakima shrugged. "Where the hell else do I have to go?"

She narrowed an eye. "Are you toying with me, gringo Indio? Are you being serious?"

Looking down at her, he slid her hair back from her cheek. "Yeah."

Leonora smiled, her brown eyes glinting dully in the

starlight. She splayed her fingers across his chest, then, smiling up at him beguilingly, slid her head slowly, devastatingly down his belly to his groin.

The Gatling gun's brass chasing shone in the buttery mid-morning sunlight that washed over the bald eastern ridges.

The bandoliers of spare cartridges were coiled beside the platform that Yakima, up at the first smudge of dawn, had built from an old packing crate and to which he'd fixed the Gatling's tripod with large-headed nails hammered through the holes in its steel-shod wooden toes. The foot-long cartridge clip was in place atop the barrel. The wood-handled crank stood upright and ready.

The wagon was a big Murphy freighter with wide iron-shod wheels, a reinforced undercarriage for steep mountain travel, and a log chain attached to the doubletree for steep cornering. A heavy, high-sided wagon, it would need the four stout mules Yakima and Leonora had just finished hitching to it while Jason O'Shannon's men finished carrying the silver ingots out of the church and hefting them into the box.

The men arranged the silver carefully around the gun platform, giving the Gatling as much support as possible, as Yakima would likely be firing it while the wagon was tearing down the mesa toward the desperadoes at a breakneck clip. Leonora had opted for the unenviable job of driving the wagon while Yakima manned the Gatling gun in the box behind her, shooting over her head and the horses and Cleve O'Shannon hunkered beside him with his sixteen-shot Henry repeater, a couple of revolvers, and a Winchester.

Jason's first lieutenant, the man in the deerskin vest and shabby sombrero whom Yakima and his two cohorts had met last night, would pitch the dynamite sticks over the side of the wagon. The man's name was Spade Reilly, an ex-army scout who'd signed on with Jason just before Obrégon had begun threatening the mine. Reilly had done his share of prospecting before and between stints with Kendall's Apache-fighting troop of the Sixth Cavalry, and he professed familiarity with the dangerous and intoxicating magic powder.

Yakima sipped the coffee that Stella O'Shannon had brought to him and the others as he continued to rake his eyes over the gun and the wagon and the mules standing impatiently in the traces.

"We are ready, then, huh?" Leonora said behind him, holding a tin coffee cup and smoking a long, black cheroot that she'd plucked from Cleve's shirt pocket.

"Looks that way."

"She's a heavy wagon, not made for fast travel. I hope she doesn't break in two when we're halfway down the mesa." The señorita blew cigar smoke through her lovely nostrils as she stooped to look beneath the wagon. "And look how high. She's top-heavy. If those mules jerk sharply to the right or the left, she's liable to . . ."

The señorita stopped when she saw Yakima smiling at her. She chuckled and shrugged as she sipped her coffee with a look of chagrin. "So we might die bloody . . . What else is new?"

When the wagon's tailgate was closed, Jason O'Shannon's men mounted their horses, which stood fidgeting and blowing as the light grew and swallows darted over the mesa searching for breakfast. The younger O'Shannon helped his wife into the saddle of Duke, her white barb horse, while Cleve finished adjusting his roan's saddle and glanced apprehensively toward the north.

Behind the group, Padre Sandoval stood like a stone statue of an aged saint before his little church's open doors, holding a small silver crucifix in his age-gnarled hands. A morning breeze tousled his thin, curly hair and lifted the dust about his sandaled feet. His lips moved in a nearly silent prayer.

Jason went over and shook the priest's hand, promising him that if they made it off the mesa alive and with the silver, he would reimburse the man for his hospitality. The old padre waved his hand and shook his head, objecting, and Jason turned and stepped into his saddle beside his wife.

Stella O'Shannon wore a simple plaid shirt under a black leather vest, a wool riding skirt, gloves, and a light green felt hat thonged beneath her chin. She also wore a Colt .36 in a holster high on her right hip, and her eyes, to Yakima's mild surprise, were solemn but unafraid.

He hadn't gotten a good look at her last night, but now he saw that she was even prettier than he'd thought, with freckles splashed across her tan cheeks. Her eyes were dove gray, with the certain, straight-on cast of the native Westerner. While her lips were thin, they were not prim.

If she'd thrown in with her ex-lover, Guy Obrégon, neither her eyes nor her demeanor betrayed it.

Stella thanked the padre for all he had done for her and her husband and leaned down to kiss him good-bye. Meanwhile, Yakima glanced appraisingly at all fourteen of Jason's riders once more, noting that while they looked haggard from their two-month ordeal, they also appeared relatively fresh and up to the task at hand.

If Yakima shot effectively without wasting ammo, most of the work would be up to Leonora and the others in the wagon anyway, with Jason, his men, and Stella bringing up the rear.

Yakima tossed his empty coffee cup into the wagon's box and climbed inside. Leonora followed, and then Cleve O'Shannon and Spade Reilly. The men doffed their hats and hunkered down—Cleve to the left of the gun, Reilly to the right—while Yakima took up his position behind it, atop the crate that stood three feet above the cargo box, well above the sunken driver's box.

The barrel of the gun cleared the top of Leonora's head by two feet, giving Yakima a three-directional field of fire. He could even swing the gun around and shoot behind him if he needed to. He'd hammered rawhide toeholds into the top of the crate to keep his boots from sliding around as the wagon raced down the mesa.

Yakima glanced at the O'Shannon riders behind him. "Stay behind me till we reach the top of the trail. I want another look down the mesa before we start down."

Jason O'Shannon nodded. He rode at the front center of his men, while Stella rode behind them on her white barb.

"I hope this works, Mr. Henry. We're staking a lot on it, Cleve and me."

"Don't feel like the lone crusader," Leonora snarled as she regarded the man over her left shoulder.

Yakima said, "Okay," and Leonora shook the ribbons across the backs of the stocky mules. The wagon creaked forward, one wheel squawking slightly in spite of the grease Yakima had given it, the mules blowing and shaking their heads. Behind the wagon a horse whinnied sharply, likely sensing the anxiety of its rider and the other men around it.

Dust swept across the flat-topped mesa. Yakima squinted through it to the north, where the rolling, dun-colored, cactus-spotted desert below slid slowly toward him as the wagon approached the mesa's edge.

Where the trail began dropping, Leonora drew back on the mules' reins.

Yakima rose up on his toes to peer ahead. The trail dropped away from them for a mile, falling gradually—a natural bridge connecting the mesa with a rounded hill five hundred feet lower on the desert floor. From a previous reconnaissance the half-breed knew that the sides of the trail were sheer until, at a point about fifty yards down from the mesa, they gentled out and became strewn with boulders and cedars.

This was where Obrégon's men were hunkered down—amid those boulders, with here and there a ribbon of smoke betraying a cook fire. Yakima had seen few men through his field glasses earlier, but he had to believe that all of Obrégon's men—aside from those who'd been taken to the dance last night—would roil up from those rocks and shrubs and start slinging lead the moment they saw the horseback riders and the wagon barreling toward them.

Yakima glanced behind at Jason and his bearded, unkempt riders—both Mexicans and Americans—sitting their saddles looking at once eager, excited, relieved, apprehensive, and scared shitless.

Yakima swung around to face the Gatling gun and the trail. He gripped the handhold at the left side of the barrel, clutched the crank with the other. He shoved the toes of his boots into the rawhide stays atop the crate, setting his feet, then freed the barrel's locking mechanism so it would turn when he started cranking.

"Let's go to work," he said.

Chapter 27

The O'Shannon riders galloped down the mesa in a cloud of dust, whooping and hollering and waving their arms like the James-Younger Gang after a bank heist in some sleepy Yankee village. They triggered revolvers and rifles over their horses' bobbing heads, sending up a din of gunfire that nearly covered the drumming of their horses' hooves.

The gang wasn't forty yards down the hill before the senorita bellowed raucously and flapped the reins over the mules' backs. Yakima clutched the Gatling gun with his hands and the rawhide foot straps with his boot toes as the wagon lurched forward, jerking violently a few times before starting down the gently falling trail and rolling smoothly behind the lunging, galloping team.

Yakima glanced over his shoulder. As planned, Stella O'Shannon was keeping pace thirty yards behind the wagon, where she'd be as far from harm's way as possible.

The hundred thousand dollars' worth of silver bars and the Gatling gun were no light load, but the mules handled it easily, as did the wagon. It helped that they were going down instead of up, and Yakima prayed that the desperadoes had placed no obstruction in the trail that he had not been able to see earlier with his field glasses.

When the wagon was fifty yards down the trail, with Jason's men fifty yards ahead, the desperadoes realized what was happening and started returning fire from the rocks along the trail. Several bounded up—bearded, scruffy-

looking Mexicans wearing sombreros and wielding Spencer
or trapdoor Springfield carbines—with looks of surprise,
shouting at their brethren that O'Shannon was trying to
make a run for it.

Smoke puffed from among the rocks. The horses of
O'Shannon's riders whinnied, and one of the men shouted.

"Fall back!" Leonora shouted as she urged more speed
from the mules. "Fall back! *Rap-idooooooo!*"

All at once, Jason and his men hauled back on their
horses' reins, skidding to a dusty, whinnying halt on either
side of the trail, making way for the roaring, clattering
wagon. Yakima squinted through the sunlit dust at the
bleached-out natural bridge straight ahead—about thirty yards
wide and sheathed tightly on both sides by boulders and
tufts of wiry brown brush.

The desperadoes had done what he'd expected them to
do when they saw the charging riders. They'd hustled out
onto the trail, laying themselves wide open to the Gatling
gun.

RAT-A-TAT-TAT-TAT-TAT-TAT-TAT-TAT!

As Yakima cranked, the Gatling belched smoke and
flames, sending a hail of .45-caliber lead over the bobbing
heads of the mules and into the small bunches of desperadoes aiming rifles or extending cocked revolvers.

Dust and rock shards blew up around them. Bullets
smashed into leather or deerskin tunics or striped serapes.
They clanked off cartridge bandoliers, ripped hats off heads
or ricocheted off raised rifles or pistols and smashed into
faces that burst like ripe tomatoes. One man—a bare-
chested, nearly black mestizo wearing a broad red bandanna taut against his forehead—dropped his rifle and
bellowed like a wounded bear as one of the Gatling slugs
smashed through his kneecap and puffed off a rock behind
him.

Two more men went down, pinwheeling and screaming
and tossing away their rifles. As the wagon continued
plunging down the trail behind the galloping mules, O'Shannon's rifle barked quickly, finishing off the wounded des-

peradoes. Meanwhile, whooping and hollering, Spade Reilly sent one dynamite stick after another hurtling down both sides of the trail, where the dynamite exploded around clumps of Obrégon men bounding up the slope with their rifles across their chests, and threw them, screaming and cursing, in all directions.

The explosions sent rocks and boulders tumbling down the slope toward the tents and cook fires of the besiegers' bivouacs. More Obrégon men shouted as they tried to dodge the thundering rocks, some able to do so, some smashed to pulp against the slope, hats and weapons flying.

When the wagon was halfway down the trail, Yakima held fire and looked around wildly. He spied only a couple more men crawling around the rocks behind the pounding Murphy. A few others, managing to dodge the bouncing boulders, ran up from the canyons on both sides of the trail. Others, some half dressed, some running up from a small cottonwood-lined stream below one of the bivouacs, ran around aimlessly, shouting and cursing as the boulders tumbled over or around them and into the valley below, several narrowly missing the rope-corralled horses. They stared in shock and fury at the wagon and riders racing across the natural bridge, heading for open desert. O'Shannon's men galloped along behind the Murphy but fired only a few sporadic shots.

The Gatling gun had quickly and cleanly cut down the desperadoes guarding the trail. A dozen or so others had been torn to smithereens in the savage blasts of the dynamite sticks, a dozen more finished in the rockfall. As Yakima had hoped, they'd been taken by surprise. An all-out run down the bridge, with a blazing Gatling gun and exploding dynamite, had been the last thing they'd expected this sunny summer morning, in spite of last night's skirmish.

The wagon continued hammering along the trail toward cactus-stippled hogbacks, the Obrégon bivouacs a good hundred yards behind and the gap opening with every racing second. Yakima saw a half dozen Mexicans sprinting toward a remuda of horses tied in a cottonwood clump. One man stood barefoot outside a tent, wearing only gold-embroidered black charro slacks and a white undershirt beneath suspenders. His long dark brown hair wisped about his shoulders as he pointed toward the horses and shouted furiously at the running men's backs.

"That's Obrégon!" O'Shannon said, pointing. "Looks like he's sending riders after us!"

"What did you expect him to do? Wave good-bye? He'll shade us all the way to El Paso . . . unless we finish the son of a bitch."

Spade Reilly held a capped and fused dynamite stick close to his chest, as though he was just dying to light it with the cigar protruding from the side of his mouth and throw it. His other arm hung over the side of the wagon, and the wind blew his thin, dark brown hair. "How in the hell you propose to finish him?"

"We'll have to spring a trap on him!"

"Sure, we'll trap him and blow him to hell and gone!"

Leonora glanced over her shoulder at Yakima, a question in her eyes. Yakima pulled his boots out of the rawhide thongs, then swung the Gatling barrel straight down toward the wagon floor. He picked up his Winchester and glanced behind at the riders galloping after him. They didn't appear to have lost anyone. Stella O'Shannon brought up the rear on her galloping barb, her hat flapping down her back.

Carefully, jostling from side to side, Yakima moved forward over the silver ingots lumped beneath their burlap covering, then crawled over the box's front panel and into the driver's box. He sat down beside Leonora and held his Yellowboy across his thighs.

Leonora regarded him with a mix of awe and admiration, and he felt the heat rise in his cheeks. His exhilaration must have shone in his face, all memories and thoughts of tomorrow swept under the rug of his consciousness by the hullabaloo.

Like she'd said, he was in his element. And he wasn't in a hurry to move on.

"Do you want to drive, Wild Man?" The silver crucifix jostled to and fro in her deep cleavage. His blood warmed beneath his belly, and he felt the urge to stop the wagon and haul the senorita off into the rocks and piñons and ravage her savagely, endlessly.

The thought coming at such a time made him smile.

"What?" Leonora asked. "Are you all right? You weren't hit, were you?"

"Shut up and drive."

"*Mierda!* The man's gone loco on me!"

Eventually the mules slowed under the weight of their load. Yakima knew there would be no outrunning Obrégon's men unless they abandoned the wagon. And since the silver the wagon was hauling had been the reason for this charade in the first place, they would all die before they abandoned it.

Jason O'Shannon had put his horse up beside the Murphy, near where his brother knelt, shifting his gaze from their back trail to the front and back again.

"We'd better stop the mules soon before you kill them!" Jason called toward the driver's box.

A gap in the high bluffs and the saw-toothed ridges appeared just ahead on the left.

Yakima pointed at it. "There!"

Leonora glanced at the sunlit opening, then at Yakima. "What if it's a box canyon?"

"That's what I'm counting on."

As she angled the team toward the gap, she tossed Yakima a skeptical frown. "Please don't go loco on me, Wild Man. I need you, okay? I've got a few good years left, and—"

"Shut up and drive."

"Shut up and drive," the senorita repeated under her breath, shaking her head. *"¡Jesús santo, el bastardo loco va a conseguirnos matados todo!"* Holy Jesus, the crazy bastard is going to get us all killed!

The canyon, indeed, dead-ended about a hundred yards into the cut. A waterfall trickled down the canyon's rear wall onto black volcanic boulders jumbled below, tumbling from a deep stone trough it had cut over eons. At the very bottom was a shallow pool that ran off over a gravel bed and down into a brushy ravine in the canyon's middle.

The canyon was bottle-shaped, with the front being the bottle's neck and the back being the bottom, which stretched sixty yards between a steep stone ridge on the right and a slightly less steep brushy ridge on the left.

"Madre Maria," the senorita breathed, looking around as she set the wagon brake and wrapped the reins around the handle. "Well, I will tell you one thing, amigo, this place is a trap. But for whom—them or us? That is what I'm wondering."

"I take it you're proposing an ambush," Jason O'Shannon said as he reined his prancing mount up beside the wagon. "The quarters are too close here for the dynamite. We'd bring that ridge down on top of us."

His men halted their horses behind him and, leaping from their saddles, levered rounds into their rifle breeches while they led their horses behind a cabin-sized boulder fronting the falls.

"Anyhow we can do it, we might as well shed them right here and now," Yakima said, standing up in the wagon's driver's box and looking around at the ridges rising on both sides of him.

The quarters were too close for the Gatling gun, too. In the canyon the need for accuracy would outweigh firepower.

Cleve O'Shannon and Spade Reilly leapt over the sides of the wagon and looked around anxiously through the dust kicked up by the mules and the horses.

"We have no idea exactly how many men Obrégon has left," Cleve said. "What if he has more that we have bullets for?"

"I'll have an answer for you soon."

Yakima jumped from the wagon to a rock ledge on the canyon's sheer wall. He stopped and turned back toward the men holing up behind rocks, boulders, and shrubs on the canyon's other side and around the falls.

Stella rode up to sit her horse beside her husband's dun, regarding him anxiously.

"You two go up near the falls," Yakima called above the water's steady rattle. "Let 'em get a look at you as they round that last bend."

Stella O'Shannon shot Yakima a sharp look. "What? You want us to bait them *in*?"

"You got it." Yakima put his face to the rock wall and climbed to another ledge six feet higher, grabbing a twisted piñon for leverage. "They won't have time to get a shot at you before the rest of us start throwing lead at 'em. If all goes well, this should be like shooting cans off fence posts. But no one shoots before I do!"

In a minute, O'Shannon's men were hunkered down along the wall or perched behind cover several yards up the sides. A couple of them crouched in the brushy ravine running down the canyon's middle, where the slow stream reflected the light from the midday sky.

Cleve O'Shannon knelt behind a cedar opposite where Yakima hid behind a stone spur jutting from the rocky wall. Beside Yakima, the senorita knelt on one knee behind another, smaller spur, her chest rising and falling heavily as she held her two cocked pistols in her hands and peered back through the canyon's narrow gap.

Dust continued to sift through the air over the canyon, butter-colored in the noontime light.

The falls rattled and clattered down the wet black wall and over the boulders below, drowning out all other sounds except the infrequent screech of a hawk hunting the timber up the brushy ridge to the south.

Yakima and the others waited.

Gradually, the steady, hurried clomp of hooves rose above the rattle of the falls.

Yakima tightened his grip on his Winchester and adjusted his boots beneath him. He would let as many of Obrégon's men into the canyon as possible before the first riders smelled the trap and started shooting. Jason and Stella, sitting their horses side by side near the falls, would give the desperadoes a moment's pause as they wondered what they'd ridden into.

Two riders appeared, coming around the last bend and into the canyon. The one on the left was Obrégon himself— a tall, rangy mixed-blood Mex with long dark brown hair, matching sideburns, and a spade-shaped goatee. He did not wear a hat, but a soiled, sweaty red bandanna around the top of his head, the tails of the knotted cloth falling with his hair down his back. His right cheek was badly scarred from an old bullet wound—a twisted white gash that contrasted with his otherwise hawkishly handsome face.

A rifle hung barrel down behind his back, and Yakima saw a wide knife handle jutting up behind the desperado leader's neck. In his right hand Obrégon held a brass-chased Colt Navy revolver, while the man beside him—short and stocky and wearing a ratty straw sombrero—wielded a Spencer carbine.

Obrégon's jaw dropped when he saw Jason O'Shannon and Stella. He jerked back on his pinto's reins with one hand and raised his Colt with the other.

Yakima bored down on him, planting the Yellowboy's sights on his sweaty, dusty bandanna.

Stella O'Shannon's voice rose sharply above the prattling falls. "Nobody shoot!"

Yakima lowered the Yellowboy and peered down and to his right. As before, Stella O'Shannon sat her barb beside her husband's dun.

But now she was holding a cocked pistol to Jason's ear.

Chapter 28

"If anybody shoots, I'm going to kill my darling husband," Stella O'Shannon said, keeping her .36 leveled on Jason's right ear, evoking a look of tongue-tangled surprise on her young husband's face.

She looked around the canyon, as did Yakima, tickling his Yellowboy's trigger with his gloved right finger. All eyes were on Stella and Jason as the men peered from their covering rocks or shrubs or humps of gravelly ground.

"Stella!" Jason barked. "What the hell are you doing?"

"Put the guns down, amigos," Obrégon said with a cat-like grin. "Or your fearless leader is going to have a larger than usual ear hole."

Yakima was vaguely surprised to hear Obrégon's precise, nearly unaccented English.

"What does it look like, honey?" Stella said, ominously accenting "honey" and offering a frigid smile on her pretty, heart-shaped face. "Guy and I have been . . . how would you put it? Stepping out on you."

"Why?" the younger O'Shannon fairly screeched.

"Shut up, Jason, you scholastic little twerp," Obrégon said, holding his cocked Colt on Jason's chest while glancing around at the O'Shannon men. "Have your men throw their weapons down, or it'll be a corpse they haul back to El Paso."

Yakima looked again at the shocked, enraged faces of the O'Shannon men peering out from their cover. They held their rifles or pistols tightly as they shifted their nervous gazes from Stella and Jason to the entire Obrégon gang, now sitting their horses in a dust cloud just inside the wide part of the canyon. Cleve peered out from behind his covering boulder with the look of a man who'd discovered the stew he'd just eaten had been cooked with rat meat.

"Why should we toss them down, Obrégon, you filthy dog?" Leonora Domingo shouted from Yakima's right. "Go ahead, *keeel* him! I don't intend to die for that fat-faced gringo. What I want is the silver!"

"I don't think this is the time to call his bluff," Yakima said tightly, keeping his eyes on Obrégon. "I don't think he's bluffing."

"Maybe not," the senora snarled. "But I'll be damned if I'll die for the gringo." She tossed her head to indicate Jason.

"The senorita's got a point!" one of the O'Shannon men shouted from behind a cracked rock and a juniper shrub. "We toss our guns down, we're all dead! You'll kill the boss anyway and ride off with the silver—slick as snot on a doorknob!"

"Amigos," Obrégon said, chuckling, "I give you my word as a gentleman of the border country! You throw your guns down, we let you and your fearless leader"—he glanced, grinning, toward Leonora—"and the lovely Wildcat of Sonora . . . ride away unharmed."

Yakima glanced quickly toward Leonora. "Your reputation precedes you, dear."

"I hope you're not offended, lover."

On the canyon floor, Stella lowered her .36 and spurred her white barb over to the Mexican gang, turning the mount so that she sat just off Obrégon's right stirrup. She sat straight-backed and high-chinned, proud and defiant, her eyes on her husband. "You'd only spend the money foolishly, Jason. Trying to live the high-society life you and Cleve come from. To show your foolish father how successful you are. You'd blow it on risky speculation, and Cleve'd blow his share on cards and women."

"Oh?" Cleve said, as his brother seemed too much in shock to speak. "And how do you intend to spend it, sister?"

"We intend to spend it taking over this part of Mejico!" Obrégon shouted in the woman's stead. "And living the good life forever more!" He reached over, grabbed Stella around the waist, and kissed her. *"Viva la Mejico!"*

A rifle flashed in the sunlight as it snaked out around a boulder on the far side of the canyon. One of Obrégon's mounted men jerked toward it. The revolver in his hand exploded.

The rifleman grunted and staggered out from behind the boulder, clutching his right temple with one hand while the rifle dropped to the ground and fired, the slug tearing into the ground and spraying rocks and gravel.

"Hold your fire!" Cleve rose from behind the boulder and tossed his rifle down. "Nobody shoots. That's an order!"

"Bullshit," Leonora said quietly beside Yakima.

"Hold on," Yakima grunted.

"You hold on, Wild Man. I don't care about these sons-abitches. Last one to the silver must stand me a whole bottle of the best tequila in Mejico!"

Unlike the senorita, Yakima felt an allegiance to the men who'd hired him.

"Hold your damn fire," he said tautly, staring over his cocked Winchester's trigger into the canyon. "Let's see how it plays out."

Obrégon was speaking, waving his pistol for emphasis. "I have asked you politely, Senores. And now I am going to ask you again. Throw down your weapons. Please. Or watch your employer die in the last few seconds you yourselves have left on this earth."

Yakima wanted to know what O'Shannon's men would do. Personally, he had no intention of turning his rifle over to the desperadoes, who would surely line him and Leonora and the O'Shannon riders up and shoot them down like cows with Texas fever. His allegiance to no one went that far.

But he didn't get a chance to find out what O'Shannon's men would do.

The whip crack of a rifle sounded from the slope on the far side of the canyon. Stella's head snapped back and sideways, as though she'd just been slapped by a powerful hand. She dropped her horse's reins, the barb shifted nervously, and all heads in the canyon swung toward her, including Obrégon's.

The desperado leader's eyes were wide with shock.

At the same time, he and Jason O'Shannon shouted, *"Stella!"*

Jason spurred his horse forward. His dun hadn't taken three strides before another rifle cracked on the slope on the far side of the canyon. Jason was punched sideways with a scream, and as his dun continued galloping forward, he pitched down the horse's side, hit the dust and brush, and rolled, clutching his upper right arm.

Yakima peered up the opposite slope, and bells tolled in his head. Men were spilling down from the high timber, smoke puffing from rifle barrels, evoking shouts and screams from the canyon floor, where Obrégon's men were cutting loose on O'Shannon's men, several flinging shots up the slope as well, shouting in a red-eyed rage, "It's a trap!"

It was a confused, flabbergasted frenzy, no one knowing—as Yakima did not himself—what in holy hell was going on. If this was a trap, who in the hell had set it?

Slugs buzzed around Yakima's ears and slammed into the rock wall behind him. Men from the canyon as well as those from the far slope were flinging lead toward him and Leonora.

"Who the hell's that?" the senorita shouted above the din, cutting loose on the canyon floor with her revolvers but glancing at the newcomers across the way.

"Looks like someone else wants to be dealt into the game!" Yakima returned fire at Obrégon's men below, gutshooting one and blowing another out of the saddle of his prancing, screaming Arabian.

Chaos reigned in the canyon. Yakima and the senorita returned fire on Obrégon's men on the canyon floor as well as on those streaming down the far slope. Because of the powder smoke, it was tough to distinguish between the two groups, and Yakima fired only at targets he was certain of.

Obrégon's men were caught in a deadly three-way cross fire between those shooting from the slope, the O'Shannon riders in the canyon, and the half-breed and Leonora. They twisted and pivoted every which way as bullets stormed around them, clutching themselves as lead cut through them.

Horses whinnied and ran wild among the men, some taking bullets and going down while others found their way out the narrow corridor, whinnying shrilly and bucking as they fled in sifting dust clouds.

Obrégon's men were quickly cut to ribbons and lay sprawled in bloody heaps. O'Shannon's men faired better, for they had the help of Yakima and Leonora, and also the cover at the base of the far canyon wall.

With all of Obrégon's men dead or dying, O'Shannon's men, including Cleve and Jason, who crouched beside the same rock, Jason with a bloody right arm, turned their attention to the newcomers. Half of the bushwhackers lay dead along the slope, for there wasn't much cover below the timberline and Yakima had killed at least ten handily with as many shots from his Yellowboy.

There hadn't been that many more of the interlopers to begin with, and now the others died, falling and rolling into the canyon as O'Shannon's riders finished them off.

Yakima snapped off one more shot, drilling a man on the slope as he lifted his bloody head as well as his revolver from the ground to fire a last shot into the canyon. Yakima's bullet puffed dust just behind the man after it had drilled through his right eye and out the back of his head.

The man's head snapped back, beard-encircled mouth forming a large O, and then he slumped forward and rolled into the canyon, where O'Shannon's men had stopped firing to look around, weary, wary, and thoroughly addled by the bloody skirmish.

Yakima cast one more cautious gaze into the canyon and

across the canyon floor already splashed red with blood from both Obrégon's and O'Shannon's dead. No more than five of the O'Shannon riders, not including Cleve and Jason themselves, were upright and peering up the slope through the powder smoke.

Thumbing fresh cartridges into his Yellowboy's loading gate, Yakima rose, squinting across the canyon. To his right, Leonora straightened as well, holstering one of her smoking pistols and emptying the spent cartridges of the other onto the ground around her boots.

As she reloaded the gun from her cartridge belt, she kept her gaze before her, swiveling her head occasionally, prickly as a hunted cat, for anyone moving down the bank behind her and Yakima.

"Christos!" she exclaimed under her breath.

Yakima began making his way down the steep slope, throwing one arm out for balance. "That's what I say."

Rocks and gravel clattered out from under his boots, and then he leapt the last few feet to the canyon floor, shuttling his gaze around the heaped and strewn dead men. The smell of blood and cordite was heavy in his nostrils. One wounded horse whinnied and tried to clamber to its feet, but it was lung-shot, and Yakima ended the beast's suffering with a single bullet to the back of its head.

"You all right, brother?" Cleve O'Shannon said.

He knelt beside Jason, who was down on both knees, holding his wounded arm as he stared at his dead wife lying half under Guy Obrégon's bloody corpse. Jason's hair was mussed, his beard caked with grit. His eyes were blank with shock.

His lips moved slightly. "Stella . . ."

"Jason," Cleve muttered.

The younger O'Shannon jerked his arm free of his brother's grasp and heaved himself to his feet. He stumbled over to where his wife lay on her back, arms and legs thrown wide. Her lifeless, wide-open eyes stared skyward.

Those eyes . . .

Yakima turned away and gritted his teeth, remembering

another pair of lifeless eyes staring into space as though in cosmic amazement that her vital life had been snuffed so quickly.

"Stella!"

The cry echoed around the canyon as Jason dropped to both knees and leaned awkwardly over his dead wife, snaked his good arm under her neck, and lifted her head to his chest, sobbing.

The other men stood around in hushed silence as the smoke began to rise and the dust sifted back toward the canyon floor. A couple of them helped the few living wounded, and Leonora, with a significant glance at Yakima, strode around the dead Obrégon men, taking the extra precaution of kicking guns away from the bodies.

Yakima glanced once more at Jason O'Shannon clinging desperately to his dead wife, Stella's arms hanging straight down to the ground beneath her. Yakima snorted to clear his own remembered images, trying to ignore the saw working at his intestines and wishing to Christ the man would stop his infernal sobbing and get hold of himself.

Muttering an annoyed curse, he looked around for Wolf. Grateful that the stallion wasn't among the dead horses mingled with the dead men, he started walking past the wagon toward the canyon's narrow neck.

A scuffle sounded to his right.

Leonora cried, *"Ay, mierda!"*

One of the "dead" men had lunged to his feet and, blood staining one shoulder, grabbed the senorita from behind, crooking an arm around her neck and raising an obsidian-gripped stiletto inset with glittering jewels to her smooth throat. Yakima recognized the long silver hair and beard and the tailored vaquero attire of Don Ungaro's first lieutenant, Alberto Espinoza.

One of the bushwhacking newcomers, he must have sneaked down the hill during the deadly cross fire, trying to make his way to Leonora.

"For the murder of Don Jesus Ungaro, *puta* bitch and fornicator with dogs, I consign you to—"

BLAM!

Yakima had switched his Yellowboy to his left hand and palmed his .44 with his right, a blur of motion that ended in the stab of smoke and flames from the revolver's barrel and a neat round hole appearing just above the silver brow over Espinoza's right eye. The man's head snapped back as if jerked by a rope from behind, both eyes widening. The hand holding the blade dropped.

"Ach!" the senorita grunted as she tore herself loose from Espinoza's fading grip.

As the man shambled backward, Yakima's revolver roared twice more, the bullets puffing dust from Espinoza's collarless pin-striped shirt and his puma-skin vest. Espinoza groaned as he twisted sideways, staggered a few feet toward the slope behind him, then fell onto his right shoulder and hip and lay there, staring sightlessly at the blood from his open brow dribbling onto a wiry sage shrub beneath his cheek.

The Wildcat of Sonora stared down at the man in awe. "It was Ungaro's yellow dog, come nipping at my heels."

"Loyal bastard. I'll give him that," Yakima said.

Leonora swung toward him, rage in her eyes and a flush in her high, tapering cheeks as she pounded her breast. "I told you *I* wanted to keel him, damn you, Wild Man!"

Yakima scowled at her, incredulous. With a caustic snort, he twirled his .44 on his finger, dropped it into its holster, and continued tramping down the canyon for his horse.

Epilogue

Nearly a month later, after a journey complicated by only two skirmishes with Mexican banditos and one with a small band of Chiricahua Apaches, the dusty, weary, desert-scorched band led by Yakima and Leonora Domingo stopped on a sage-covered knoll in the heat of a dry Texas afternoon.

Ahead, the sun-blasted village of El Paso sprawled in its broad desert valley bordered by burnt orange rimrocks.

"Why are we stopping?" Jason O'Shannon asked, sitting beside his brother on the silver wagon's driver's seat. The Gatling gun, for which they had only about five cartridges remaining, jutted like a giant brass bug from the box humped with burlap-covered silver ingots.

"End of the trail," Yakima said, staring straight ahead at the bustling burg, dust rising from the wheels and hooves of wagons and horseback riders threading the town and the broad, powdery trails around it. The rails of the Southern Pacific line shone like quicksilver at each end.

"What do you mean?" Cleve said. "That's El Paso down there. That's the end of the trail."

"Nope. This is the end for me."

Yakima glanced back at the two O'Shannons staring at him, befuddled, Jason still wearing the bandage around his upper arm and keeping the arm in a sling fashioned from a red polka-dotted neckerchief. Their five surviving outriders had stopped their horses around the wagon and were squinting at Yakima with equally dubious looks.

"Don't much care for a city the size of El Paso," Yakima said, gigging Wolf back toward the wagon. "I'll take my cut now."

Cleve scowled. "I don't have that—"

"Yes, you do. I've seen that overstuffed wallet of yours. Just give me a thousand. Any more than that I'll just use to get myself in a bind so snug I'll never see daylight again."

"Me, too." The senorita rode her steeldust gelding up beside Yakima and extended her hand toward Cleve. "I'll take my cut. I never cared for El Paso much either. Or Texas in general."

Cleve looked at both Yakima and the senorita in bewilderment. Then he glanced at his brother, who only arched a brow. Since the death of his beloved but traitorous wife, Jason O'Shannon hadn't had much to say to anyone, including his older brother.

Cleve sighed. He reached down for the cowhide satchel tucked beneath the driver's seat. He set it on his lap, opened the flap, and pulled out a thick wad of greenbacks.

"Some mighty nice bathhouses in El Paso," he said, looking up at the riders before him as he counted out the bills.

Your wife will be there, too, Yakima thought with a wry inner chuff. He wasn't concerned about Ashley O'Shannon, however. He could handle her and her husband. He wanted some time alone in the open spaces to try to sort his life out. In El Paso he would only find himself in trouble and in jail in probably less time than it would take to have Wolf scrubbed and fed.

"I'll get a bath in the river," Yakima said. "Nice cool one, and a free one to boot."

He reached out and took the money Cleve extended. Leonora followed suit. Yakima didn't bother counting his, but only stuffed the wad in his saddle pouch. Leonora, on the other hand, counted hers twice, glancing over the shuffling notes at the gambler as she counted in Spanish under her breath.

"*Sí*," she said, seeming surprised. She stuffed the money down between her breasts. "It's been a grand time, amigos. Next time you're in Mexico, look me up, huh?"

The senorita backed her horse away, and Cleve looked at Yakima. He shrugged, embarrassed by the moment. "Well, *muchas gracias*, Yakima," he said. "Keep your guns loaded. I have a feeling you'll need 'em. Especially if you head back to Mexico."

"Who said I was heading back to Mexico?"

Both O'Shannons glanced at the senorita walking her steeldust slowly south. By now it was roundly known among the group that she and Yakima had been rolling up in the same blanket, and the half-breed had been the target of more than a few envious looks because of it.

"That there's a free-range filly," Yakima said. "And I might just head north as soon as south." He pinched his hat brim at the brothers, then backed Wolf away from the wagon. "See you around."

When the wagon and the riders had continued on toward El Paso, Yakima glanced around, squinting his green eyes as though expecting one of the far horizons to beckon.

"Hey, Wild Man!"

Yakima glanced behind him. Leonora sat her steeldust sideways to him, grinning. The horse's tail blew out in the hot breeze, and the senorita's dusty hair blew back from her sun-browned shoulders. The wad of greenbacks stuck up from her cleavage.

She narrowed an eye and canted her head toward the chalky western bluffs through which the Rio Grande snaked.

"Head over to the river for a bath and a tumble?"

Yakima snorted as he removed his hat to sleeve sweat from his forehead. Setting the hat back on his head, he glanced around once more.

No direction beckoned just now. But the prettiest *bandita* in all of Mexico and perhaps even Spain just had.

He chuckled again, shook his head, and turned Wolf

around to face the Wildcat of Sonora's smiling, beguiling countenance.

"Couldn't have put it better myself."

They spurred their mounts westward, whooping and hollering like trail-weary waddies on Saturday night, dusting the sage for the Rio Grande.

The raptor did not know whether the man was dead or alive, and the man wasn't sure himself.

The man knew only darkness and burning misery and tooth-splintering pain that worsened occasionally, like the sudden raucous upbeat of a drunken four-piece Mexican band on a Saturday night in some smoky border-country cantina.

The raptor, a turkey buzzard, hovered low over the wagon being drawn by two burly mules across the sun-hammered sage flats toward cool blue mountains that rolled back against the northern horizon.

The man lay spread-eagle on his back in the wagon box.

He wore a beaded buckskin vest over a brown wool shirt, a white-checked red neckerchief, patched dungarees, and worn black boots without spurs. His wide, seamed face was drawn taught with torment. Thick auburn hair flopped across his forehead with the wagon's pitch and sway. His brushy, soup-strainer mustache was the same color as his hair, and his eyes were squeezed shut, carving deep lines up into his temples. His cracked and swollen lips were stretched so that his large white teeth peeked out from beneath his mustache.

Blood leaked from his right side—a large, matted mess of it staining his shirt and vest. It was this that the raptor sensed, as well as the fluid leaking out around the man's hands and ankles, which had been nailed into the wagon's scarred oak bed. The man resembled a frontier Christ crucified not on a hilltop but to a wagon bed and sent, lurching and squawking and clattering, across southwestern Colorado.

The land around was pocked with sage and cedars and ringed with craggy mountain peaks, some still tipped with snow.

The hungry raptor decided to take its chances.

Lifting its dusty black wings, it dropped down over the bouncing wagon. It lowered its spidery legs and lighted atop the man's broad, sweat-soaked chest, keeping its wings half-spread to balance itself as the mules continued doggedly pulling the wagon across the meandering desert trail.

It cocked its bald head and stared with pelletlike, copper-colored eyes up into the man's taut face as though waiting to see if the man would react to its presence.

He did.

One eye opened, showing a frosty blue iris and red-veined white around it. Both eyes bulged. The man said through gritted teeth, just loudly enough for the bird to hear above the wagon's din, "Get off me, you filthy bastard!"

The man winced at the pain in his nailed palms and ankles as he tried, with minimal success, to arch his back and shake the bird from his chest. The bird only spread its wings slightly farther apart and canted its head to one side as it continued staring into the man's eyes.

"I said," the man raked out, tears of misery rolling down his sun-blistered cheeks, "get the hell off me, *vermin!*"

As if in mocking defiance, the bird skittered down to the man's flat belly, dug its three-pronged feet into his shirt and vest, and lowered its long, hooked beak toward the half-jelled blood on the man's right side, just above his cartridge belt and empty holster.

He dropped his chin to watch the bird, horror showing in his eyes and tension tightening his jaw. "Don't you— goddamnit! *Don't* you . . ."

As the bird ground its sharp beak into the wound, the man's angry, desperate rasp broke off, and a shrill scream rose from the wagon to careen across the sun-seared valley.

The echoing cry startled the mules into lopes.

Two line riders from the Blackbird Canyon ranch spied the wagon an hour later as it wound into the rocky, piñon-studded foothills of the Lunatic Mountains. By this time the wagon was nearly filled with the flapping wings and bobbing bald heads of turkey buzzards. Their squawks and barks could be heard from a mile away. A half dozen of the raptors hovered over the wagon like a cloud of giant mosquitoes.

The line riders rode down a steep slope and onto the switchback wagon trail in the shade of a sprawling boulder, stopping the mules and hazing away the enraged raptors. Most of the birds fled to the ground or a lightning-topped cottonwood nearby, squealing and moaning with proprietary anger.

As the mules snorted and stomped, twitching their ears suspiciously and occasionally lifting a shrill, anxious bray, the riders rode up on either side of the wagon and stared down at its grisly contents.

"I'll be damned," said Billy Roach. "Ain't that . . . ?"

"Trace Cassidy," said the other rider, a potbellied, sombrero-hatted man named Ralph Appleyard. "It sure as hell is. The old gunslinger himself. Or what the buzzards left of him." The middle-aged drover grimaced as he regarded the bloody, pecked-over remains of Cassidy, from his nailed wrists to his nailed ankles. "Someone sure gave him his due."

"For what, you s'pose?" asked the younger Roach, whose black-and-white-checked neckerchief buffeted in the dry breeze lifting from the Sapinero Valley.

"For whatever he did. Had to be a while ago. Trace hung up his guns when he moved out here to take up ranchin' with his woman—a childhood sweetheart from Tennessee, I heard tell, though I never met her." Appleyard nodded toward the higher, fur-covered slopes of the northern mountains. "Has him a ranch up high in the Lunatics, another two hours from here."

"Key-*riist*, Hooch—someone sure had it in for him bad. I don't know I ever seen a man treated this ugly, and I punched cows two years in Apache country!"

Appleyard stared grimly toward the northern peaks, now obscured by late-afternoon clouds from which a couple of thin, gauzy rain curtains danced. "They sure as hell must have. And they must have some mighty big *cajones*, too, sendin' ole Trace back into them mountains like that."

"How's that?"

"Mountain people," Appleyard said, his eyes grave as they

roamed the distant slopes and fissured ridges. "They take care of their own. Not folks to mess with. When they see that someone sent one of their own back to 'em in that condition, hell's gonna pop. Mark my words. Them mountain folks stick together and yield trail to no one."

Billy Roach followed Appleyard's gaze deep into the Lunatics, and his young eyes grew pensive, wary. He fingered the sandy down above his chapped upper lip.

"Come on, Billy," the older drover said, turning his horse down trail. "We got a herd to tally. Best leave these mules to their work."

When Roach sat his claybank mare beside Appleyard's, several feet behind the wagon, Appleyard raised his .44 Colt Navy, then winced as the revolver roared, blasting black smoke into the sky.

The echo rolled across the valley.

The mules brayed and bolted forward, leaning hard against their collars, the wagon once more jouncing and clattering behind them. Mules and wagon raced off up the slope.

Appleyard stared after them, seeing Trace Cassidy's head bouncing and wobbling on its shoulders, the man's auburn hair sliding in the breeze. Screaming like a pack of enraged witches fresh from the bowels of the Devil's own Hell, the buzzards flapped clumsily into the air and headed after the wagon. It didn't take them long to catch up to it.

The old cowboy was glad when the wagon and its grisly entourage disappeared down the other side of a rise, its clatter and the buzzards' barks dwindling with it.

Then there was only the ratcheting of cicadas, the soft rustle of the dry breeze against the rocks and yucca plants, and the ominous rumble of thunder over the Lunatics.

Colter Farrow jerked up his head from his pillow and reached for the Remington .44 he'd hung from the horn of the saddle lying beneath his cot. He thumbed back the hammer as he aimed the gun at the line shack's plank door and shallowed his breath, listening . . .

He heard only the raucous braying of the cattle that he and Chance Windley had brought up from Mourning Squaw Creek.

Some of the calves had been separated from their mothers

during the drive, and they were calling to one another desperately while the two big, burly bulls were snorting and bugling and jostling for position with the bellowing heifers. Through the cabin's single front window Colter could see a couple of yearling calves wrestle around and mount each other like drunken cowboys in a cheap whorehouse. A thin smile shaped itself on the young man's lips.

In his sleep he'd thought he heard a horse whinny, and that could mean anything—from something as benign as a rider from a neighboring ranch moseying up for a cup of belly wash and game of cards, to Ute braves looking to steal some beef and skewer a white drover with arrows fletched in distinctive Ute fashion.

An Indian would take Colter Farrow's long shock of dark red hair and hang it from a war lance to show the pretty Indian princesses around the lodge fires tonight, maybe buying himself a frolic between cool cherry-colored legs under an old buffalo robe.

Dropping his stockinged feet to the floor, the skinny young cowboy remembered the run-in he'd had with one such Ute three days ago on the drive up here. He'd caught a stocky, scar-faced brave in tattered deerskins and an army blue bib-front cavalry blouse trying to haze off two heifers and a calf.

Galloping toward the brave on his brown and white pinto, Colter had fired a warning shot over the Ute's head.

The Ute, armed with only stone-tipped arrows and a war hatchet thonged at his waist, ducked with a start then, abandoning his mewling booty, rode to the lip of a dry wash, and waved his arms and shouted at Colter, insanely enraged.

What little of the Ute tongue Colter had picked up in his years here in the Lunatics—fully half of his sixteen years—told him the brave had been threatening that, the next time they crossed paths, Colter's red hair would be hanging from the bow he'd been holding high above his head.

Shouting hoarsely in his guttural tongue, the Ute had pointed at the bow, then at Colter, and had reined his pinto pony around sharply and galloped up a pine-covered ridge toward a rocky rim.

Colter had had run-ins with Utes before. Few drovers hadn't in the Lunatics, the tribe's ancestral hunting ground.

But he'd never encountered one with eyes quite as poison-mean as this one's. Colter had a nettling suspicion he'd regret just shooting over the loco warrior's head and not plunking one through his brisket, which was what his older partner, Chance Windley, had warned him he should have done.

"Shit, we coulda just buried the red bastard in a gully, caved the lip down on top of him, and no one would be the wiser. And you wouldn't have to worry about losin' that pretty mop of hair o' yourn!" Windley, who figured he was about nineteen years old, had given Colter's hair a tug at the back and taken a long sip of his rye-laced coffee. "And we'd have us a fine Injun pony to show the girls at the dance barn!"

It was the angry brave who Colter now watched and listened for as, dressed in only his threadbare longhandles and socks, and holding his cocked .44, he stepped outside the line shack into the dusty yard scored with his and Chance's horse tracks and liberally littered with fresh cow plop.

The smell of sun-baked shit and sage hung heavy in the hot midsummer air.

Chance couldn't be out here, as Colter had watched his partner ride off toward the higher Sanderson Meadow with a dozen cow-calf pairs around noon, just before Colter, who had nighthawked the herd, had lain down for a snooze. No one *should* be out here except for Colter's string of cow ponies and the cattle he was up here to tend.

The young puncher had just turned to his left to start circling the cabin when a wooden rasp sounded behind him. He wheeled, raising the cocked Remington toward the cabin's far corner.

Holding fire, he lowered the gun once more as a cinnamon heifer scratched her neck against the ends of the hand-adzed logs, rolling back her big, dung-colored eyes with bliss.

Colter released a held breath, his hammering heart slowing. "Good way to become beefsteak, Momma," he told the cow.

As if in response to the waddie's warning, the cinnamon heifer stopped scratching her neck suddenly. She stood with everything but her head and a few inches of neck sticking out from behind the cabin. She turned her head slightly to one side, glancing behind her.

With a startled snort and a sudden thump of hooves, she

bolted straight out from behind the cabin and went running into the front yard, mewling indignantly, tail curled and back legs scissoring stiffly. Beyond, her black calf turned toward her and mooed. The heifer replied as it slowed near her off-spring and began to graze calmly, lowering its tail. The calf moved toward her and dropped its head to suckle.

Colter stood frowning at the cabin's far corner. He'd raised the Remy again and once more his heart quickened.

What had frightened the heifer?

The enraged Ute?

Colter didn't doubt the brave had been piss-burned enough to have followed him to the line shack. Maybe he'd been lurking around out in the pines, waiting for his chance to strike and give the young waddie one of those Ute haircuts he'd heard so much about in the bunkhouse back at the ranch headquarters.

Slowly, wincing as his right stockinged foot came down on a thistle, Colter backed away from the cabin's open front door. When he made the corner opposite the one the cow had been scratching on, he leaned back slightly from the waist to glance down the cabin's east side.

Nothing but sage, the side window, and the old sled Norman Holliday had hauled up here last winter for skidding logs up to the cabin for sawing and splitting. The sled was grown up with needle grass and fescue. A mouse or chipmunk was scratching around beneath it.

Deciding to circle the cabin and come up behind whatever had spooked the heifer, Colter glanced once more across the front of the cabin, flies swirling around the open front door, then turned and started down the side. He passed the sled, stopped at the back wall, and edged a cautious glance around the corner.

Nothing behind the cabin either, except for the one-hole privy and the overturned corrugated tin tub that the line-shack waddies used occasionally for washing their clothes and, less frequently, themselves.

He slipped around the corner and scurried on the balls of his feet toward the cabin's opposite side. Halfway there, he stopped.

Someone had kicked the sled.

Colter's pulse quickened. His hand grew slick around the

handle of his .44 as an image flickered behind his eyes of the tall, skinny Ute in the cavalry blues creeping up on him with his war hatchet poised for a killing blow. Wheeling, Colter crept back to the cabin corner he'd just left. He drew a deep breath and, squeezing the Remy in his hand, edged a look around the corner.

He caught a brief, fleeting glimpse of long chestnut hair and a denim-clad backside slipping around the front corner of the cabin, heading toward the door. As he stared past the sled, Colter's red eyebrows beetled over his light blue eyes, and a pensive cast entered those eyes a half second before they brightened devilishly, and the corners of his thin lips rose.

He scurried back toward the other rear corner and pressed his back to the cabin's back wall, cocking an ear to listen.

Boots crunched brittle grass and gravel on the cabin's west side. Denim cuffs scratched together as someone walked toward the back of the cabin—slowly, furtively.

Biting his lip, Colter reached down and picked up a stone. He listened, gauging the position of the person moving toward him along the cabin's west wall, then winged the rock up over the roof.

He heard the rock thump up near the front.

The footsteps stopped abruptly.

Colter gently set his .44 on the ground near the base of the cabin, then peeked around the corner. Quickly but quietly, moving on cat feet, he ran up behind the figure now moving away from him—a slender, chestnut-haired figure in a blue wool shirt, black denims, and tan felt hat—and grabbed her around the waist.

The girl's scream turned to a groan as the young man's thin but long-muscled arms squeezed the air from her lungs. She raised her pointy-toed stockmen's boots and curled her knees toward her chest as Colter said, "Tryin' to sneak up on me, eh, Miss Claymore?"